MALE/FEMALE/MALE AND ROMANTIC HEDONISM
Two Erotic Novels

ALSO BY KELLY CARR

Male/Female/Male
Romantic Hedonism
Husband Swap & Roughing It: Two Dirty Stories

MALE/FEMALE/MALE AND ROMANTIC HEDONISM
Two Erotic Novels

KELLY CARR

Abernathy and Monroe

For those of us who are romantic at heart.

This edition published in 2009 by Abernathy and Monroe.

Paperback ISBN-13: 978-0-9841957-2-5
Paperback ISBN-10: 0-9841957-2-6

First published by New Tradition Books in 2004.

Published by Abernathy and Monroe.

eBook ISBN–13: 978-0-9841957-3-2
eBook ISBN–10: 0-9841957-3-4

Male/Female/Male
A Story of Ménage

Toe-curling good.

"Whenever you're ready, Katrina," Wes said.

Whenever I was ready... Whenever *I* was ready. It was up to me. They were waiting on me. They wouldn't move until I told them to move. A sense of power, of pure unadulterated power, washed over me just then. It was good to know that I was calling the shots. I was in total control and it made me feel like the most special woman in the world. And the mightiest. Right then and there, I was the only woman in the world to them.

My eyes turned to Wes and then to the Zack. I couldn't help but grin mischievously. I was so naughty. The thought of what we were about to do was making me feel like a bad, bad girl. It was good to be so bad. Especially in this case and especially with these two men who sat patiently waiting for me to do what I was going to do.

They wouldn't even move until I told them to!

Like good little boys, they sat at the foot of my bed, each keeping their distance from the other as their eyes devoured me and my skimpy outfit. Their eyes were all over me, penetrating me, almost making me *feel* their stares. I was dressed in a tight black tube-top and a short denim mini-skirt. My heels were nearly four inches off the floor and pushed into a pair of clear plastic stripper platform shoes, which had been a gift from Wes. The tube-top had come from Zack and the miniskirt was from my own closet. We had dressed me tonight, each of us picking out our favorite article of clothing.

I wasn't wearing any underwear.

I knew I looked like a total slut, which was kinda the point. But I liked looking that way, for them. Ordinarily, I just looked like a normal young woman going about her business. But on our special nights, I dressed up for the part so I could *become* the part. My make-up was heavy and my long, dark hair was curled and piled on top of my head. I looked good and they loved the way I looked. I could tell from the way they stared at me.

The main reason I liked the outfit was because I didn't normally dress like this. Not at all. I was usually a very conservative dresser but this was their preferred outfit. I wore it to please them and to please myself. But mainly I wore it because it was short, it was skimpy and therefore, it allowed for easy access. It was the kind of outfit a man wanted to rip off a woman's body—with her permission, of course. It was the kind of outfit that made their mouths water and their skin tingle and their dicks stir. It didn't take much imagination to visualize what was beneath the clothes. Their hands could find their way easily underneath to grope me. And it could come off in seconds.

There they were, my men. Two of them. One. Two. One plus one is two. Plus one is three. There were three of us. Three of us getting geared up for our next threesome, our next foray into the magical world of group loving. We were headed into our next excursion of sinful delights that would leave me panting and begging for more and fantasizing about our next time, about when we would do it again. And I wouldn't be satisfied until it occurred and then, when it was over, I would want it again and again.

They were still waiting on me to make the first move. Both of them. My men. *My* men. Waiting on me to give them the cue. Waiting on me to seduce them with my mind and with my soul, but mostly with my body. I felt like such a goddess then. It was such an addictive feeling.

I smiled at both of them, quite sure of myself, quite sure of them, and got out of my chair. I took my time walking over. I took my time to study them, like the way they studied me. I knew they liked what they saw. Knowing that gave me power to move forward, power to quicken my pace. They liked my face and my blue eyes. They liked the freckles across my nose and they liked my plump red lips. They liked my petite but strong body. They liked my breasts which were squeezed into the tube-top but spilling over, inviting them to take a good look and tempting them into taking a good feel, then they could suck them, grope them and pleasure me. They liked my legs which looked longer in the heels and gave them more curve then they already possessed and they possessed quite a bit. They liked all of me and I liked all of them.

Their eyes were all over my body then, as if they couldn't get enough of it, of me, as if they were fearful that it might suddenly disappear without them getting the best look they could. Their eyes skimmed it before they concentrated on a leg or a cheek or a lip before they began to scan it again. They didn't want to miss anything. Men are such visual creatures. I loved giving them the visual they wanted. I loved being their pin-up girl, their sex goddess, their one and only.

Wes smiled at me. The corners of his intense blue eyes crinkled a little when he smiled. He was so handsome, so unbelievably handsome, with dark hair and olive skin and a sharply defined jaw-line. He was dressed in a blue button down shirt and a pair of black slacks. He always dressed like that. He always took care with the way he dressed and always shaved for me. He was a handsome man who was made more handsome by his great personality. He knew how to make me smile and he knew when to let me talk. But mostly, he knew when to hold me and when to let me go.

Zack didn't look so bad himself. He was lighter than Wes; his hair was dirty blond and he purposefully wore it messed up. He had a goatee and nice, masculine lips I loved to nibble at whenever he was around me. He was tall and he was strong. His shoulders were wide and his arms big. He was a good guy and was better than most I'd met.

They were both so wonderful. I don't know how I ended up with them, but I wasn't about to ask any questions, lest I tempted fate. I would not, could not screw this up. It was the best situation a woman could find herself in. I knew a good thing when I saw it and so I accepted it, as they accepted me.

They were motionless at the foot of the bed, sitting still, waiting on me to make the first move. I continued to walk slowly and allowed them to devour me with their eyes. That look they gave me, powered by lust, gave me a surge of energy. It was so nice to be wanted in this way.

I would think of nothing else from this moment on other than what they were doing to my body and what I doing for theirs. It was time to get the show on the road. I couldn't take the suspense any longer. I was about to jump out of my skin from all the excitement, from all the anticipation. No formalities were needed. We all knew what we were here to do and we were all here to take care of me. It was totally selfish but that made it all the more divine.

As I neared them, Wes got out of his chair and stood, taking me into his arms. He began to kiss me softly and slowly, really taking his time to get my juices flowing. He didn't have to bother. I had been hot for this all day. I had fantasized about it at work and while I was taking my bath and while I was dressing and at dinner. I had thought about nothing since the last time we did it, besides thinking about when we would do it again.

Wes bent me back and began to suck at my throat. A deep moan came out of my lips and my pulse quickened. That was Zack's cue to join in. He came up behind me and bent down behind me, running his hands over my ass, running them up my skirt until he was playing with my pussy. I was so wet I was dripping. He began to gnaw at me. I shuddered as he began to bite at my legs. It was coming and it was coming strong and it was coming to take me over. It was that good feeling that was entrenched in my body and begging for release.

But not until I said so. I was totally in control. They were my stud boys, my men and they did what *I* wanted. I called all the shots. Neither looked at the other as they both began to paw at me with their big hands. They acted as if the other wasn't in the room. They never acknowledged each other's presence except for a friendly handshake before and polite goodbye after. They weren't there for each other. They were there for me, to give me pleasure. It was about me, not about them.

I pushed Wes back onto the bed and got between his legs, standing. In a second flat I had his pants unzipped and was bent over him. I grabbed his dick and began to give him head, using a little pressure at first, which was what he liked best. As I sucked him, Zack got behind me and tore the skirt from my body and then he was sucking at me—at my pussy—like I sucked at Wes. *Ohhhhh, Goodddd!* Wes held my head as I went up and down on his hard cock. It throbbed slightly and I knew I was doing too good a job. If I kept it up, if I sucked any harder, he would come. And I wasn't ready for that. The night was early and we'd just gotten started.

I ground my pussy against Zack's face for a moment before I stopped and jerked my head towards the side. He grinned and went and lay down across the top of the bed positioning himself so he could take me. I laid on my side beside him with my back to him and then Wes was in front of me, making me the meat of the sandwich. They were both at me, taking me, taking all I had to offer and I had a lot. Their hands were all over my body and Wes jerked the tube-top down and began to suck on my breasts. He moaned and grunted a little as he did so, as if he couldn't get enough. I loved that sound coming out of his mouth, coming from deep inside him. I stared at Zack over my shoulder and loved the way he was playing with my pussy with one hand. He slid it in sideways, opening up my ripe lips, and then bent down to lick at my neck. I turned over to Zack and he totally took over my pussy. He kissed his way down my body and pushed open my legs and began to lick and suck at it. He did that so well. He gave perfect head. But then again, so did Wes.

But right now, Wes was sucking on my tits as Zack sucked on my pussy. A sharp moan escaped my lips and I threw my head back as all these sensations took me over. I felt the first little orgasm; it was on its way. I moaned and a grunt came out from inside me and I pressed myself onto his face, grinding. I could help myself. I was done in. I was coming, bucking up off the bed as I came and I began to purr as it dissipated then went away.

The best part came next.

I turned to Wes and opened my legs wider and he got between them, his hard cock pointing at me. I grabbed onto it and stroked it and then helped him put it in. I almost gasped. He was good-sized man; his dick had to be at least eight long and hard inches and it took up every square inch of my pussy as he shoved it in.

Zack moved until his cock was in my face. I grabbed onto it and began to suck with all of my might as Wes fucked me. He gasped and pulled back a little. I slowed down and gave it a lighter suck, which he liked and nodded with approval. I winked at him and then I began to feel another orgasm, this one much bigger. When I was this turned on, I could come at the drop of a hat but I knew if I prolonged it, I could have a bigger one, a more intense one that came from deep down inside me and erupted slowly. Those were the best. I wanted one of those, so I grabbed onto Wes and slowed him down a little. He slowed and bent to suck at my tits. I threw my head back and went back to concentrating on Zack's cock. I sucked and stroked it until I tasted his precum.

I pulled back a little just as Wes began to pound me harder. I was going to come sooner than expected if he kept it up. But I couldn't control myself. If I didn't focus on it, I might lose it, and I didn't want that. So I forgot about everything else as it began to play with me, tease me. It was coming just like I wanted it to. I shouldn't ignore it. I gave myself over to it and a slight scream tore out of my throat as it hit me and it hit me hard, so hard I was bucking up against Wes and nearly grunting in my passion. I couldn't get enough then. I couldn't get enough of the moment or of my passion or of them. *Them.* I loved them both.

That was their cue to get things in motion. It didn't take Wes long to come and he was coming hard. It was still tickling me, the orgasm. A funny little squeak erupted from my lips and my toes began to curl as I was being fucked, as I fucked back as Zack was pumping into my mouth then and all of a sudden, I exploded with another orgasm. I came and it came at me in spurts: one, two, and three. I shook with each spurt and Zack came just then, came in my mouth and I sucked him dry as I came and then I felt the last of Wes's cum exploding inside my body.

I shuddered. It was over. My eyes fluttered open and then I smiled at both of them. They smiled back. We smiled with satisfaction. There's nothing like good sex. Nothing. I never believed life could be so wonderful. It's good to be wrong about a few things, but I knew one thing for sure. I was one lucky bitch.

The Thing.

I know what you're thinking. Well, maybe I don't. Regardless, let me set the record straight. I never thought I would be in a relationship with one good man, let alone two. I never thought I would ever be involved in a male/female/male threesome nor did I think that I would get off on it so much. Like most people, I thought those threesomes were not only about the woman getting off but about the men getting off as well—*with each other.* Not appealing to me, to say the least, but if that's your bag, then that's your bag. But that's not what this story is about.

Not to say that I didn't have any preconceptions about three-ways, either. When I was younger I did, but then I watched a few pornos and realized that, no, that wasn't the way it worked at all. It was all about the woman and her pleasure. Sure the guys got pleasure too, but *not* from one another. They got it from the woman. And the woman, in this case, was me. *Me.* I loved that. There was so much sexual power in it. Yeah, power. To know that

I could say who, what, when, where and how, and they'd oblige, was the best feeling in the world. It was beyond bliss. It was downright addicting.

It's all really dirty. Not dirty in a bad way but dirty in a good way. Dirty because it felt good to be so damn bad and to get *off* on it. Dirty is a good word. A very, very good word.

I loved that *I* was the one both of them wanted and that they saw me as this totally sexual creature. They knew that I would do anything to sustain and sate my passions. My passions. Sounds a little soap opera-ish, but, hey, that's the right word in this case. A few years ago, I wouldn't have even thought I had anything like passions to worry about. I was just trudging along, living my life like anyone else and not really concerned about sex or getting off. Now it's all I think about. It just started one day, right out of the blue. One day, it was like I didn't care about sex and the next, I *really* cared about it.

Well, it happened right after I turned thirty. I like to call it The Thing. And boy did The Thing happen. It was like I was suddenly awake. It was like I was suddenly alive. I just began to quiver all over. I awoke from a fog and felt such sexual energy that I began to tingle, just *tingle,* with the thought of doing it. It was hard to contain it, too. I just had to start having sex all the time. I began to feel really, really...well, horny. Sure, I had sex before all this and I enjoyed it, but to be honest, I could live without it. I rarely fantasized and I didn't even masturbate. Now I do it all the time. Sometimes even when my boys are watching. They love to watch me play with myself and then they race each other to the bed to see which one gets me first.

When I hit my thirties, I began to feel really sexual and horny all the time. I call it my dirty thirties. I wouldn't go back to my twenties for nothing now. I was a bore in my twenties and bordering on being a prude. Now I couldn't imagine going without sex even though when I was younger, I went without it quite a bit. That may have been what led to my divorce. But looking back on it, I suppose we had good sex. He seemed to enjoy it anyway.

Oh, yeah, my divorce. I am, as they say, a divorcée. I came to Las Vegas with my then-husband, Tony. He had gotten a job at one of the casinos doing some logistical thing. We left our small, hometown Tennessee town with a U-Haul and some pretty big dreams.

Once we got to Vegas, Tony began to work these really long hours. Well, that's what he told me. He did work a lot, but he was also partaking in the delights of Vegas. He was partying his ass off and kicking up his heels and generally having a good time. Without me.

Not that he didn't ask me to join him occasionally. He did. He'd say, "Hey, a bunch of us are going out to a club. Meet me there." Sounded nice, but there were things to do like setting our house up and looking for a job. Once I landed a little gig as a receptionist at an insurance company, I didn't feel like partying after the long hours I was putting in. The bosses at the insurance company were slave drivers and, being the people pleaser I once was, I thought I had to put up with their demands. So I did.

I did feel resentment that Tony was out having a good time while I was working my ass off and we got into a bunch of fights over it. But he told me, "Look, this is why we moved here. Besides, I have to make contacts and be available. That's part of my job now."

So I let it go. I guess Tony got tired of asking me to join him because after a while the invitations stopped. I didn't notice nor did I care much as I was usually exhausted after I got home from work. It didn't really matter to me what time he came home as long as he *came* home. I, being the good little stay-at-home woman with a full time job, let him enjoy himself. Besides we had been married forever so I never suspected he would cheat and if he did, I never suspected it would mean anything.

Nevertheless, when he found his true calling as a party animal and decided to leave me, I was somewhat devastated. No, I was beside myself. I think I cried for a month straight. *What am I going to do without him?* Blah, blah, blah. And it just seemed to come out of nowhere. One day we were married and the next, he wanted a divorce. The question of why was stamped on my brain. I couldn't get past it. I was hung-up on "why." *Why did he do this to me? Why wasn't I good enough? Why was this happening? Why all of a sudden? Why doesn't he love me anymore? Why? Why? Why?* I thought if I could understand why then we could work it out. But it doesn't work like that.

I remember saying to him, "But *why*?"

He just stared at me, looking sadder than I felt. "I don't know, but I just want to be free for a while. It's really not you, honey."

But it felt like me. It felt like I had done something wrong. Something terrible. Why else would he want out? However, there was nothing I could do about it. Yeah, I have to admit I did all the necessary begging and pleading but that didn't hold him. Because we'd married so young, he wanted to sow his wild oats. It was as simple as that and looking back on it, I understand. Who could blame him? There was nothing I could do. Not one damn thing because when one person wants out of a marriage, there's nothing for the other one to do but step aside. If you're lucky, it will only hurt for a little while. Most of us aren't that lucky. I hurt for nearly six full months. But after that, I was okay. I was okay because in the midst of all this awful pain, I began my transformation.

After the divorce, I was awarded alimony because we'd been together for over ten years. Tony didn't like that much, but then again, he'd been the one to initiate the divorce and there wasn't a damn thing he could do but pay. I was also awarded our house and most of the furniture. Not that I reveled in it or anything. I was lonely and if Tony had wanted to come back to me, I would have welcomed him with open arms.

It was hell living without him. I felt all alone in this new, bigger city and even considered moving back home. I stopped going to work and lost my job. I lay around the house and did nothing but flip the channels on the TV. But being miserable gets *old* after a while. Sure, misery loves company, but I was tired of being its buddy.

One morning I woke up early, looked around my bedroom at all the boxes that still needed to be unpacked and felt... I felt like unpacking them. They had been there for months, ever since we'd bought the house. I was tired of stumping my toes on them and I was tired of their staid, ugly brown appearance. I wanted those boxes out of my life.

I got up out of bed and went to the boxes, tore them open and started to sort through the junk. I decided most of it was crap and that I should just throw it away. I picked up the box, took it outside and put it on the curb. I stared at the box sitting there and

I felt satisfaction. I felt like I had accomplished something. It was a good feeling so, I turned on my heel and went back inside and went through the entire house. I moved junk around and tore through boxes and closets until I had the entire house almost emptied and sitting outside in the driveway waiting for the garbage men.

After I had delivered the last box out of the house, I noticed something odd. There was a woman going through the boxes. She caught me staring at her, jerked and smiled like she was embarrassed. I couldn't help but smile back. What the hell was she doing?

"Hey, are you having a yard sale?" she asked.

I just stared at her but then thought, *what a wonderful I idea.* I shrugged and said, "I guess."

"You've got a lot of stuff here," she said.

"Mostly junk."

"Oh, no, it's good stuff."

It was?

"How much do you want for this?" she asked and held up an old vase *I'd* bought at a yard sale.

"I dunno," I said. "A dollar?"

"For this?" she asked. "You know its milk glass, don't you?"

I didn't. I knew I hated it and wanted to get rid of it for years but Tony liked it and told me to hold onto it. But Tony wasn't here now, was he? No. And I could sell the damn thing for a dollar if I wanted to. In fact, most of this crap I'd kept because of Tony, who was the world's biggest packrat. Now I could get rid of it all! And there were all kinds of junk in the garage he said he'd pick up. It had been there since the divorce. Why not get rid of that, too? It was the best idea I'd had in years.

"Cool," she said and smiled. "I'll take it."

"Okay," I said, not sure what the hell was going on.

Just then, a car drove up, stopped and an older couple got out and immediately began to sort through the boxes. I just stood there and when they asked how much something was, I told them. After everybody dispersed, I had about twenty bucks in my pocket. I looked down at myself. I was still in my pajamas.

I ran inside the house, changed into a pair of jeans and a t-shirt and ran back out. There were about five people going through the boxes now. I smiled widely. This was going to be a good day.

I worked all day on selling my old crap. By two o'clock, I had made almost a thousand bucks off my impromptu yard sale. I could afford a new couch! And maybe some new pots and pans. I could change my life by changing my surroundings.

A middle-aged man asked me, "Are you moving?"

"Uh, no," I said and smiled at him.

He eyed me. "Oh, I just though if you had any furniture you wanted to sell..."

Boy, did I ever. I hated my furniture. I hated the old couch and the ugly coffee table and my cheap dining room set. I decided it had to go, all of it.

"You can have a look," I said and jerked my head to the front door. "If you see anything you want, let me know."

He smiled at me and went inside the house just as a woman pushed a wad of cash in my hand.

"That's for this," she said and pointed to two boxes.

I nodded. "Okay, thanks!"

She left and was replaced by a little girl who held up an old teddy bear that Tony had given me for Valentine's years ago.

"How much is this?" she asked sweetly.

"For you," I said and bent down to her eye level. "It's free."

She smiled and thanked me, then skipped over to her mother. I wished I had a better teddy bear to give her than that old thing, but she seemed to like it.

The man came out of the house and said, "I'll give you a couple a thousand for it all."

No way! I couldn't believe my luck! My mouth dropped. "You will?"

He nodded.

I said hurriedly, not giving him time to change his mind, "I'll take it. When can you get it?"

"I can have a truck here in a few hours," he said. "I own a used furniture shop."

So that was that.

I worked all afternoon and into the night. The people just kept coming and buying all my old crap. I guess everyone loves a yard sale. The man came back with a big truck and he and two other guys took all my furniture. After they left, I began to pick up trash from the lawn and pack the rest of the crap up into garbage bags. Another man came up to me and told me he would take the rest of it for fifty bucks. I was so relieved that I was going to get rid of the rest of it, I readily agreed.

It was about nine that night before I realized that all I had to eat all day was a banana and a coke. I was starving. I went inside and ordered a pizza, got myself a beer and took a tour through my now nearly empty house.

As I walked through the house, I smiled. It was such a relief to be rid of all that junk. I had cleaned it out and now I could start over. I stopped walking and stood taller. It, just then, occurred to me. I was going to start over; I was really going to start afresh. I was going to *move on*.

Wow. Tony really wasn't here with me anymore. It suddenly hit me. I was alone. But being alone meant I would never have to pick up after him again! I would never have to "remind" him to mow the yard or to clean up his messes. I would never have to worry about him pissing me off by not helping out around the house ever again!

I was free.

I threw my arms open and ran through the house. I was free! It was then that I realized that being married really hadn't been that great. It was kinda a pain in the ass to be honest. I stopped and thought about it. Many times I had felt like I was the one suffocating, wanting out. But when you're married, you work through that stuff, even if you don't want to. Tony had actually done me a favor! I was free and I could do whatever I wanted. I didn't have to worry about reporting to someone again. I didn't have to worry about shit. I was free, free, *free!*

I grinned to myself and walked into the empty bedroom. I didn't have a bed anymore. That made me smile because if that was my biggest problem, then I was doing alright.

Mourning time, over.

The next morning, I awoke in my sleeping bag that had somehow escaped the yard sale and I felt different. I realized something was missing in my life and it wasn't just all the junk I had sold at the yard sale. And, like the junk, it wasn't something I wanted, either. I realized that the pain was gone. I was finally over Tony. I didn't care if he wanted to come back now. As a matter of fact, he could kiss my ass. I didn't want him after all that emotional pain he'd put me through. My mourning time was over.

I danced around my bedroom for a few minutes after I had my breakthrough. I shook my ass and felt alive. I was so happy. I hadn't felt this good in *years*. I danced around the room and made it to the bathroom where I picked up my toothbrush and danced some more. I danced until I caught myself in the mirror.

Oh, good God.

I stopped, turned to the mirror and my mouth fell open. Was that me? I shook my head and opened my eyes wider. It was me. And I was fat! No wonder Tony had left me! I had to be at least forty pounds overweight. I looked terrible. I had rolls of fat hanging off me and, dear Lord! I had back fat! I had never had back fat before in my life but I had it now! How long had I let myself go and why had I done it? Well, depression will do that sort of thing. Also, eating vats of chocolate to ease the pain doesn't help matters.

I guess I hadn't noticed I was getting fat because I had stopped caring about myself. And I had avoided mirrors like the plague. But now I couldn't avoid it any longer. As I stared at myself, I realized I used to look pretty good but now I looked like... I looked like a bitter divorcée. I looked like a woman who didn't give a shit about herself.

I had dark circles under my eyes. My face looked blotchy from too much caffeine and sugar. That's all I ate, that's what I lived on. I didn't care about myself and I abused my body because of my misery. And now it pissed me off. I was so pissed off at myself for letting myself go, I could have spit. Why had I done that? Over a man? Sure, he had been the love of my life, but did that mean I had to basically deny my existence once we were done? No, it didn't.

I took a stand. Right then, I took a stand to better myself. Tony might have left me but that didn't mean I had to live like this. I didn't have to be overweight. I didn't have to have blotchy skin. And I didn't have to wear frumpy clothes. Frumpy clothes...?

I raced to my closet. Oh, dear Lord! It looked like the wardrobe of a grandmother on her way to her Florida retirement home! I didn't have dresses hanging in there, I had tents! I needed new clothes, a whole new wardrobe. But why should I buy a new wardrobe for this body? I didn't like my body; I didn't like all the fat on it. I had to change it first.

When had I decided to stay fat? I thought about it. Well, I knew I had gained about five pounds a year for every year I'd been married. We'd been married almost ten. Fifty pounds! I was at least fifty pounds overweight! Surely that couldn't be right.

It was right. I weighed almost 174 pounds. I jumped off the scale as if it had bitten me. *When did this happen?*

And just what the hell was wrong with me? I had acted like once I was married my life was over. I had turned into my mother! Oh, God, that was my worse fear! My mother was miserable! She hated her life. She was fat. She told me I shouldn't move to Vegas.

I didn't have to be like my mother. I could change. I could do it. I didn't have anything to lose, did I? Nothing to lose but this fat off my body. Nothing to lose but the misery. And, most importantly, nothing to lose but the grandmother's wardrobe hanging in my closet.

I made the decision that I was going to change my life. I didn't ask for this. I didn't ask for my husband to leave me. I didn't ask to be alone. I didn't ask to be fat. I was going to change it all. Everything in my life was going to be better. I was tired of being tired. I was sick of feeling bad, of being miserable. And I was going to do something about it. And it started on that day.

I looked around the bedroom. I really needed to buy a bed. After that, I'd get started on all the other stuff.

I was nervous and embarrassed when I went to the gym for the first time but, oddly enough, the people who worked there were nice. I had expected them to be assholes because they were skinny, good looking and in good shape. But they weren't. They were happy to help me. They set me up on an exercise program and even told me what to eat to lose weight.

I got hooked on exercising and would go to the gym nearly every day. Something just overcame me and I couldn't help but go along with it. In a few months time, my weight was down and I was getting in great shape. I was still overweight and I had a long way to go, but I was determined. I even became friends with the people who worked there. I also became friendly with the other people like myself who were trying to get in shape. The owner of the gym noticed how well I got along with them and offered to send me to a fitness instruction class so I could work for him. So, in addition to a new body, I got a new career. And one that paid a lot more than I was making being a receptionist.

It didn't stop there. Why should it? A new body deserves a new wardrobe. I had put it off for a long time but the day finally came. I emptied my closet, cringing at all the sad mistakes I'd made when I was unhappy. Or, rather, when I didn't care what I looked like. I had a freakin' dress jumpsuit in there! Or was it called a romper? Whatever, it was basically a onesie, like the kinds babies wear. I had a onesie! And it was in floral print!

Out, out, out. It all went into the garbage. As I was purging my closet, I was purging my soul, getting rid of all that crap in there that brought me down and made me miserable. No more! No more unhappy, lonely nights! No more knit pants! No more crying myself to sleep! No more being the victim.

I was a new woman. And I got a new wardrobe to go with along with it. I went out and spent a small fortune on new clothes. I bought only hip and stylish things and if they happened to cost a little bit more, then so be it. I'd never spent money on myself before but the times were changing. I was changing into a new woman who was going to live a new life and she *had* to have some new clothes to go along with it.

I refurnished my house and only bought things I liked. It was nice to not have to get someone else's opinion, too. I bought hip, stylish furniture and new mirrors and pictures for the walls. After I was done, I had one groovy pad that included a Chesterfield leather sofa I'd picked up at an antique store, beautiful wool loop rugs over the hardwood, two red slipper chairs upholstered in yummy fabric and a new gorgeous flat-screen TV that sat on top of a beautiful tiger-oak credenza. I also did the rest of the house, too, and even splurged on an upholstered sleigh bed which I covered in an expensive comforter and sheets. My dining room table was the coolest farmer's table I'd picked up at a flea market and well worn. The chairs were French provincial and added a quirky elegance to it. Yeah, it looked really good. However, new furniture usually comes with new debt, which meant I had to work a lot of overtime. But I now had the kind of home I'd always wanted even thought I didn't get to spend that much time in it. Kinda ironic.

Even so, I started going out at night, hitting clubs with my friends from the gym. Men hit on me left and right. It was great. I was having the time of my life. I was suddenly happy. I was glad Tony had divorced me; otherwise, I wouldn't have known the joy of being able to flirt with other men. I wouldn't have known how good it felt to be free. Maybe Tony had been onto something. Besides, he was out having the time of his life, so why shouldn't I?

It's like this. They say things happen for a reason, right? Something bad happens but then, hey, life goes on and so did mine. I kissed my ex goodbye and took a class in fitness instruction, got a pretty good job and then all of a sudden, I'm in demand. Success was mine for the taking. All of a sudden, I had a client base that grew almost daily. It felt so good to know people wanted me to help them get in shape. People are always talking about how I transformed their bodies and their attitudes. I made a difference in people's lives. Me! Before I couldn't even help myself but after this one bad thing happened, my world opened up.

So I had this great job and I loved it. I loved pushing people to get in shape and I loved the adrenaline rush from a hard workout. I made a good living doing it, too, and in addition to the alimony I got from Tony, I have a nice little life. I would get up early, go to work and after work, I would go out with some of the girls and hit the clubs. As I said, I had married young and had never really experienced single life before and I can tell you, I loved it.

And the men loved me. They loved my firm little body and my long brown hair and my blue eyes. They loved my Southern accent and would always get me to "talk" for them. "Say y'all," they'd beg me. "Alright, y'all," I'd say and shake my head. "That's they last time I'm saying that!" They bought me drinks and dinners and all that good stuff. And the thing was that they didn't want anything from me. We were all just having a good time and good times sometimes meant good sex and sometimes it meant "please leave before I wake up."

Like I said, it's those damned dirty thirties. I now knew how teenaged boys feel. It's like you *have* to have it. If you don't get some, you *will* go crazy. Just thinking about it was enough to send me over the edge sometimes. Sex, sex, sex. It's all I had on my mind some days and on those days I couldn't get through the day without getting some. Sometimes I got so horny I could have humped a tree. But I didn't have to hump trees. I could hump real men instead and that's because I developed this great thing called confidence. And once confidence was back on my side, the world was my oyster.

That was about two years ago. In two years, I went from being a fat, frumpy housewife to a sex kitten. I went from a person who was miserable and found happiness in a candy bar to a person who laughed and enjoyed life. And all it took was me getting up off my ass and changing my attitude. All it took was a sight change of circumstance to show me what I was capable of.

It was like my whole world opened up once I took the blinders off and allowed myself to see outside of the box I was living in. I was so glad I didn't let the bad times get to me. I was so glad I waited them out and transformed my life; otherwise I wouldn't have my boys now.

Oh, yeah, getting back to my boys, Zack and Wes. Wes and Zack were like a godsend to me. They gave me anything and everything I wanted and all I had to do was ask. And they both tolerated one another and, though they weren't really friends or anything, they got off on the threesomes as much as I did. It's not a big deal. We only did it occasionally. Well, at least once a week. I have to have it at *least* once a week and the rest of the week was up to them.

Wes once said, "I get Monday and Tuesdays for sure. He can't have you on those days."

Zack agreed and said, "I have to have Friday nights so we can go to a club or two and I can show you off."

So, it worked out fine. They shared me, I shared myself. And we enjoyed our fun.

It's funny, but none of us were that jealous. Of one another, I mean. Sometimes I would see them checking out other women but I didn't mind. Sure, I'd get a little pang of jealousy, but I'd ignore it and just chill until it went away. I didn't have ownership issues. I knew they were independent of me, each of them breathing from a different set of lungs than I was. I knew that someday it could end and it could end badly. So, I enjoyed it for what it was and it was good fucking. This ownership thing people have with one another is crazy. I don't get it. However, I do admit that if one of them wanted to bring in another girl, I might have freaked out. Maybe not. But this wasn't about another girl; it was about me being their girl and their slut in the bedroom.

So life was good. Life was so fucking good that I wanted more and more. And then I wanted to share it.

Goodbye, party-time.

Before I met Zack, there was Wes and Wes only. We were an item. We were together. There wasn't talk of threesomes or anything like that. It was just he and I in our own little world. We'd been together every day since the first moment we'd laid eyes on one another. We didn't need anyone else.

We had met in a club and that had been it. Once I saw him, no other guy mattered. It was like, *who is that?* There seemed to be this magnetic force pulling us together. We eyed each other for a few minutes before he made a move. I just stood there and waited. And I waited because I knew something phenomenal was about to happen.

"Hello," he said finally.

"Uh," I stammered. "Uh, hello."

"I'm Wes," he said, extending his hand.

"Katrina," I replied and felt more nervous than I had ever felt in my entire life. Who *was* this guy? Where *did* he come from? And *how* could I get him into my bed? But I was almost afraid to touch him. I might get an electric shock. That's how strong the connection was.

He smiled at me, leaned in and whispered in my ear, "Wanna get out of here?"

Wanna get out of here? Hell, yeah, I did. But then, I felt weird. I'd just met this guy. I stared at him, at his handsome face and before I could let bad thoughts of him possibly being a weirdo take over my brain, he smiled at me. In that smile, I saw something. I don't know what it was, but it was like I knew I could trust him. I wanted to trust him. That's what life is sometimes about, isn't it? Trusting someone. I didn't get a bad vibe off of him in the least. It was like I had been waiting on him to show up. And then, there he was.

Before I could change my mind, I nodded and followed him out of the club. Yeah, just like that. I didn't question it. That would have been stupid. I felt really nervous around him but at the same time, at ease. Like I'd been waiting around and wondering when he'd show up and then when he did, I knew. I knew he was *the one.* I don't know how I knew, but I just did.

We didn't say anything as we left the club and got into his car. What could we have said? "Nice to meet you" wasn't in our lingo. It's like we knew we were going to go fuck each other's brains out. And we knew we couldn't do anything about it.

He took me back to his house. It was great place in the suburbs with a huge entranceway. It was also tastefully and stylishly decorated. I didn't give a shit about the house. I was all about him. I couldn't wait for him to touch me.

He didn't wait long either. As he prepared us a drink, I sat on his couch and sized him up. He was probably the best looking guy I'd ever seen. Tall, dark and handsome. He had a great smile, which he used often. His hands were large and I was willing to bet his dick was too.

He handed me my drink and I threw it back. He chuckled and sat down right next to me. I was so nervous I could have jumped out of my skin and run away. I almost wanted to. But I couldn't. He was going to take me somewhere good. I couldn't wait to go.

"How long have you been in Vegas?" I asked to break the silence.

"Let's talk later," he said and took the glass out of my hand, placed it beside his on the coffee table and then we just jumped at each other. No need for small talk. No need for anything but touching and kissing. And groping.

I moaned as his lips met mine for the first time. They were cool and strong. They pressed against mine until my mouth opened and his tongue came in to play with mine. I moaned again and felt him push me back on the couch. I went willingly and lay down as he settled on top. We were pawing at each other, tugging and ripping at our clothes. He grabbed my shirt and ripped it open and dove in for my breasts which were waiting and *needing* him to play with them. It felt so good when his big hand finally closed over one and squeezed, then his mouth was on my nipple, sucking it into his mouth and playing with it. His tongue stroked it as he sucked and before he pulled back, he gave it a little bite.

"Ahh," I moaned. "Don't stop."

He wasn't about to. He was making a path down my body with his mouth and hands and tongue. No inch was left untouched. I arched away from the couch when his face stopped at my pussy. The anticipation was too much. It was unbearable. To have his face and his lips on my pussy, on that part of me, was like heaven. My skirt was off in one quick motion and his face was pressed between my legs, just pressed and then he breathed me in, breathed my smell in. That made my juices flow even more. I was so turned on by this man.

He took his time to explore my pussy, to explore every single inch of it, like he wanted to know what it was all about. All the while, he was giving me this immense pleasure, this deep, yet light pleasure that just felt right. There was no better feeling in the world than to know he loved being down there, between my legs, sucking at me and licking at me and telling me he loved everything about me, about my body that he'd do something like that to prove it.

The orgasm, the first one of the night, was quick. Before I knew what I was doing, I had grabbed onto his head and was humping his face. He went with me, not letting my pussy or clit away from his mouth or tongue until I was spent. He kept at it until I was nearly howling from the pleasure and then he grabbed onto my ass, scooped me up and gave me one final lick, a long one right down my slit.

I was so turned on I could have came again from that.

Before I had a chance to do it, he was on me, in me, pushing his big, hard cock right up in me, not letting me move one single inch as he gained control of me. And he was in control. I loved that. He could have it. He did a good job with it and we both knew that where fucking was concerned, there could only be one chief. And it was him. He was fucking me, fucking my brains out. My senses were all on fire and I just wanted him, all of him, on me and at me and touching me and groping me and kissing me all at once.

"You're so tight," he moaned into my ear and licked it. "Such a tight pussy."

"Your cock is so big," I moaned back and sucked on his neck, then gritted my teeth because it felt so good. "God, I love your cock!"

"I love your pussy," he said and fucked me harder. "I'm gonna fuck it."

"Oh, fuck it, baby," I moaned and suddenly felt the orgasm. "Don't stop! Please, don't stop!"

He didn't stop. He couldn't have stopped if he wanted to. He fucked me so hard and for so long, my legs were trembling. It's like they had turned to jelly. I fucked back, squeezing his hard cock into my pussy for everything it was worth. I loved fucking him as much as I loved getting fucked by him, with his hard cock. We were both coming at the same time and the couch was shaking, the window panes were shaking and then the eruption and then the peace after it filtered away.

Afterwards, we couldn't do anything but lie there and pant. After the panting subsided, the kissing started again and then the touching and before I knew what was happening, he had me up on all fours and was fucking me doggie style and I was taking every single inch of his hard cock.

This went on half the night and we fell asleep in each other's arms. And we've been together ever since.

★★★★★

Just let me stop here and say that Wes had the most beautiful fuck face in the world. I loved his fuck face and I was beginning to love him. He was so good. He was one of those guys girls dream about when they dream about their dream guys, *that's* how good he was. He gave me flowers and backrubs and gifts to show his appreciation and devotion. He bought me a trip to a spa because he said I was working too hard and needed a break. He cooked dinner for me on a weekly basis. He called if he was going to be late or couldn't make it for a date. He took me out, he kept me in, and every night that we were together, he fucked me good.

He was getting ready to do just that now. I was the happiest woman in the world.

He began to undress me, taking his time. I loved that he did that, that he took care with me, that he rubbed my bare skin before bending down to kiss it. He paused. I wondered if something was wrong.

"I love you," he said out of nowhere.

I jerked myself out of good-feeling land and stared at him, mouth agape. "What did you just say?"

He smiled and kissed his way back up my body. "I said I love you, I love you, I love you."

I was dumbstruck.

"I mean it," he said before kissing me on the lips. "I love you."

I felt all… I dunno, butterfly-ie. It was a wonderful feeling, don't get me wrong, but did this mean my party days were over? Was my good-times lifestyle gone? Had my party-time ended? We'd only been seeing each other for a few months and hell, I just got divorced. This was all…all of a sudden. It scared the crap out of me.

He stopped kissing me and swallowed hard. He was waiting. He was waiting for confirmation. He had put himself out there and now he wondered if he was going to get burned.

I didn't know what the fuck to do.

I looked into his eyes and felt… So good to have him staring back at me. So what if my party-time was over? Big deal. So what if I'd only had a good year to get my groove on with a few other men? I didn't have good, intense orgasms with them. But I did have Wes and he was worth a thousand men, or in my case, five or six. Maybe seven. And he was so good. He was kind and sweet and cute and had a great set of arms and he had a great job and knew a lot of groovy people. He drove a Jaguar and made me breakfast in bed and… Well, you can see why I didn't want to let him get away. Any man that brings a girl breakfast in bed is a keeper. Especially if he prepared eggs the way Wes did. He always sprinkled a little shredded cheddar on top.

"I love you, too," I said and felt it, really felt that love inside of me for him. I was ready to move on. Tony had moved on. He and I had kept in contact and had actually become really good friends. But he had his permanent sweet thing so it was only fair that I should have mine.

A look of relief swept over Wes's face and he grinned. I grinned back and opened my arms to him. He fell onto me and hugged me tight. I sighed with happiness. How fucking good life was. How fucking good.

"Phew," he said and kissed my neck. "I was beginning to wonder."

"Sorry, I kept you waiting," I said and licked his ear a little.

He pulled back and said, "You mean it, don't you?"

"Of course, I mean it," I said and felt a little shock that he would think I *didn't*.

"Sure?"

"Yes, I'm sure," I said and almost giggled. "God, you're so serious right now!"

"Sorry," he muttered. "You had me worried for a minute."

I wrapped my arms around his neck and said, "You're not worried anymore, are you?"

He shook his head happily.

"Good," I said and pushed my face towards his for a kiss.

"Mmm," he moaned and kissed me. "I think we should get married."

I froze. He stopped kissing me and pulled back just as my eyes nearly popped out of my head. He couldn't be serious. No way. He held one finger up for me to wait, got out of the bed, raced out of the room and came back with a ring box. A little blue ring box from Tiffany. Seriously? Was he serious?

He was serious.

"Will you marry me?" he asked and opened the box.

I stared at the ring. It was gorgeous. It was platinum and diamond and large and everything I could have ever wanted, had I wanted to get married right then and there. I stared at him. "Are you serious?"

He nodded.

I stared back at the ring, then back at him and then, it all made sense. Even though I'd already been married once and it ended badly, even though it made me nervous to think about doing it again, even though I liked being single, it all made perfect sense. Maybe because he was the one asking. Maybe because that ring was the most gorgeous thing I'd ever laid my eyes on.

"Yes," I said.

"Really?" he asked, grinning.

"Yes!" I squealed and threw my arms around his neck and began to kiss his face. "Yes, yes, yes!"

"Then let's do it."

I grinned at him. This was too perfect. And it was a little too easy. There *had* to be a catch. I batted my eyes a little and muttered, "You really wanna marry me?"

"Yes, Katrina," he said. "I do."

Huh. So, goodbye, party-time. Hello… I stopped and thought. Oh, hell. Hello, marriage. Again.

"Uh, Wes?" I said.

"Yeah?" he asked and moved in closer to me.

I breathed in his smell, loved it. It made me horny, his smell. He always smelled so good. Oh, forget it. Forget about asking stupid questions. Forget about ruining the moment. Forget about everything but this.

"What is it?" he asked and pulled back.

"Oh, nothing," I said and wrapped my arms around his neck and pulled him close to me. "Let's fuck."

So we did.

The catch.

We didn't set a date or anything like that. We didn't move in together. He kept his house and I kept mine and our schedules remained the same. Sometimes, he'd sleep over at my house and sometimes I'd sleep over at his. Sometimes, we'd go a day or two without seeing each other. This was great because once we hooked up again, the sex was out of this world. Being skin-starved for a few days always makes the sex so much better.

I kept my own life and he kept his. We met in the middle of it all. Nothing much changed besides the fact that I wore an engagement ring. It's like we just decided to get married and then decided not to do much about it. Sure we talked about it from time to time and I even tried on a few wedding gowns. Well, I bought one but I hid it in the closet. I know it was stupid but the dress was perfect. My first wedding consisted of a plain white dress and a cake in a church reception room. I wanted this one to be better. So I bought the dress because not only was it perfect but I knew if I waited, it would be gone. Or just in case Wes wanted to run down to the Little Chapel one day. I wanted to be prepared. I knew the pictures in that dress would be phenomenal. I imagined plastering them all over my house.

But as time went by, I began to notice that something was off. Wes began to act a little differently towards me. He didn't withdraw or anything like that, he just stopped talking about getting married. I didn't let it bother me. I was in no rush to get married again. But if I did get married, I wanted to marry him. Still, it was puzzling.

"Katrina, I have something to tell you," he said over dinner one night.

I nodded and looked around the crowded restaurant, then back at him. "Okay, honey."

He gave me a tight smile and said in a rush, "I love you, I think you know that. You're fantastic and everything I've ever wanted in a girl, in a woman. You're smart, beautiful, bold and vivacious."

Vivacious? Well, if you say so. I couldn't help but grin like a fool. I was vivacious! Me!

"I love that about you," he said and took a breath. "In fact, I love everything about you. It's not that."

I nodded, smiling at him. *Keep talking baby, this is all good.*

"I love that we get along so well," he said. "We don't fight like other people, you know? And we don't crowd each other, either."

He was so getting a blowjob tonight.

"It's not that I have a problem with our relationship or anything," he said. "It's not that at all. It's just… It's just I have this one problem."

I sighed, not really listening to what he was saying anymore. Flattery always made my short attention span kick in.

He kept on, even though I wasn't paying attention, "But there's one problem. I don't want to spend the rest of my life not ever sleeping with another woman. I have to have that."

He finished and gave me a shy smile, as if to seek my approval. I smiled back. "You think I'm vivacious?"

The smile slid off his face and he said, "Uh…yeah, I guess…"

I grinned. "Wow."

"So?" he asked.

I shook myself. I was still hung up on the "vivacious" part and all the other stuff. He thought I was vivacious! Vivacious. That's a good word. All that other stuff he'd said was good, too but vivacious was great.

"Katrina?" he asked.

I sighed happily, still lost in my thoughts. I'd finally found him. Mr. Right. There he was, sitting right in front of me. Tall. Dark. Devastatingly handsome. He said nice things about me. We were going to get married! I was going to look so good in that dress.

He cleared his throat and seemed a little agitated. "Katrina, did you hear me?"

No. I hadn't. I was in La La Land. I liked being in La La Land. He gave me a little glare and crossed his arms. What was wrong with him?

I sat up and said, "What'd you say, honey? I'm sorry, I didn't hear you."

He didn't allow his agitation to take over. He stared me dead in the eye and said, "If we get married, I plan to continue sleeping with other women."

Of course I had been taking a sip of wine and as soon as the words were out of his mouth, I almost choked. Wes got up and slapped me on the back a few times.

"Are you okay?"

Was I? I took a breath, rubbed my watering eyes and nodded. After I got my breath back, I shook my head at him and muttered, "Wha…?"

"Are you okay?" he asked again.

"I'm fine," I said and coughed. "What did you just say?"

He sat back down and stared at me. "You heard me. Didn't you?"

"I don't…" I began. "I mean… Did you just tell me that you want to sleep with other women?"

He nodded, and then quickly said, "Not now. I'm talking about in the future."

In the future? Wait a minute. Was he…? Did he…? I sat there for a moment, confused, then I got it. What the fuck? Now I was good enough but soon he'd tire of me? Is that what he meant? That's what he meant. What a bastard! What the hell was going on here?! What happened to my happy world? How could he do this? I was having so much fun with all this relationship bliss I must have gone dumb. Suddenly, I was angry. I was good and pissed off. I knew it! I knew there was a catch! *This* was the catch! He wasn't perfect and he never would be! He was just like Tony, just like every other man out there!

Wait a minute. Maybe I had read it all wrong. Oh, hell, I knew I hadn't. And why had he told me this here? In our restaurant? The one he always took me to on "special" occasions. The one where we sat in the secluded horse-shoe shaped booth in the back. Was this a special occasion? No, he'd said it here because he didn't want me to freak out. We were in public and that meant I'd have to behave like a good little girl. *The bastard!* Who did he think he was dealing with here? An imbecile? A stupid girl? Oh, he had another thing coming.

But…maybe I had read him wrong.

"What exactly do you mean?" I asked innocently.

He glanced around the restaurant, nodded at someone he knew, and then looked back at me.

"Well?" I asked, getting slightly agitated at him.

"It's like this," he said and lowered his voice. "I can't settle down. I mean, I can. I can give you everything you want. I can give you that white picket fence, I can give you kids, money to shop or do whatever you want to with. But I can't give you *every*thing."

"Really?" I said and thought about why I had agreed to marry him. Hell, I was having a good time being single, too! But I didn't want to have sex with any other man besides him. He was perfect. He was a good lover. And that's why I'd agreed. He was fucking perfect! I wasn't about to let him go. I'd put too much work into him, into this relationship. I'd read all the fucking books, done the research. I was a good, if not great, lover. At least above average. I gave head on a consistent basis. In fact, I liked to give head. I especially liked to give it to him. Now I didn't want to.

"Katrina, I just want to be honest with you," he said and grabbed my hands. "I can't give you my loyalty. I can't be faithful to only one woman. I've tried. I've been married once before, you know that. It didn't work out because I cheated. And I cheated because it's in me to cheat."

And because all the women in the world were throwing themselves at him. The bitches.

"But what *are* you saying?" I asked, near tears. "You don't want to get married?"

Oh, God! I'd paid a fortune for that wedding dress! I'd had it altered, too, so I couldn't get a refund. I was so stupid.

He sighed as though he was trying to come to terms with himself. And with me. He finally said, "I want to marry you."

"So do it."

"I won't do it unless you agree."

"Agree to what?" I asked, exasperated.

"To allowing me my freedom."

That stung. *I want you as long as I can fuck around on you.* Oh, shit, shit, *shit!* It was true, wasn't it? Men were all bastards. They were all dogs. They were all hell-bent on ruining the lives of all women!

"Listen," I said slowly. "If you want to break up with me, you can come out and say it."

"I don't want to break up with you."

"Then what the fuck do you want?" I hissed and several people glanced over at us. Oh, fuck them anyway.

"Shh," he said. "Keep your voice down."

"I won't keep my voice down," I hissed. "I've spent a fortune on a fucking dress that I'm not going to get to wear!"

"I'll pay for it."

"Ah ha!" I snapped. "You do want out."

He was letting the agitation seep through just a little bit. "No, I don't want out. I want to marry you. I love you."

"But I'm not enough," I snapped. "Is that it?"

He shook his head. "Yes. No! You're turning it all around on me! I don't know! I mean, you're enough right now. You're everything to me. Right now. But it all changes, honey."

"We can be different!"

"No, we can't," he said. "I thought the same thing with my ex-wife—"

"Please stop bringing her up!" I hissed. "I don't talk to you about Tony!"

"I'm trying to make a point."

"So make it. You're beginning to piss me off," I said, though I was hanging on his every word, on every syllable. What if he was my last chance at a good man? Good men were so damned hard to find and if you were lucky enough to find one there was always, always a catch. They had twelve kids from previous relationships or were just plain crazy. I was thirty-two. If I didn't get married soon, I'd be one of those pathetic women out there who had pictures of their cats in their offices instead of their kids. 'Cause they didn't have any kids! They had cats! I was terrified of being a Cat Lady.

"Do you love me?" he asked.

That threw me. My mouth fell open but I managed to say, "Of *course* I love you."

The waiter was nearing our table with our food. We spotted him at the same time. I pulled back from the table just as he put the plates in front of us.

"Fresh ground peppercorn?" he asked and produced a big brown pepper grinder thing from thin air.

"No, thanks," I said and suddenly couldn't take it anymore. The walls were closing in on me and I was having trouble breathing. I suddenly wanted to run from the restaurant and disappear.

He held the thing out to Wes, who shook his head. He asked, "Is there anything else I can get you?"

"The check," I said and pushed my plate away.

"Is there something—?"

"No," I said and threw my napkin on the table dramatically before I hurried out. "Nothing's wrong."

"Of fuck," I heard Wes mutter as I made my way out.

My ex-husband, Tony, and I were really good friends. How weird was that? A few years ago we were ready to kill each other over our divorce but after a while, we became best friends. We shared everything. Well, most everything. We didn't have sex anymore.

As soon as I got home, I picked up the phone and spilled my guts to him. He listened, contemplated, sighed, coughed and gave pause. When I was done, I wiped the tears from my eyes.

"Marry him," he said.

"You're only saying that 'cause you're sick of paying me alimony!" I snapped.

"Yeah," he said slowly. "But he seems like a nice guy."

"You did too, asshole." I lit a cigarette and smoked as I said, "I'm going to call it off."

"No, you can't do that."

"What can I do, then?" I asked.

"Marry him," he said. "And stop complaining."

"Oh, you men are all the same," I said. "I bet you wanted something like that."

He didn't respond.

"Tony?"

"Well, I thought about bringing it up but, but then..."

"What?" I asked.

"I didn't think you would go for it."

"Why?"

"I just didn't."

I rolled my eyes before responding, "Whatever."

"Look at it this way," he said. "He's a man and at least he's willing to admit he's a man. He's being honest about it."

I was stumped.

"You know?" he said.

"But, Tony," I said, about to start crying again. "He said he won't be faithful to me!"

"No one can ever be faithful to another person," he said.

"Especially in *your* case," I couldn't help but say, but then felt bad about saying it. "Sorry, I didn't mean it like that."

"Then how do you mean it?" he asked and sighed.

"I just didn't mean to be a bitch."

"Listen, Katrina, people screw around, we both know that firsthand," he said. "Life isn't like the movies. We're human and humans like to fuck."

"What the hell are you talking about? You haven't turned into a swinger, have you?"

"Nooo," he said slowly. "Think about it. An affair broke us up. Maybe we didn't have to break up."

"But you fell in love with her!" I snapped.

"But I still loved you!" he snapped back. "I told you that but you told me to leave."

He's right. I had. But then I told him he could stay. He left anyway.

"I'm talking about you facing up to reality," he said more calmly. "You've got a good guy and you're gonna kick his ass out, just like you did mine, so you can—"

"I didn't kick you out, ass," I said. "You left."

"Well, if I had stayed, you wouldn't have made it easy on me."

"Why should I have made it easy on you?"

"I don't know," he said. "And then you go and get beautiful and then..."

"Oh, shit," I muttered. "Tony, shut up."

"Well, why didn't you lose that weight when we were together?"

"You're awful!" I exclaimed. "Anyway. What about my situation?"

"Marry him," he said. "You do love him, right?"

"Yeah," I said. "But what does that have to do with anything? He'll still cheat on me."

"He's gonna do it anyway," he said. "And then you can kick his ass out. And for what? Because he admits to liking pussy? Newsflash—men like pussy."

"*Tony!*"

"Well," he said. "It's true. Men love pussy."

Sometimes I wished we hadn't remained friends.

"You let him go, Katrina," he said. "And I can guarantee you of one thing."

"Of what?"

"Of being alone."

I froze. He was right. Sure, I'd get another guy, then what? Maybe fall in love with him? Maybe not. I'd settle. If I let Wes go, I'd have to settle on some guy who couldn't match his socks, who listened to top forty radio *all the time*, who forgot to shave on weekends, who would never, ever be as good as Wes was. Cause Wes I loved. I loved him so much. Not just his looks or money—

though those were fine attributes—but loved the way he talked and smoked and fucked and... Oh shit!

"This isn't helping me!" I yelled.

"Well, it should. You need to stop being so stubborn."

"I will not marry a man that will cheat on me."

"Then you aren't never gonna marry again," he said. "And if you do get one that doesn't cheat, don't think he isn't thinking about it."

I scowled at the phone for a good minute. I could tell he was scowling back. I hung up. Fuck him anyway. I stared at the phone and grabbed it, dialing his number.

He picked up, and knowing it was me, said, "Think about it like this. What if it were your idea?"

"My idea?"

"What if you were the one who brought it up?" he asked. "You told me yourself that you didn't necessarily want to be married again. Think of it like that. You get married and you can still have fun."

"I don't know..." I sighed. "Everything's fine as it is. Why should either of us screw with it?"

"*Because* people get bored, just like we got bored," he said. "That's the way it goes. At least you both know upfront what you're dealing with."

There really was no going back. There really was no knight in shining armor. No perfect man. They didn't exist. Wes did admit it to me, so if it happened, *if* he cheated in the future, it's not like I hadn't been warned. Why was life so fucking complicated?

"Well, I gotta go, Tony," I said.

"Just think about it," he said. "He seems like a good guy."

And that was the whole problem.

Caved.

So, I caved. Though I really didn't feel like doing it, I figured I could do something about the cheating situation later on. I told Wes I had reconsidered and I would agree and then we made up. But I felt uneasy about the whole thing. I just didn't want to share him. I wanted him all to myself. I deserved him!

"What do you think about us getting another girl?" Wes asked later that week.

I screeched, "Wes!"

He recoiled as if I'd slapped him. "Just kidding. Why are you so edgy?"

"Because," I said slowly. "You told me you couldn't be faithful to me and it's still freaking me out a little."

He nodded. "Did you want me to lie?"

"Yes!"

He sighed. "Is this really bothering you that much?"

I nodded. "Yeah, it is. And I don't want it to. I mean, I'm not a kid anymore and once you're married things change. I mean, I was married before."

He nodded. "Maybe it's just too soon."

"Too soon?"

"Us getting married," he said. "Maybe we should wait."

Great. I knew it was too good to be true. He'd want to "wait" and to "postpone" and then he'd leave me a fucking note on the kitchen counter one morning: *"Dear Katrina, It's over. Bye. Wes."*

"I don't want to wait," I muttered. "I mean, it's complicated and I just don't think it should be this hard."

He took my hand. "I think *you* need to wait, baby, not me. I know what I want and I want you but I don't want this to eat you up inside."

"It isn't eating me up inside!"

He eyed me before responding, "Yeah, it is. Jealousy can do that."

"I'm not jealous!" I yelled. "Why are you saying that?"

"You're not jealous now," he said. "Because I'm not doing anything but what if I came home one day and told you I had hooked up with someone else?"

The thought made me nauseous. It really did. But was it my problem it made me sick to my stomach? Yeah, it was. I was more afraid of how I would react than I was afraid of his actual doing it. I was afraid I couldn't handle it and would sink into a deep depression after I found out. I was just, simply, afraid.

"See?" he said when I didn't respond.

"See what?" I said and felt tears stream down my cheeks. "I just want us to be together."

"And that's all I want, too," he said.

"I'm just afraid it will all change, Wes," I said.

He nodded. "The thing is, baby, that fear is just holding you back. Well, it's holding both of us back. I want to be with a woman I can share everything with. I thought you were that woman. When we met, I thought, *she's perfect!* I could see us together for years and years. I felt so comfortable with you that I thought I could bring up the fidelity issue."

Boy, that made me feel like crap. It's like he had this image of me being this free spirit and I'd crushed it. He thought I was more open than I actually was.

"Were you disappointed in me?" I asked quietly.

"A little," he said. "But if that's the way it goes, then that's the way it goes. I mean, I want to be with you. I can give you almost everything but you can't have it all. I want something for myself. Otherwise, we'd both go crazy, baby."

I swallowed hard. He was right. Why make an issue of it? More importantly, why deny it? We were built this way, we weren't built for monogamy. If we were, Tony and I would still be together, happy in our ignorance of all the other things—and people—out there.

"Am I not good enough?" I cried and felt it, felt so low and undesirable and just bad. This was killing me and it hadn't even happened yet. Love was so close to pain. There were on the same level, love and pain. One moment, happiness, another moment, pure dread and misery. It was almost enough to make a person not want to mess with any of it. I stared at him. He was worth it, I knew that. But how could I get through this without hurting both of us? I should just be happy he'd been so honest with me. But I wasn't.

"Of course you are," he said. "You're better than good."

"You don't really think that."

"I do," he said and pulled me into his lap. "I really do. Listen, let's forget about it. Let's take it slow. Let's wait a year so we'll grow and we'll know for sure. I shouldn't have rushed you."

But I had wanted to be rushed and swept off my feet. I just didn't want Mr. Honesty ruining my fairy tale. But was it better that he had told me before or if he'd just cheated? I didn't know but I did know I wished he'd just kept his big mouth shut.

"Is that okay?" he asked and kissed my cheek. "Wait a year and see?"

I nodded.

He grinned at me and pulled my face to his and we kissed. And then it didn't seem to matter. Maybe I could change him. That wasn't going to happen. Leopards don't change their spots. Maybe *I* could change. But I knew that probably wasn't going to happen, either.

Cat and mouse.

The year seemed to fly by and before long, I was caught up again in that magical feeling of love and hope and all that crap. I was so happy that when this happened, I was jolted back to reality.

It was a nice reality, don't get me wrong. Just totally unexpected.

"Hi," he said. "I heard you were the best."

I just stared at him, at this stranger. At this man. *Who was he?*

"I mean, best trainer," he said and seemed to blush. "*Trainer.*"

I kept staring at him. Who was this guy? And where did he come from? It was like he was perfect. Nothing was wrong with him. Had a factory assembled him? If so, I wanted to buy stock in it.

And he wanted me to train him? He was already in great shape and those arms, oh, my God! I hadn't seen a set of arms like that in years. Wes had great arms, but this guy's were bigger and stronger and... Oh. Me. God.

"So do you think you can help me?" he asked.

I started to say something, but then realized I had merely squeaked instead of answering him. I cleared my throat and managed to get out, "What's your name?"

"Zack."

"Oh," I said and smiled up at him. He was *so* tall. "I'm Katrina."

"I know your name," he said and leaned in towards me. "They told me you were the best."

"They?"

"The people at the front counter."

I stared past all the fitness equipment and in the general direction of the front counter of the gym. "They" must have been

Nick and Helen. They worked the front counter and trained part-time. Sometimes all three of us went out and got shit-faced. Since I'd been seeing Wes we didn't do it that much.

He nodded. "So can you help me?"

I stared at him. He had big, beautiful green eyes—oh, wow, I'd never seen eyes like that—and a masculine jaw line and just looked good enough to eat. He was tall. He was well built and...I was getting married. I was in love with Wes. *Hello!?*

"So," I said, slipping into business mode. "What is it you want?"

He stared at me and I felt his eyes. Like what he wanted was me. I shook myself. No. He didn't want me. He probably had to beat the women off. But so did Wes.

Wes. Good. Yes, think about Wes. Wes who was going to marry me. *Some*day. Wes who respected me and loved me and never mentioned the cheating thing again after our talk about it. Now the cheating thing didn't seem like such a big deal. If he got to cheat, would I get to cheat, too? And could I start with Zack? I shook myself. *Stop it!*

"I just want to work on my cardio," he said. "I heard you do running hikes."

I nodded. "Yeah, sometimes at Valley of the Fire. It's really hard. Not that you couldn't do it or anything...I mean, you look healthy and... Yeah."

"That's what I want."

"Okay," I said. "But I have to tell you, we have to meet very early and—"

"I don't have a problem with that," he said.

"Oh? Oh. Good."

"So can we do it?" he asked.

"Sure," I said, nodding. "I'm not sure when I can do it, but I can schedule you in. I'll have to get back with you, though. I'm kinda busy right now."

"That's cool," he said, then pulled out his wallet and handed me a business card. "There's my number."

I took it and looked it over. Zack Parsons was his name. Parsons? Where had I heard that name before? Parsons... A lightbulb went off in my head. Oh, he was a *Parsons*. He was from the Parsons family and they owned a bunch of casinos! He was filthy stinking rich. Wes was well off but he wasn't rich like this guy and—

I was going to marry Wes because he and I loved one another and this guy was probably gay anyway. Look at him. He was dressed well, even for the gym. Of course, he wasn't training today and his outfit of a nice button-down cotton shirt and jeans and leather shoes were… Nice. He looked damn good. Damn it. Why did I have to already be in love with someone else?

"Cool," I said, not knowing what else to say. "Let me check my schedule and I'll get back with you."

He nodded and headed towards the door, then stopped, turned and said, "It was very nice to meet you, Katrina."

So formal. I couldn't help but grin at him. He was trying to impress me. I liked that. I liked being impressed. I liked that he was the one doing it.

"You, too, Zack."

"So," he said and smiled shyly. "Just give me a call, okay?"

"Will do," I said and watched him leave the building.

I took Zack to the Valley of the Fire the following Thursday morning. I was usually off on Thursdays but I made an exception for him. Not because he was Zack Parsons or because he was cute or anything like that. I did it because I could use the extra money. My old dishwasher was on its last legs and I wanted a new one, preferably one that didn't sound like a rocket launcher whenever I turned it on. I could have bought one on credit, of course, but I'd finally paid my debt off and was hesitant to get back in. From now on, I wanted to pay cash for everything, if at all possible. So, it had nothing to do with Zack. At least that's what I told myself.

We met at the gym around five in the morning and he insisted on driving his SUV. I climbed into it and felt a little uncomfortable. What if he kidnapped me? What if he did something gross and I wanted to get away from him but couldn't? What if he left me in the desert with no food or water?

But the real question was *what if he makes a pass at me?*

And that made me nervous. What if he made a pass at me? I would remain strong. I wasn't a cheater. I had been cheated on and it was a bad, bad thing. Besides that, I was a professional. I never dated my clients. Never.

However, none of my clients were as cute as him.

We made it to the Valley of the Fire in about an hour. The place was breathtaking—lots of big, red rocks and open desert terrain, a few rabbits and a few cactuses, or cacti. Lots of space that was one-hundred percent deserted at this early hour. It was a little chilly out as well. I almost wished I hadn't agreed to this.

I shook myself and we got out of the SUV and told him, "Let's start with a little warm-up."

"Okay," he said and grinned.

I demonstrated a few leg and groin stretch and then we did a few sprints. After that, I said, "Now take it slow at first because you don't want to overexert yourself all at once. We're going to go up and around the rocks, mostly running on the sand. This is really good for your calves."

He leaned back and checked out my calves. "Do you do this a lot?"

"Sometimes," I said.

"Your calves are great," he said and got another look at them.

"I hate them," I said.

"But they're so shapely and muscular."

"Yeah, but when I try on a pair of knee-high boots, I can't zip them up over them."

He smiled. "You should never cover those things up."

I blushed. Why he was making such a big deal over my calves? I knew they were nice but all the same I almost wished he'd shut up.

"Anyway," I said. "You ready?"

He was still staring at me.

I stared at him. "What is it?"

"You have such a tight little body," he said and stood back from me. "I mean… Wow! Look at you… Wow."

"Well, that's what I get paid to do," I said. "You ready?"

He nodded and we began to jog. He kept sprinting ahead of me and then would jog in place until I caught up. It was annoying as hell. I was the trainer, okay? Just because your legs are longer than mine doesn't mean I'm not in charge. We did this for about twenty minutes. Then I told him to slow down and walk for a while, then we'd speed up.

"Sounds good," he said and started sprinting off again.

I let him go and decided he really didn't want to train. He wanted to play. I let him get ahead one more time and, when he stopped to wait, I sped up and flew past him. He immediately took off after me. Of course, he caught up in no time. I turned around to look at him. He held out his hands like he was a monster after me and I started laughing. He was laughing, too. We were like two little kids playing hide and seek. Except neither one of was hiding.

But I couldn't help but think, *let me get this straight, this guy wants to work out but all he does is act stupid. Why?*

I knew why. I knew exactly why. I also knew the game wasn't hide and seek. It was cat and mouse.

I picked up my speed and managed to get ahead, though I was still laughing. I was laughing so hard I didn't even feel myself trip over the rock. All I knew was that there was an incredible amount of sand in my face and my knee was throbbing.

Oh, fucking shit.

"Are you okay?" Zack said and rolled me over.

"Ow!" I screamed as pain shot up through my leg. I didn't want to look down at it. I didn't want to see how bad it was. I peeked. Oh, God. My knee was red and swollen and that meant I would be out of commission for at least a couple of days. *Great.*

"Does it hurt?" he asked.

"Yeah, you could say that," I said sarcastically.

"Do you need to go to the hospital?"

"No," I said. "I'll be okay. I just need to pack it in some ice and take a few aspirin."

"We can do that."

I almost smiled gratefully at him but winced instead as another pain shot up through my leg.

"Here," he said and, in one fell swoop, picked me up. "Let's get you back to the truck."

I pushed against his chest and said, "No, it's okay. I can walk."

"Like hell you can," he said and carried me all the way to his SUV. And it was a good distance, too—almost a mile. He carried me the whole way, never stopping to rest. He carried me like I weighed only a pound. I never felt so girly before in my life than I did up in his big, strong arms.

He put me in the back seat, told me to stretch out and then he drove like a bat out of hell until we got to a convenience store where he went in and purchased some ice for my knee and a bottle of water so I could pop a few aspirin.

I watched in amazement as he pulled his t-shirt off and ripped it apart, then packed ice into it and placed it on my throbbing knee. I sat up and held it over my knee and he pulled back, leaning in the frame of the door. All of a sudden, I really noticed his body and almost became mesmerized by it. His body was fantastic. It was hot. His chest was tanned and wide and tight, and so masculine. His pecs were defined to perfection. I glanced at his shoulders and arms which were just as perfect as his chest. I imagined being snuggled up in his arms; they were so big and strong. My eyes went lower to his stomach. He had a six-pack. For a brief moment I imagined my hands sliding down his chest to his stomach and then to his—

What the fuck was wrong with me?! My knee throbbed again and I groaned with pain. Good. Pain takes away the bad thoughts.

He grinned and opened my water, handed it to me and said, "Anything else?"

Yeah, just lean in here for a minute and let me touch your big arms. Just for a moment. I'll be quick. I shook myself and said, "Actually, I'm dying for a cigarette."

"You smoke?"

I nodded. "Yeah, but don't tell anyone. Trainers and smoking aren't exactly supposed to mix."

"I smoke too," he said and grinned like we had this great thing in common. *Let's be unhealthy together! Yay!*

"Light us up one, then," I said.

He dug into his glove compartment and pulled out a pack, lit us one and as I smoked, he got back into the driver's seat and drove back to Vegas, a little slower than I would have liked. I knew I wasn't in that much pain, but he was driving like grandpa.

As he drove, he chitchatted, telling me all kinds of things about himself. I nodded and occasionally winced from the pain in my knee. I once started to ask him to speed up but then realized why he was taking it slow. He was taking it slow so he could prolong the trip. It made me a little uneasy, but not enough to call him on it. I liked listening to him talk.

"Want me to drop you off at your house?" he asked.

"No, just take me to my car," I said. "I can drive."

"I'll drop you off," he said. "Then I can get someone to run by and get your car."

"Zack," I said. "I'm okay. Just take me to the gym."

"I'll take you to your house," he said.

I groaned and gave him the address and in no time he was pulling up in front of my little stucco house. I always smiled whenever I saw my little house, mainly because it was mine. I took so much pride in it. Once Zack carried me inside, he looked around and told me how nice he thought it was. I grinned. I loved compliments on my house.

"Thanks," I said. "You can put me on the couch."

He lay me down gently and asked me where the blankets were. I told him and he came back with the comforter from the bed and my pillow. He propped me up and then handed me the remote control and then went for another aspirin, some alcohol to clean the scrapes and some bandages. I watched in amazement as he cleaned my knee, bandaged it and handed me an aspirin.

After I took it, I said, "You don't have to make a fuss over me."

"No," he said and sat down in a chair. "I want to."

I smiled and said, "I know you must be busy."

"Actually, no," he said. "I'm free today."

I nodded. Was he planning on hanging around with me all day? He still had his shirt off. He still looked *so* good. I shook myself and said, "I have to say, you're very good at this."

"At what?"

"Taking care of me," I said.

He shrugged. "I like to help people."

"Well, you know what you're doing."

"Thanks," he said, grinning. "Why don't I order us a pizza or something?"

I checked the clock on the wall. It was almost noon! My stomach grumbled almost on cue and I nodded. He ordered the pizza and tried to get comfortable in my ultra-modern but not so comfortable chair. I loved that chair. It looked good but no one ever sat in it, not even me.

"You can sit over here," I said and scooted up on the couch. "That way we can both watch TV."

He grinned and came over to the couch. He settled in and I flipped the channels until I came to my favorite talk-show.

"I like this one, too," he said.

I stared at him for a second, then back at the TV. "Don't you have a job?"

"Oh, yeah, I work for a casino," he said. "I'm just taking a leave of absence for a few months."

"Nice life," I muttered.

"It is," he said and grinned.

I shook my head at him and we watched as a transvestite came between lovers.

"Is your knee okay?" he asked.

I nodded. "It feels a lot better."

"Good." He stared at the TV and then back at me. "You want me to rub it?"

All of a sudden, I knew *why* he was hanging around. Oh, yes! Oh no! No, no, no! I had an urge to slap my wrist in shame. But I knew I'd have to set him straight. Even if I didn't want to. I stared at his bodacious body. Why did I have to have a boyfriend? It was so unfair!

"Zack," I said. "You know I have a boyfriend, right?"

His head dropped then he looked back up at me. "I kinda figured a girl like you wasn't on the market."

"A girl like me?"

"Yeah, like you," he said. "Listen, that's okay. I just want to be...friends."

I almost cracked up but caught myself just in time. "Okay, we can do that. But really, if you have something to do, I can take care of myself."

"No, I don't mind," he said. "And I'm not trying to...you know. I just thought if you wanted me to rub your knee, it might help."

"Well, if you want to."

He nodded eagerly. "I'd love to."

And I'd love you to, I thought.

He pulled the comforter off and lifted my legs, slid under them and rested them gently his lap. He began to rub my knee ever so gently and I lay back and relaxed, really loving the feeling of being pampered, the feeling of him easing the pain with his big hands. I must have dozed off because the next thing I knew, he was rubbing both of my legs, using long strokes. His hands were threatening to get closer and closer to my shorts. I started to sit up and push him away but then I thought why not see what he was going to do. Yeah. Why not?

I knew what he was going to do. I had fantasized about it since the day we met. I wanted it and I wanted it bad. And if meant I was a bad person, then that's what it meant.

His strokes were lighter now as he neared the leg of my shorts. And then he just lifted them with the tip of his finger and began to rub under the fabric. I shuddered with delight, with anticipation. The finger was making its way to my panties slowly, so slowly I was about to come from the buildup. And then it was under the panties, then on my pussy, sliding between the lips and resting on my clit.

I moaned.

He moved and leaned over me and our lips brushed. We moaned in sync as our mouths opened at the same time and his tongue slipped into my mouth as his hand stayed there, on my pussy.

I moaned and he began to move his finger a little and I found my hips moving too, moving rhythmically to the movement of his finger, to the beat of my heart and before I knew what was happening, I was coming. As I came, a little wail escaped my lips.

That must have been his cue. He got down between my legs, slipped my shorts off gently as not to hurt my knee and dove in. His mouth clamped onto my pussy and he sucked at me until I came again and this time it was a little more vicious, as if the orgasm didn't want to come out and I had to make it. I screamed as I came because it hurt a little to let it go.

And then he was on top of me, his mouth on mine, me smelling myself, tasting myself, tasting my pussy on his mouth. We ate at each other's mouths and I began to stroke his hard cock through his pants. He was about to come out of them when the doorbell rang. We jerked and stared at each other.

"I'll get it," he said.

"No!" I exclaimed. "It might be someone! Get off me! Quick!"

He pulled back and I jumped up, howled in pain and hopped around. He tried to make me sit but I pushed him down on the couch and threw the comforter over him to hide him and hobbled to the door. I peered through the peephole to see the pizza delivery guy.

Thank you, God!

"Hold on!" I called and grabbed a twenty and a five out of my purse, opened the door a crack and slipped it though. He took it, slid the pizza sideways through the crack and thanked me before he discreetly left.

"Time to eat," I said and turned around.

Zack threw the comforter off, jumped up and ran at me. I just stood there and waited. He grabbed me up in his arms and our lips locked. I dropped the pizza. He carried me all the way to the bedroom where he threw me down on the bed and began to eat at my body, at all of it, not missing one single inch. I just lay there and panted and began to want him until I thought I couldn't stand it another moment, couldn't stand it until he was inside me, fucking me.

He pushed my legs open with his knee, bent over, sucked my nipple in his mouth and as he nibbled at it, he pushed his hard cock into my tight and wet pussy. I gasped. He was a good, good size. He filled me up with his cock and he began to ride me, fuck me, fuck my brains out. I pushed back at him and wriggled and writhed and moaned and shook.

"Wrap those strong legs around me," he whispered in my ear before licking it. "Come on, wrap them around me."

I wrapped my legs around him and he went in deeper. I gasped and he really began to fuck me. He overtook me. He took me over the edge and I began to come almost instantly. I squeezed my pussy around his cock and rode it until the orgasm stirred deep within me and then all I could do was hang on as it erupted inside my body, slowly at first and then with more force. He was coming and he was coming as hard as I was. The entire bed shook as we came and both of us grunted until it was all gone and there was nothing left to do but gasp for air.

After I stopped gasping, I realized what I'd just done. I turned to him and said, "I think you'd better go."

"Not just yet," he said and climbed back on top of me. "We've got more business to take care of."

I couldn't help but grin and wrap my arms around his neck and pull him in close to me. I muttered, "Well, if you insist."

"I insist."

I nodded. I might have insisted on it myself if he hadn't.

No pleasure without consequence.

As soon as Zack left, I was beside myself with anxiety and worry and pure and utter self loathe. I had just cheated. *Cheated.* I was a cheater! I was so bad. I was just like Tony! What I did was wrong. So wrong. I didn't know what to do. I paced the entire length of my house, smoked a half pack of cigarettes and cursed myself. Why had I done that? Why hadn't I sent him away? Why did I have to fall? Why had he been so chivalrous? Why did it feel so good?

Since I wasn't getting anywhere with myself, I called Tony.

"Hey, what's up?" he asked.

"Are you sitting down?"

"I am not sitting down," he said slowly. "What's wrong?"

"Tony," I said and took a deep breath. "I just cheated on Wes."

"I knew you would do it!" he exclaimed.

I was taken aback. I told him so.

"No," he said. "You're not getting off so easy, little lady. Admit it."

"Admit what?" I asked annoyed as hell at him.

"Admit what I was saying is true."

"And what was that?" I asked and tapped my foot.

"That people want to fuck around and it doesn't really have anything to do with loving the other person."

Fuck! He was right! Damn him!

"So, anyway," I said. "How's it going?"

"Not going to admit it, are you?"

"Listen, what I did was wrong, Tony. I know that and I just wanted to ask for you advice. Do you think I should—"

"No," he said, cutting me off. "Don't tell Wes."

I was aghast. "Why *not?*"

"Do you want trouble?"

"No," I said. I definitely did not want trouble. But I had started it so I would have to face some sort of consequence for it, right? No pleasure without consequence. Right. I hoped I was wrong.

"Katrina," he said as if he were humoring me. "I wasn't going to tell you when I had my affair. But then I started feeling guilty. So I told you and now I wished I hadn't."

"Fuck, Tony," I snapped. "This isn't about us."

"No, I don't suppose it is, but in retrospect, I wished I had just kept my mouth shut."

"Why?" I asked.

"Because I hurt you and I never wanted to do that."

"So why did you tell me?" I asked.

"Because I knew it would make me feel better," he said. "It was a selfish thing to do."

I was stumped.

"So," he said. "Just forget about it. Don't tell him. Move on with your life and pretend it never happened."

An image of Zack and me doing it doggie came to me. How in the hell was I supposed to I forget about *that?*

"Are you sure?" I asked. "Because I'm not so sure."

"I'm sure."

I left it at that. He was right. So, I kept it to myself. When Wes called later that evening, I told him about falling, but left out the part about Zack driving me home. I left out a lot of other things, too, but, hey, Tony told me it was the best way.

I was beginning to believe it, too.

"Do you need me to come over?" Wes asked, all concerned.

He was too good for me. I was such a louse! But it wasn't my fault. It was Zack's fault. No, it was all because of those damn dirty thirties, The Thing. I just couldn't control myself anymore. Maybe I needed medication or something.

"No," I heard myself saying. "That's okay. I just need to rest."

"Okay, sweetie," he said nicely. "Call me if you need anything."

"I will," I said and made sure to add, 'I love you."

I could tell he smiled. "I love you, too, baby."

Not an hour later, a big basket of flowers arrived from Wes. The card read: *Get well soon! You know how horny I am!*

I fell to the floor and wanted to kill myself. *Louse!*

Instead, I went to bed early and tried to ward off any sexual fantasies about Zack. Not an easy task considering he had fucked me two ways to Sunday. I tossed and turned and then couldn't stand it anymore and had to get out my vibrator and get happy before I could sleep.

I woke up several times during the night with a sense of dread coming over me. I tried to shake it off but couldn't. I knew I had just fucked up something so sweet and delicious with Wes. But I was human! That didn't make me a bad person!

Or did it...

I groaned and got up out of bed and started to get ready for the day. Wait a minute. I didn't have to get ready for the day. I'd called work and they told me to take as much time as I needed, that they'd reschedule all my appointments and to let them know if there was anything they could do.

Yeah, there was *something* they could do. They could give me my clean conscience back, that's what they could do. But they couldn't. I hated having a guilty conscience.

I went back to bed and hid under the blankets for a while. I tried to fall asleep but couldn't. I was such an early bird. Well, no sense lying there awake. I figured that I should at least brush my teeth. I did that and then started to walk into the kitchen for some orange juice when I heard a horn honk. I looked out the window and saw Zack pulling into my driveway in my little convertible. Oh. Shit. I had forgotten about my car! It had been at the gym since yesterday! I had also forgotten about him telling me he'd drive it home for me. I'd given him my keys without hesitation.

In less than two seconds, he was knocking on the door. I wasn't about to let him in. If I let him in, then...well, *that* would probably happen again. So, he was staying outside that damn door. And I was going to have him banned from the gym, too. He was way too much temptation for me.

I kept the door chained and opened it just enough to hold my hand out and said flatly, "Give me my keys."

"What's up with you?"

"You're not coming in here," I said calmly. "Now give me my keys."

"Why can't I come in?" he teased.

"Because you're a bad man," I said. "Now give me my fucking keys."

He chuckled and said, "What makes me a bad man?"

I groaned and said, "I think you know. Keys—give me my keys. Please."

He slipped them through the crack and said, "How are you feeling?"

"Why are you here?" I asked.

"I came to doctor you," he said and grinned. "And to bring you your car."

"Zack," I said. "I'm engaged."

"You don't have to be," he told me and slid his hand in and grabbed my arm. I shivered just from his touch, from that ultra light, but firm grip he had on me.

"Stop it," I said and wriggled away from him.

"Open the door."

"Zack, I can't see you."

He shrugged. He wasn't going anywhere. Not after that. Not after what we did yesterday. He wanted a repeat. So did I. But I couldn't. It wasn't allowed.

"Come on, baby," he whispered. "I just want to check your knee."

I just stared at him. But, maybe... Well, in *that* case. *No.*

"And I brought you a little something," he said and pulled a little gold box of chocolates out of his jacket. Oh, my God. He was too good. But so was Wes. Why couldn't I have both of them? One sent flowers, one chocolates. Together, they were more than perfect. I would never want for another thing in my life if I had both of them.

I stood my ground and told him, "You have to leave."

"Don't you want your chocolates?" he asked and shook the box.

I snatched the box out of his hand and said, "Thanks. Now leave."

"I will after you let me see your knee."

I was wavering. I really wouldn't mind him checking it out. It was swollen and blue today and it still hurt. I had to take care and not walk too fast or I might pop the kneecap right off. Didn't want that. He might be able to give me some pointers on how to keep the swelling down.

"Okay," I said and unchained the door. "But then you have to leave."

He came through, kicked the door shut with his foot, swept me up in his arms and carried me all the way to the bedroom. I screamed and yelled and fought him the whole way.

As he put me on the bed, he said, "Calm down. I have to have you lying down to check it."

I glared at him. "I don't like you man-handling me. And we're not playing doctor here!"

"I like to play doctor," he muttered and bent down to inspect my knee which was covered by my pajama bottoms and said, "Take off your PJ's."

"No way!" I snapped. "Now get out of here."

Of course, I was just acting angry. If he left, I would have chased after him. But I didn't want him to know I wanted it or anything. He'd have to work for it.

Thankfully, he ignored me, bent over me and in one swift motion, my PJ bottoms were off and on the floor. And he was staring at my knee and at my black panties. He wriggled his eyebrows and said, "Oh, those are sexy."

God! That pissed me off. Like I had worn them for his benefit or something! Maybe I *had*, but still. I jumped up and began to beat my fists on his back. He allowed me for beat him for a moment but I could tell he was trying not to laugh. That pissed me off even more.

"Get out!" I yelled at him and tried to push him off the bed. "Now!"

"Keep that up and you'll have to be spanked."

He did not. *No.* He did not just say that to me! The bastard! I was about to hit him again but he caught my hand, flipped me over and I was suddenly aware that I was across his lap and he was spanking me! Like I was some little kid! Like I had done something bad!

Maybe he was my Karma. Even so, I yelled, "Stop it, you pig!"

"How about a little spank?" he said. "Oh, she likes to be spanked."

Actually, it was kinda nice, I mean… No! I didn't like this. No one had ever done this to me and I hated that he was doing it now. The bastard! He was slapping my ass, spanking me. *Why was he doing this?*

I knew why.

"Zack!" I screamed. "Stop it!"

He gave me one last whack and said, "Did you like that?"

"You fucker!" I hissed. Actually, no I didn't like it. It stung like hell. But it felt kinda nice, too. I wouldn't let him know that. I rubbed my ass and groaned, "Why'd you do that? It hurt!"

He bent down and began to kiss and lick the places he slapped. Then he slapped it again. This time harder.

"Ow!" I said.

"Just wait."

"For what?" I asked. "For you to make me black and blue?"

"No, crybaby," he said. "Just wait."

I waited and he gave me another slap. This time, it felt...different. It felt...sexual. Something stirred within me. I felt it stir and then I felt myself, my pussy, grow warm, hot even.

"Feel it?" he whispered.

I nodded and he gave me another slap, this one got my juices flowing. I shuddered with passion.

"Oh, that little ass," he said and bent to kiss it. "It's so perfect. I love your ass."

"Zack—"

"Shh," he told me. "I'm talking."

I shut my mouth and waited.

"Your ass looks so damn good," he said and ran his hand over it. "I love your ass."

I lay there and tried to contain myself, tried to control myself. It took everything I had to not jump up, push him back on the bed and fuck his brains out. But I waited. There was something cool about to happen soon.

"I'm going to fuck your ass, baby," he said and grabbed it, squeezed it and then ran his hand between its cheeks. "I'm going to fuck it. Would you let me fuck your ass?"

He didn't even have to ask.

"Yeah, you'd like that, wouldn't you?" he whispered and pulled my shirt up and began to kiss my back. "What else would you like me to do?"

"Just what you're doing," I breathed.

"Oh, this?" he asked and began to play with my ass. "You like that? Are you a dirty girl? Tell me you're a dirty girl."

I couldn't believe I was saying the words as they came out of my mouth, "Yes, I'm a dirty girl."

"I thought you were," he said and slapped my ass, this time harder than before. He pushed me up on the bed and got between my legs and began to eat me, slurp at me, fuck me with his mouth and tongue. I laid there and shuddered, loving it all, loving the way he was doing it, loving that it was dirty and nasty and felt so good. I felt the first orgasm almost instantly and wailed a little. It felt so good I had to bite at my fist to keep from screaming.

Without a word, after I was finished, he positioned himself behind me, opened my legs and drove it in. He drove his hard cock right up in me as I lay there and panted and felt pain and passion and pure, unadulterated lust coming out of me. I felt it in my pussy and I felt it in my ass as he fucked me there. He grabbed the back of my head and pulled me to him so he could suck on my neck as he fucked me, as he fucked me in this dirty but ultimately satisfying way.

I moaned and found my hand between my legs, resting on my clit. I began to hump my hand. His hand went to my pussy and he fingered me there as I fingered myself as he fucked my ass. Then I felt it, this enormous orgasm. It began to tickle me, taunt me and it was coming at me from all over. My entire body, my entire being just felt it. Just felt alive and active, like every single cell in my body was being raised and told to tingle. I couldn't contain myself. I was lost then, lost inside that orgasm, so lost that it was controlling me, as I lost control. I began to howl like a wild animal and the sound ripped out of my throat and came out like a mad cry. And it was madness; it was so good it was almost dark and scary. And he began to cry out, too, but not in the same manner as me, but because he was about to come. No, he *was* coming as I was coming. We were both coming at the same time and each of use felt each other, each other's bodies and mind and souls and desires at that instant. And we fucked like that until neither of us could hold onto it anymore and we collapsed to the bed, with him lying on top of me.

"Damn," he said. "That was good."

I nodded but couldn't speak. I was at a loss for words. And I was still out of breath. We *had* to do *that* again.

"Yeah," I breathed and snuggled in the crook of his arms. "It was."

He sighed and said, "I think I love you."

I froze.

"I do," he said.

"That's a little…sudden," I stammered and sat up. "What the hell do you mean by that?!"

He sat up and said, "I don't know. It just came out."

I glared at him. "Don't fuck with me."

"I'm not fucking with you," he muttered. "It's like I thought it but I said it too. It was weird."

"Listen," I said. "This is about sex. And that's all it's about."

"I don't know," he said. "It's different."

"No, it's not different, Zack," I said and jumped off the bed. "Don't make it different. I already have one boyfriend!"

He swallowed hard. "So? What's so special about him?"

"He's my boyfriend!" I said. "He doesn't have to be special!"

"What?"

"I mean," I said and grabbed my cigarettes off the nightstand. "I don't have to explain why he's special."

He looked away and nodded. "So I can't be?"

"What?"

"Special to you," he said and turned back to me.

"I didn't say that."

"You didn't have to," he said and got out of bed.

"Zack, don't," I said and grabbed his hand.

He jerked it back and hissed, "Listen, I don't go around saying stuff like that. It just popped out, okay? You don't have to spit on it."

"I wasn't spitting on it!"

"Yeah, you were!" he yelled and bent to grab his pants.

"Zack, please, just listen. I—"

"I don't want to listen," he said.

I threw my cigarettes down and went at him, grabbing him by the waist and stopping him. He allowed me to hold him for a moment before he pushed me away and I fell on the bed.

"You bastard!" I yelled and before I knew what I was doing, I had jumped on him and was beating the shit out of his back. I don't know why he inspired this little rage in me but I hated the fact that he was bigger and stronger than I was and that meant he could throw me around like a sack of potatoes. But at the same time, I loved it. Maybe I wasn't trying to hurt him; maybe I was trying to get him to put me in my place. So he would fuck me again.

He spun me around, threw me on the bed and tried to hold me off him. But I wasn't having it. I slapped at him until he grabbed my arms, pinned them behind my back and got in my face.

He hissed, "If I want to love you, I will. You can't stop me."

"You better let me go, you bastard!" I hissed and felt spit fly out of my mouth and onto his face.

He jerked his head to the side, faced me again and pressed his lips against mine, pushing me back on the bed. I tried to scream and struggled against him but there wasn't much I could do. He was one strong son of a bitch. We fought all the way to the bed, all the way down and in one quick motion, he kissing me, pushing me down and I was responding, letting it take me over. And then nothing mattered. It didn't matter because we were soon fucking.

It was a slightly vicious fuck, slightly maddening because we bit at each other as we panted with lust and anger. He pounded against me so hard I gasped. I pushed back against him, and then sucked at his mouth until it opened and then I sucked at his tongue. He moaned and I opened my eyes. He was staring at me. I stared back and we began to fuck, slowly fuck, slowing down to feel it, really *feel* it. I squeezed my pussy and sucked his dick more deeply into me. He moaned and held still so I could ride it, ride his hard cock until I felt something stir, then erupt, then explode inside me. Intensely it exploded and I bit down on his shoulder and he cried out in pain, in pleasure, and he rode me harder and rode me until he came and there was nothing left to do but ride it out and then hold each other as the feeling of euphoria slowly faded away.

I noticed we didn't move one single inch away from each other. We stayed like that for a very long time and we stayed like that because it felt right not to move away, not to experience the shame that comes with finding our clothes and covering our nakedness and our souls.

He said, "I love you."

I turned to stare at him and though I felt bad about saying it, it felt right to do it, so, I had no choice and I couldn't deny my feelings. I had to say it because I felt it. So, I said, "I love you, too."

He smiled. He smiled because he knew it already. I'd just confirmed.

Plaything.

I decided that Zack, because he was so rich, was just bored and I was his plaything for a while. I would happily remain his plaything until he got tired of me and moved on to another plaything. I liked being his plaything. And because I was his plaything, I didn't have to give up Wes.

I was getting so good at denial, I was starting to scare myself.

Zack came by in the mornings and then I saw Wes at night. Because I had already fucked like crazy and was still turned on by it, by the time dinner was over, I was jumping on Wes. My hormones were out of control. The more sex I had, the more I wanted. No. The more I *had* to have. All I could say was thank God for the pill.

I was such a bitch. Bitch, bitch, bitch.

But what could I do? I had two great men and just let me say, that was a damn good feeling. I was so happy I was listening to Barry White all the time. I'd crank up his greatest hits and just feel good about everything. About life and love and sex. I felt good about my body and about the blue sky and about the warm, desert wind. I felt good about helping my clients at the gym. I felt good about smiling all the time and about being so happy.

I was one lucky bitch and I knew it. So, I rode it out. I devoured life like a person should devour it. I loved my life; I loved everything about it and that's because I was sated. I was getting satisfaction on all levels. Both of my men gave me just enough space so I wasn't going crazy trying to schedule them into my daily routines. And both fit perfectly into my life. It wasn't like I was neglecting Wes for Zack. Zack and I met in the mornings and Wes and I met at night. Sometimes Wes would go away for business and Zack and I had an occasional night together. Sometimes Wes stayed over and Zack knew if his car was in the drive not to come in. Wes got more attention from me and because I felt awful for cheating on him, I didn't pick fights and I made sure to agree to go to his favorite restaurants and to wear his favorite dresses.

The guilt was bad. But it didn't stop me. I couldn't help myself. It just felt right to have an affair with Zack just like it felt right for me to be with Wes. Sure, it was downright deceitful and not a nice thing to do, but I couldn't stop it. I'd prepare a speech for Zack, outlining all the reasons why he had to get out of my life, then he'd show up with a box of chocolates and I'd be back to square one.

Then I began to rationalize it. Why not play it out and see what happened? What *could* happen? Wes could find out and break up with me. Then I'd have Zack. Zack could get bored and then I'd just have Wes. Deep down, I wanted both of them. Selfish, I know, but that's what I wanted. So, I kept it a secret and was very cautious on all levels. I didn't want to hurt Wes anymore than I wanted Zack to stop coming over. But, in the meanwhile, I was so happy about it all I was in a perpetual state of bliss. It was not a bad place to be.

Well, I knew what was eventually going to happen and it happened before I was ready for it. But doesn't it always?

One night, I had Wes over for dinner and I noticed he was being really quiet. Like he was mad about something. Dumb me, I didn't think the obvious. Maybe it was because I hadn't seen Zack that morning and I had a lot of other things on my mind. Maybe it was because I was still thinking it was too soon for anything to come to a head. Maybe it was because I was such a dumbass.

"So how was work?" I asked and smiled at him.

"Okay."

"Do you like the chicken?" I asked. "I marinated it then I grilled it. Like in that recipe I told you about."

"It tastes fine."

"Oh," I said and sighed. "I'm thinking about getting my hair cut. What do you think?"

"Leave it alone."

He always said that. *Don't cut your hair. It looks good. Leave it alone.*

"So," I said. "Wanna go see a movie later on?"

"Doesn't matter to me," he said and sat up straighter in his chair. "We could ask your boyfriend to come with us, if you like."

I didn't immediately get what he was getting at. No, I was a dumbass and thought he was joking, so I joked back, "And maybe we could ask your girlfriend, too. Have a little group sex or something."

He glared at me for a few moments before he spat, "Sure, except *I* don't have a fucking girlfriend."

That's when I knew something was up.

"What's wrong with you?" I asked.

"Damn it, Katrina," he hissed. "Don't you fucking play games with me."

"*What?*" I asked, getting slightly irritated. "What are you talking about, Wes?"

"I saw you!" he yelled.

"Saw me what?!" I yelled back.

"You and your boyfriend, that tall motherfucker!"

Oh, no...nooooooOOOOO! I was shocked beyond belief. Who? What? When? Where? *WHY!?* Why, why, why, oh fucking why?! Oh, shit. Shitmotherfuckingshit! All good things must come to an end. And usually they come to a bad, bad end.

"What are you talking about?" I asked, trying to look innocent. I knew of course. I knew he knew. The big question was how long had he known. And what was he going to do about it?

"You and that...that..." he said and angrily threw his napkin down on the table. "You and that motherfucker kissing on your porch at six yesterday morning!"

Oh, shit. I had allowed Zack to stay over if he promised to leave early. He was going to be out of town for a week or so and I had made an exception. An exception that apparently wasn't the wisest choice to make. It was my undoing.

"What were you doing here at six in the morning?!" I yelled.

"I came by to give back your Barry White CD," he hissed.

Damn Barry White! Barry White was my undoing!

"I was going to put it in your mailbox and not wake the princess from her fucking beauty sleep! I didn't know the princess was already awake!"

"Don't patronize me!" I yelled.

"I'll do what I damn well please," he hissed and got up from the table and began to pace, throwing his arms around like a madman. "And here I thought you were working all these extra hours! Here I thought you were tired and that's why you didn't want to stay over at my place as much. Here I was feeling sorry for you! But the real reason you're so tired is because you've got another boyfriend!"

I felt like one hundred percent grade-A shit. Nevertheless, I exclaimed, "I don't have another boyfriend! You're my boyfriend!"

"Oh, please," he scoffed. "I just can't believe you're such a slut!"

I stared at him. He was really beginning to piss me off. Here he was telling me I was a slut because I liked having sex! What did that make him?

"Wait a minute!" I yelled back. "Don't you dare call me that! Just because I'm a woman and I like sex doesn't mean you can classify me as street trash!"

"Well, that's what you're acting like!" he hissed.

Oh, God! That flew all over me! I wanted to scratch his eyes out! I wanted to do him some damage, some real damage. So what if I liked fucking? Big deal. Better than being a prude. Prudes were miserable and I should know. I had played that part well in my marriage. Wifey shouldn't like sex. Wifey is good, kind and pure. Wifey knows the way to a man's heart is through his stomach and doesn't have anything to do with his dick. All lies to make all wives miserable. To make all of us women feel like shit for being sexual beings. All lies made up by men to make us stay in our place. Don't get any ideas about being what you want or acting out your sexual fantasies because it's all about the man. And I had bought into it. I had bought into it so much, it had destroyed my marriage. Tony wanted me to be more sexual, I just couldn't. I had society on my back forcing me to be good. *What will the neighbors think?* Wes didn't understand because he was a man and men were never made to feel bad over liking sex. Why did men want to make us feel bad over it? It's not like men could do it by themselves unless they jerked off and, really, what was the fun in that? Wasn't doing it with a woman much better? Sure, they could do it with each other but most of them didn't want that. They wanted a woman to do it with, not a man. I mean, sex is usually about a man *and* a woman. It takes two to tango.

"I just can't believe you," he said and shook his head. "I just can't."

I was so over this shit. How dare he talk to me like that? I had broken out of my shell and was just coming into my own sexually. And there he was telling me it wasn't okay. It wasn't okay for me to want more sex. All I could do was have was sex with him. Just sex with him. Then... Then I remembered our conversation just after we got engaged. He couldn't be faithful. He didn't want to lie to me, all that shit he fed me. Bastard! *He* couldn't be monogamous, but he sure as hell wanted *me* to be. Can you say hypocrite three times fast? Hypocrite, hypocrite, hypocrite!

"Well," I said calmly. "It *was* your idea."

"What do *you* mean?"

"Oh, you don't remember telling me you couldn't be faithful? And that you were sorry and all that shit but—"

"I didn't mean—"

I finished for him, "For me to do it."

He glared at me. "No, I meant in the future when our obsession with one another wears off."

"No, you meant when your obsession with *me* wears off."

He glared at me but didn't respond.

"Isn't that right?" I hissed. "You knew one day you would want someone else to fuck and wouldn't want a nagging wife and—"

He held up his hand and said, "Katrina, I've heard enough."

"Well, I'm not finished, you hypocritical bastard!" I screamed and knew I should have never admitted it to him. I should have stonewalled him. Denied everything, told him he was hallucinating or that he had gotten the wrong house, the wrong girl and the wrong man. God, this was getting a little too complicated. Here he was pissed off as hell and *he* was the one who brought up having sex with other people. Of course, he never said anything about me doing it, had he? Oh, no, and why would he?

Of course, I had been the one to "talk" him out of it. Boy, what a stupid move on my part! I just didn't have any idea it could be as sweet as it was. But now I knew and I couldn't live without it. If that made me selfish, then that's what it made me. I wasn't going to start denying myself. I'd done that for years and for what? So I could be miserable? Fuck misery and fuck Wes if he didn't understand.

"It doesn't make it right," he said.

"It's not about right, Wes," I told him. "It's about you being a hypocrite."

"I am not a hypocrite!"

"From where I'm standing, it looks like you are."

His eyes shot bullets at me. I almost felt them. We stopped speaking. One of us would make a move. We were waiting the other out. One of us would have to make the decision to leave. That would be Wes. It was in his hands. One of us would try to make up. That would have to be me and I wasn't about to. Sure, it had been wrong, but it hadn't been *that* wrong.

"I've had enough," he hissed. "But I've got one more thing to do."

I watched as he stomped out of the dining room, heading to the bedroom. What was he going to do? Was he going to...? No. He wouldn't do that. He might!

I jumped up and raced after him. He already had my wedding dress out of the closet and was ripping it to shreds.

"What are you doing?" I wailed.

"What do you need with this?" he asked. "You bitch!"

"You motherfucker!" I screamed. "I paid for that!"

"I won't let you keep it so you can marry that asshole in it!" he roared. "I'd rather die!"

"That's mine!" I cried and grabbed what was left of it. I held it in my arms and began to sob. It was ruined, just like our relationship. I watched in horror as he stomped over to me, grabbed my hand and yanked my engagement ring off my finger. He took it, threw it to the floor and smashed it to bits.

It was really over. Nothing I could do about it now. How did things get so complicated? Why does sex complicate everything? Why does it make everything bad and ugly? It shouldn't. It should be revered. It was the one thing in this world that made a person really and truly happy. And everyone shit on it. Everyone was so scared of it, of its power. And it had power over all of us and there wasn't a damn thing we could do about it but sit back and watch it tear our lives apart.

"Now how does that feel?" he asked.

I just stared at up at him with tears running down my face. "You're mean."

He got down in my face and hissed, "Yeah, now you know how I feel. Now you know how bad it hurt when you broke my heart."

"Wes—"

"Don't talk to me," he said and headed out of the bedroom. "Ever again."

And with that he left. And I with that, my heart felt dead. I didn't know how I was ever going to recover.

Nothing to do but sit back and cry. And I cried for two days. Not just over Wes and our failed relationship, but because of what broke us up. I didn't hate him, even though could have, really easily. My feelings could have turned black. But I didn't want to ruin what we had by coloring it with hate. He didn't single-handedly ruin it and neither did I. It just got complicated. Forced to look at what we were really all about, neither of us could handle it. The world was bigger than we were and once we stepped outside of our world, it came crashing down on us.

What if the shoe had been on the other foot? What if he had been the one to cheat? I knew I would have taken it badly. I would have cried and broken up with him, the same way that Tony and I had broken up. But then, I knew I would have moved on from it. *If* I felt like I felt now. If I knew what I knew now. Sex isn't bad. Having sex and loving other people isn't bad. What's bad is confronting that feeling of knowing you are not the only person in the world who can give another person all his good feelings. Knowing others can do it too is like a shot to the heart. That's where all the trouble comes in. That's where it all starts. We're so afraid of losing ourselves to someone else that when we do, we become frightened that they will take that love away. And the thought of having them lose themselves to someone besides us is terrifying. It makes us bitter and hateful. We gave it all to them and then they gave it to someone else.

But the thing was, I didn't take any love away from Wes to give to Zack. I loved both of them. I never knew I could love like that. There was so much love in me, I sometimes felt like I could burst from it.

On the third night after Wes left, he banged on the front door. I almost didn't let him in. I almost pretended not to be home. But I knew we'd have to confront each other at least one more time. There was no way around it. So I let him in.

He didn't speak for a very long time and neither did I. We just sat on opposite ends of the couch and stared at the TV, which was turned off.

"I don't know what to say to you," I said finally.

He nodded but didn't reply.

"But I am sorry I hurt you," I said and stared at him. "I never wanted to hurt you."

"Didn't you think I'd find out?" he muttered.

"Yeah," I said. "But I tried not to worry about it."

"What do you mean?"

"I mean," I said and swallowed hard. "I just wanted to live and whatever happened would happen without me forcing the issue."

"Is that right?" he asked, starting to get angry. "I just can't believe you."

"Believe me?"

He turned to face me. "I can't believe what a little slut you are."

This time, I succumbed to the anger. I couldn't stop myself. I was at him and on him and I had slapped him before I even knew what I was doing.

"You bastard!" I yelled and slapped him again. "How dare you?!"

He grabbed my hand and pulled me to him. "That's what you are, isn't it?"

"Yes," I hissed. "And fuck you!"

"Fuck me?" he snarled. "No, fuck you."

"Get out of here!" I screamed. "Now! We're over! Done! Through!"

"Why did you do it?"

"I'm human," I said. "I can't be loyal to just one man. I thought we discussed this already!"

"No, you didn't want to do that, as I remember," he said. "I changed for you and for what? So you could fuck around on me?"

"I'm sorry you feel that way," I said calmly. "Now get the fuck out of here."

"Is he coming over?"

"He has a name and it's Zack," I said. "And, though it's none of your damn business, he isn't coming over. He's out of town."

"So that's why you're alone."

"No," I said. "I'm alone because I choose to be alone tonight. Remember, I'm a little slut and I could go down to the bar and bring any old thing home if I wanted to."

"Yeah," he said, nodding. "That's true."

"Don't egg me on, motherfucker," I hissed, shaking with fury.

"Why not?" he asked. "You said it yourself, a little slut like you can go out and get fucked whenever you like."

"You're damn right I can," I said and suddenly felt myself lunge for him. He had me so pissed off I didn't even realize I was beating at his chest with my fists until he had me turned me around and pushed me up against the wall, my back to him. I couldn't believe he did that. I couldn't believe I was in that position. I was, all of a sudden, helpless.

"Wes, stop!" I yelled.

"No," he said calmly and his hand came around to unzip my jeans.

"Stop!" I yelled and pushed away from him and ran into the bedroom. He ran after me. I got to the bed and stopped, staring at him, feeling somewhat scared. What was he going to do? I could understand why he was so upset, to a certain degree, but this anger of his was something new. I'd never seen it before. And I didn't much like it.

"Isn't this what you want?" he asked and grabbed me and threw me to the bed.

"Wes!" I yelled and tried to crawl away from him. "Stop it!"

He flipped me over and climbed on top and the next thing I knew he was kissing me, kissing me viciously and dangerous and like he didn't care if I was enjoying it or not. But then I found myself responding to that hateful kiss but before I could moan and enjoy it, he flipped me over, pushed my hips up off the bed until I was on all fours and tore the clothes from my body. And then he fucked me. He fucked me hard, again like he didn't care if I was getting anything out of it but then at the same time he knew I was. And I was because he was filling me up with his hard cock and just from that I was coming and he was coming and as he came, he pulled out and sprayed his hot and sticky cum all over my back. I shuddered as it hit me and felt myself returning from orgasm land. It was a good fuck, maybe too good. It was one of those fucks that sent a person over the edge and the edge is sometimes a scary place to be.

I fell to the bed exhausted. He fell down beside me and we stared at each other for a long moment, not speaking, not thinking, just staring and feeling what we really felt for one another, love.

No matter what I did or what he said, we couldn't change our feelings.

"Do you love him?" he asked quietly.

"I don't know," I said. "But I do know I love you."

"Is he a fling?"

I thought about that. Was Zack a fling? I didn't know. I knew if he stopped seeing me tomorrow, I would be hurt. I would be okay with it, but it would hurt like hell. I had tried to guard my feelings for him and not feel any love but when you share what we'd shared—all that good, intense hot sex—it was hard not to love the person who was giving it to you. It just happened like that.

"I don't know, baby," I said and ran my finger down the bridge of his nose. "I don't want to lie to you."

He stared at me sadly.

"I mean," I said. "I like you both. I mean…I'm in love with you but with Zack, I really like him, too. I never thought I could feel like this about two men at the same time."

"But you do love me, right?"

"I do," I said and smiled at him. "I really, really do."

He nodded. "I'm sorry I was such an asshole."

"I accept your apology."

"No, I mean it," he said. "I hate that I hurt you."

"It's okay."

He shook his head and looked like he was on the verge of tears. He grabbed me and pulled me to him, kissing my cheek as he said, "I wouldn't hurt you for the world. I was just so jealous I couldn't see straight. I didn't even know I had it in me to be like that."

He was making me so sad. I felt tears stream down my cheeks. We were healing then, after we had hurt each other. It was a good feeling to heal together like that. It brought us closer to admit to each other the things we had admitted.

"Don't cry," he said and wiped my face with his thumb. "I can't stand to see you hurting like this."

"I'm not hurting so bad," I said. "I'm just feeling an enormous amount of love for you right now."

He seemed almost shocked, as if he didn't think I could ever love him after what he'd done. "Really? You feel love?"

I nodded. "I feel love. Lots of it."

He smiled, but then it disappeared as quickly as it came. "I am just so sorry."

I held his face with my hand and forced him to look into my eyes. "It's okay. It's understandable. I forgive you."

He nodded but shrugged. "I don't know what came over me. You know I would never hurt you, right?"

"I know."

He began to kiss me, kiss the tears off my face, kiss me everywhere, from my forehead to my breasts, to my legs. Soft kisses that made me tingle and want more.

He murmured something. I opened my eyes and stared down at him, kissing my feet. I said, "What?"

"What did it feel like?" he asked and stared back at me.

"What do you mean?"

He crawled up my body until we were nose to nose. "What did it feel like with him?"

Was he serious? Did he really want to know? What could I tell him? And if I told him, would he get upset again?

"It was okay," I lied, thinking that was the best route to go and smiled at him. "Not like what we do."

"Like we do?"

"Yeah," I said and wrapped my arms around his neck. "When we have sex, it's like we have a strong connection. A soul connection, like a soul fuck."

He stared at me and said, "I know what you mean. But I want to know what you felt when you fucked him."

"Just lust."

"If it was just lust," he said. "You wouldn't have let him spend the night."

That was true. But I didn't want to hurt him anymore. I wanted this to be over so we could resume our lives and get onto the living.

"You can tell me," he said and began to kiss me again. "You can tell me and I won't get mad."

His touches were becoming more concentrated and I felt them; I felt them teasing me, preparing me for the orgasm that lay ahead. I felt him bringing me under his control, like he always did whenever we were alone like this. And, as he did this, I began to feel freer and I began to tell him.

"It was hot," I muttered and felt embarrassed.

"Where did you do it?"

"On the bed."

"On this bed?" he asked and stared at it, then back at me.

I bit my bottom lip and nodded. "Yeah, here and once in the kitchen."

"On the table?" he asked and his hand went between my legs.

"No," I said. "On the floor."

"What did he do to you?" he asked and began to play with me, with my pussy which was so wet it was dripping.

"He gave me..." I stopped.

"What?"

"He kissed me down there."

"Like this?" he asked and pushed my legs open wider and gave my pussy one good long stroke with his tongue.

I shivered and muttered, "Yeah."

"Or did he do this?" he asked and pressed his mouth against it and his tongue came out and gave it another lick.

"Yeah, like that," I moaned and began to feel the orgasm.

"Or did he do this?" he said and pulled away from me and flipped me over. He grabbed my ass and raised it in the air and then pushed his cock inside me. It felt so good, I gasped.

"Yeah, like that," I moaned.

He gave a hard thrust and grabbed my head and pulled it to him. "Did he fuck you like this?"

"Yeah," I moaned. "He did."

He gave another thrust that sent me over the edge. I was *this* close to coming. I was so wound up I could have jumped off the bed and humped the leg of a chair. But I wasn't going anywhere. I didn't have to. He was going to give it to me.

"You like that, don't you?" he asked and began to ride me.

I held onto the bedpost and moaned, "Yeah, I do."

"Yeah, you like it," he said and didn't stop. "Tell me you like it."

"I like it," I moaned.

"How much?"

"A lot!" I gasped and began to come. I couldn't do anything then but hang on for the ride, hold onto him as we both began to come and we were coming hard. It was the most intense sex we'd ever had. So intense I was screaming with ecstasy and with pain. It hurt to fuck like that. But it was a good hurt.

Once the orgasm began to trickle away, we fell to the bed and he grabbed me and pulled me into his arms. He began to kiss me and I lay there and kissed back. He stopped suddenly and eyed me.

"Are you still going to see him?" he asked.

"No," I said.

"Why?"

"Because I don't want to lose us."

He sighed. "You can still see him."

"Wes—"

"No, I mean it. You can still see him."

"But I don't want to," I lied. "I don't want to see him."

"You don't?"

I shook my head. "No, it hurts you too much."

"I'll get through it," he said. "And something like sex shouldn't break us up."

"But—"

"But if you're going to do this," he said, cutting me off again. "I want something."

"What?"

"I want to watch."

"What!" I screeched.

"You have to let me watch," he said.

My mouth fell open. "Are you kidding me?"

"No," he said and straddled me, squeezing my body between his legs. "I want to see what he does to you."

I couldn't believe what I was hearing.

"But more importantly," he said. "I want to see you. I want to see your face when you're getting fucked."

I was dumbfounded.

"Don't tell him I'm going to do it," he said. "I don't want him to know I'm here."

"I don't know if I can do that," I said and shook my head.

"You can," he said. "You can do anything you damn well please. A guy like me can't stop you."

"What does that mean?"

"It means," he said and kissed my nipple. "I want you to be who you are. I want you to be free. And once you're free, I can be free and we can be happier than we ever imagined."

"So this is about you, too?"

"It's about us," he said. "Me and you doing what we want to do and what I want right now is to see you get fucked."

I was stumped.

Comedy of errors.

Even as I was setting the "date" up with Zack, I couldn't believe I was doing it. I felt devious and weird. I don't know why I even agreed but I had, so I had to go through with it.

"Just relax," Wes said. "Don't even think about me being there. Okay?"

Now that was going to be hard. How could I *not* think about him being there? He was going to be in the closet like some damn peeping Tom, for God's sake!

"This is how it will work," he said. "Invite him over here, bring him into the bedroom and do your thing. I'll watch from the closet and when you're done, make him leave."

He didn't know but when Zack came over, his visits weren't that short. We didn't do quickies.

"I don't know, Wes," I said. "This is just a little too weird for me."

"How is it weird?"

"Well, you're going to be in the closet like some pervert watching us and it's going to make me uncomfortable as hell."

"You don't understand," he said.

"Maybe I could just set up a video camera."

He seemed to like that idea, but then he shook his head. "No, I want to see the real thing."

"Why don't you just go to a sex club or something?"

"Because I want to see *you*, not some damn bimbo who's pretending she's getting off. I want to see you doing it."

"Me doing what exactly?"

"Damn it," he said, exasperated. "You getting off with another guy. I want to see what you look like while you're doing it. It's not about the act itself, it's about you."

Oh.

"It's like… Almost like you're my very own…"

"What?"

"Porno actress."

Really? Wow. I liked that idea but this was just mind boggling. I couldn't get around the fact that he wanted to see me like that. Especially after he had freaked out on me like he had. I didn't want another freak out.

"You can't freak out," I said. "If you see it and it pisses you off, you have to stay in that damn closet."

"I know," he said. "This is just as much for me as it is for you."

"Ya think?" I asked sarcastically and rolled my eyes.

"I have to get over this jealousy and I want you to help me," he said and put his arms around my waist.

"This is just so weird," I said and shook my head at him.

"It feels weird now, but once you do it, it won't."

"How would you know?"

"I just do," he said.

What did that mean? Maybe he thought if I went through it, then it wouldn't be a big deal once it was over. I didn't know what the hell he meant. All I knew was that this was going to turn out bad. I felt it in my gut. How could it have turned out otherwise?

"Okay," I muttered and left it at that. I was still feeling guilty for fucking Zack in the first place and I guess I thought if I did what Wes wanted me to, then I could make it up to him. But this felt a little extreme.

I didn't even know why Wes wanted this. It was out of the blue. At first, he was livid with jealousy and now he was curious. I couldn't get my head around it but then decided he wanted to see it so he could cut me loose. Seeing me fuck some other guy would make him fall out of love with me. It would be easier that way.

I hated it. I hated the thought of it and I almost hated Wes for putting me in this position. Even if I'd brought it on myself.

I almost considered telling Zack about it, just so he'd know, but, sensing my doubt, Wes said, "And don't tell him anything abut it. He might not be able to get it up if you do."

"What are you? A sex expert or something?"

"I've read a few books," he said.

Whatever. I guess I should have a read a few books myself. I just hoped it turned out alright. I didn't want Zack to feel like he was on display or something and I hoped he would never know what I had set up.

The big day finally arrived. Zack came over to my house right at noon, like he always did on Wednesdays. Wes had taken the day off for this special occasion. I was almost mad at him over all this. It was getting too complicated and like I said, it was just a little too weird for me. What if this happened and what if that happened? It was truly going to end up being a comedy of errors. I could almost hear the canned laughter as I imagined Zack and Wes confronting each other. "No, I'm her boyfriend," they'd both say right before I came in and got caught in the middle. *Argh!*

But I had agreed and I couldn't back out. I might as well do it and let the chips fall where they may. I just hoped they didn't fall on me. I could see how this might work out badly. I could see Wes storming out of the closet and taking Zack by surprise. I just see them beating the shit out of each other. They were both large men, both over six foot and both muscular as hell. That thought brought some sexy imagines to my head. Divine. They were both so damn divine. If I could just have both of them...

What? What was that? No. I never wanted one of those. I never even considered having a threesome. But now I was considering it and it sounded almost like a good idea. No, I wasn't. I wasn't *that* into sex. No, not me. I mean, who would want that? I stopped myself but the fantasy of both of them giving it to me came hard and I almost fell over with lust. I saw both of them pawing at me, grabbing at my body, kissing me, fucking me.

I guess I did want it. I was t*hat* into sex.

I shook myself. No. That would never happen. Things like that only happened in porno movies. And this wasn't a porno movie. This was my life. And after this was all said and done, I had a distinct feeling it was going to suck bad.

Zack came over promptly at noon. He came with another box of chocolates which he knew I couldn't eat. I mean, I was a personal trainer and if I got fat, I would lose my job. I appreciated the thought even though I'd have to throw them in the garbage. Just where our relationship/fling was going to go after today.

I mean, this couldn't work out right. It just couldn't. It had disaster written all over it. Any fool could see it from a mile away. *Danger, danger, leave premises immediately! Odd sexual behavior going on!*

Zack kissed my cheek and said, "You look absolutely beautiful today."

I blushed. It embarrassed me whenever I got compliments like that. Thanks. You don't look so bad yourself.

"Thanks," I said and let him into the house. "How are you today?"

He grabbed me, pulled me into his arms and said, "I'm horny, baby."

I laughed nervously and said, "Well, you came to the right place."

"I always do and I come the right way," he said and laughed at his dumb joke. I didn't laugh. Usually his dumb jokes cracked me up mainly because he was the one telling them. He got a slightly wicked twinkle in his eyes whenever he told one and then would wait in anticipation to see if I would laugh. I never laughed at the joke, but I laughed because he wanted me to laugh. He cracked me up, not the jokes. But today, I couldn't have laughed if my life depended on it.

"Oh," I said.

He smiled and bent to kiss me. I couldn't relax at first but then I did and started to get into it. I responded and tried to steer him over to the couch.

"No," he whispered. "Let's go into the bedroom."

Oh, boy. Here it was. Step to it.

"Okay," I said a little high-pitched. I cleared my throat and said, "Okay. Let's go."

He grabbed my hand and led me into the bedroom, pushed me back on the bed and began to kiss me through my clothes. I lay there stiffly, staring at the closet door, which Wes was peeking out of. I just felt weird, odd. I couldn't relax.

"What's wrong?" he asked and stared into my eyes. "Did I do something wrong?"

"No."

"Then what is it?"

"Nothing," I muttered and stared at the wall.

He kissed my cheek and said, "Come on, tell me."

I stared at him and felt like crying. This was so overwhelming for me. I couldn't get past it to enjoy myself. Wes was the one with the weird problem, not me. It wasn't my fault I couldn't relax and enjoy what Zack wanted to give me. And he wanted to give it to me so badly. I just couldn't allow myself to take it. That was being too selfish and maybe a little weird.

"Come on, baby," he said. "Tell me what's wrong."

"I'm just stressed out," I said.

"Poor baby," he muttered. "We don't have to do anything. We can just lay here and hold each other."

"No!" I said a little too shrilly, then calmed down. "No, I mean, we can do stuff."

"Are you sure?" he asked. "I just want to make sure you're in the mood is all."

"I'm sure," I said and smiled weakly. "Come on."

I rose up off the bed and pressed my lips against his, but I didn't feel the initial little shock of excitement, of pleasure, I normally did. He didn't seem to notice and began to kiss me.

I responded at first but I kept thinking about Wes staring at us and I couldn't get into it. I was so nervous that nothing felt good, nothing felt *right*. But what if… What if I told him that Wes was in there? What if I made Wes come out and confess that we'd set this up? It couldn't be any worse than this feeling of loathing I had. And I had it. I felt like I was deceiving Zack and I didn't like that feeling at fucking all.

I took a chance. "Hold on."

"What?" he asked and his eyes narrowed at me.

"Just sit tight," I said and went to the closet and opened the door all the way. "Come out, Wes."

No answer. This really was threatening to become a comedy of errors.

"Come on, Wes," I said and looked in the closet. He wasn't there! Where was he? I looked around the room, and then focused on the bathroom door. He was in the bathroom.

"What are you doing?" Zack asked suspiciously.

I stared at him and thought about laughing it off. But then what? I had to tell him. I hated to lie, to be devious. It just wasn't in my nature.

"What kind of game is this?" he asked and came over to me.

"It's not a game," I said. "I—"

He cut me off by kissing me and then he took me over, took control of me. The next thing I knew, he had my skirt hiked over my hips and was going down on me. I couldn't stop myself from enjoying that. I draped my leg over his shoulder and got into it, got into the cool but sweet sensations his tongue and mouth and salvia were giving me.

I glanced over at the bathroom. No movement. Maybe Wes had left. Maybe he had crawled out of the window. I didn't know but I did know I was about to have a little orgasm. It came at me and devoured me, then went away as quickly as it came. I shuddered and Zack pushed me up against the wall and I helped him unzip his pants and put his cock inside me. He fucked me standing up, up against the wall and before I knew what was happening, I was coming again. I was so caught up in the moment and the idea of someone watching—of Wes watching—was actually beginning to turn me on. I could just feel his eyes on me, devouring me the way that Zack was devouring me then, with his lips and hands and dick. I stared towards the bathroom and suddenly wanted him in there, watching me get off.

"Ahh," Zack moaned and came inside me. He gave a few more thrusts before kissing me. "That was so good, baby."

"I know," I said and kissed him back.

"Give me a minute and we'll do it again."

I stared at him and nodded, then looked over his shoulder and gasped. Wes was standing there behind us, staring at us, staring at us still joined together. And we stared at each other and both of us felt something shift in our relationship, in our hearts and in our souls. It was acceptance of me being sexual, of me being a woman and him being a man. Acceptance of both of us for what we were. This was why he wanted it, to show me how it could be, how good it could be. I was so overcome with emotion, I almost started crying.

"What is it?" Zack asked and looked over his shoulder. He saw Wes and his mouth dropped open, then he stared back at me. "What the hell is going on here?"

Before I could answer, Wes was at Zack and I just knew he was going to start a fight. But he didn't. He grabbed him by the shoulder and literally pulled him off me and then he was on me, kissing me, devouring me. I responded before I could help myself. Maybe it was because that lust I felt, that lust which surged though my body. I wanted to share that lust. I moaned and ate at his mouth as he ate at mine, then he was eating at my breasts. Then he was fucking me just like Zack had done a minute or so earlier. I don't know what Zack did, or what he was thinking. I was just overcome by Wes and couldn't think of anything besides his fucking me and me fucking back and my next orgasm, which was right there in front of me, dangling closely, letting me know I could reach for it at any time. I grabbed it and came, just like *that*. All the lust I had ever felt seemed to swell inside of me at the moment I came. I had never felt such liberation as I did then.

Wes came with a grunt and a groan and then he pulled my head back and thrust his tongue in my mouth, kissing me hard. I kissed back and moaned as the orgasm finally left me, leaving its mark all over my body, which was red and ready for another round.

Zack was staring at us. I kissed Wes and stared back. I wanted him too, I wanted him again. Right now. Something inside me had been awakened and I was ready for it to take me to the next level.

Zack shook his head and started out of the room.

"Don't go," I said. "I can explain."

"You don't have to," he muttered.

I moved away from Wes and ran after him, grabbed his hand and said, "Listen to me. I don't know what to say, but—"

"You don't have to say anything. I understand."

"You do?"

"Yeah," he said and glanced at Wes. "He gets off watching you fuck other guys. I was one of the other guys."

"No!" I exclaimed. "It's not like that."

"Looks like that to me."

I turned to Wes for help. "Tell him Wes."

"It's true," Wes said and cleared his throat. "This was the first time."

Zack stared at him like he didn't believe him.

"Really," I said. "He saw us together one day and he got really pissed off but then he wanted to… And I'm sorry if you don't like it or whatever, but…" I stopped. I really didn't know what to say.

"But," Zack said. "I thought you and I had something special."

"We do," I said. "We can."

"But you're with him," he said and jerked his head over to Wes. "And that means you can't ever be with me."

"That's not true," I said.

"Listen," Wes said. "It was just a once in a lifetime thing. It's over now. I apologize if it made you uncomfortable."

"Made me uncomfortable?" Zack said and pointed at himself. "Yeah, you could say that!"

"Zack, it's not like that," I said and held his arm tighter. "Just—"

"Leave me alone," he said and shoved me away from him, shoved me so hard, I fell to the floor and felt like a fool.

Then my worse fear came true. Wes was on Zack in a second and they were fighting, kicking, punching the shit out of each other.

"Stop it!" I screamed and tried to tear them apart. "Stop it now!"

But they weren't stopping. They were going to beat the life out of one another. I sat there and watched numbly and wondered what I could do. Wes was now punching Zack in the face. After he got a couple of punches in, Zack grabbed his arm and gave him a good one back. I was almost in awe of this fight. It was the best I'd ever seen. And, I hate to admit it, but it turned me on beyond belief. These two strong men fighting over me? Oh, God, those muscles. I couldn't watch for long or there would be nothing left of either one of them, so I did what I had to do.

I threw my head back and screamed at the top of my lungs. Screamed until I was hoarse and screamed until they stopped fighting and just stared at me. When I finally stopped, I couldn't speak because my throat was so dry.

Zack got up and fetched me a glass of water and Wes rubbed my back.

"Are you okay?" he asked with concern.

I shook my head and grabbed the water out of Zack's hand and downed it.

"Are you going to be alright?" Zack asked.

I held one finger up and he clamped his mouth shut. When I got my voice back I said, "You two have really got a lot of nerve."

They just stared at me.

"You're fighting over me like I'm a piece of meat," I hissed though I was far from being pissed off. I was too turned on to be pissed off. I couldn't let them know that, though.

They dropped their heads.

"I mean, come on," I said and pulled my skirt down. "Where do you get off?!"

Wes started to say something but I held my hand up and he shut his mouth.

"Uh uh," I snapped and resumed pacing. "I agreed to do this, Zack, because Wes was so overcome with jealousy that he couldn't see straight. Sorry, but that's why. No, we've never done this before and if you think we're a bunch of perverts, then fine. I don't give a shit."

He nodded and glanced at Wes, then down at the floor.

I turned to Wes. "And I agreed to do this for you. *You!* And you repay me by beating the shit out of him? Who do you think you are?"

He shrugged and looked ashamed. Good enough for him.

"I am not going to put up with this shit," I said. "We're here now and whatever that means, then that's what it means. Sorry, life works like this sometimes. You do crazy things and sometimes they work out and sometimes they backfire."

They nodded simultaneously.

"Now I'm going to take a shower," I said and turned on my heel. "If you like, we can talk some more when I'm done."

As soon as the warm water hit me, I began to calm down. And I began to think about them, both of them giving it to me. The idea was divine and sexy. It was a little too much and in a matter of minutes, I had convinced myself if I could get them both to fuck me at the same time, then all of this could be over. I could also give this whole threesome thing a try and see what all the fuss was about.

I got out of the shower and wrapped a towel around my body then went back into the bedroom. Wes was sitting on the bed and Zack was in a chair. They weren't talking or looking at each other. I could feel the tension. I was determined to change it and make it all better, for all three of us.

"Now," I said and clapped my hands together. "We can do one or two things. We can leave this room and forget it ever happened. Or we can move on and do it the right way."

"What?" Wes asked.

"If we're going to do this, we're going to do it the right way," I said. "And that means, both of you are going to fuck me at the same time."

They weren't the least bit shocked. Well, they were a little but I could tell the idea was just as intriguing to them as it was to me. I took the towel off and stood before them naked and as their eyes drank me in, I felt a surge of sexual power wash all over me and give me the courage to do this. I felt like such a woman then, naked but in control. I had what they both wanted. And that made me want this.

I went over to the bed and lay down. "Wes, come over here."

He came over and sat down beside me.

"Come on, Zack," I said and watched him walk over and sit on my opposite side. "Now sit back and relax and let's see how this goes."

"Katrina," Wes said. "Are you sure you want to do this?"

"Yeah, I am," I said. "And I want to see if you two can do it as well. You think you got the balls?"

They glanced sideways at each other and nodded.

To be honest, I didn't know if I could go through with it. I could tell that our first ménage a trois was going to be nerve wracking. I was apprehensive because I'd never done anything like that and I was more than sure they hadn't either. What if I pissed one of them off? What if I upset one of them by doing something the other had never seen before? If I kissed Zack first would that make Wes jealous?

I tried not to think about it and just did what felt right.

I offered Wes my mouth and Zack my pussy. Both seemed pleased with my decision and responded accordingly. I took Zack's hand and pushed between it my legs and then I pressed my lips against Wes's. His mouth opened and as our tongues touched, a deep moan came out of my lips. I was so turned on. I felt Zack's hand between my legs, touching me and exploring my pussy, fingering me. He got between my legs and pulled them open and he dove in, eating at me, licking at me and kissing at me. It felt *so* good.

Wes moved back and I unzipped his pants, grabbed his cock and began to suck at it as Zack sucked at me. I loved having it in my mouth as I was being eaten. The two sensations were thrilling. I tasted Wes's precum and I could feel myself about to orgasm.

I stared down at Zack and said, "Put it in me."

He nodded and pulled it out and pushed his hard cock inside me, filling me up and as he concentrated on fucking me, I concentrated on Wes whose head was thrown back with a look of ecstasy on his face. I smiled because then I had both of them in my control, both of them by the balls. Both of them inside of me in different but similar ways.

Zack's fucking because more concentrated and I began to focus on Wes more. I could tell if I gave a little more effort to Zack I would have come really quickly. But I wanted this to last. Both of their hands were on me. Zack had his face buried in my neck and he was kissing it and sucking on it. Wes was squeezing my breast with his hand and all the sensations mingled in the exact right way and it was overpowering. Before I could stop myself, I was coming and so was Wes. His hot cum just shot into my mouth and I sucked him dry as I came, slurped it up and wanted more.

Zack came just then and grunted as he filled my pussy up with himself, with his hot cum. I loved that feeling. I loved the dirtiness of all of this. Of getting off because you were horny and doing it because it felt good to do it. We were doing it for the pleasure of doing it. And it was a pleasure to do it.

When it was over, we fell away from each other. I noticed they didn't really look at each other. Not that much. But I couldn't take my eyes off them. Damn, they were so hot.

Wes got up and lit me a cigarette. As I smoked it, I inhaled with satisfaction and wondered when we could do it again. I was so lost in my thoughts that I didn't hear something Zack just said.

"What'd you say?" I asked.

Zack said, "We should do this again.

Wes agreed by nodding. "I mean, if you want to, Katrina."

I grinned and couldn't believe my luck. Did I want to? Were they crazy? Of course I wanted to and I wanted to as soon as I finished my cigarette.

So we did.

Double the pleasure.

So it began. So it was. About once a week, we'd meet up and have a three-way. It was so damn good. I never thought anything like it was possible. But it was. And it was happening to me.

"I have an idea," I said and smiled at Wes and Zack. "Wanna hear it?"

They nodded.

I pulled the scarf from behind me and held it up with one finger. "How about it?"

Wes got my meaning and took the scarf. He and I had done this sort of thing before. Once he even tied me to the bed. So, with a smile, he wrapped it around my head, thusly covering my eyes.

Oh, *y-e-sssss!*

He pushed me back on the bed and I felt Zack lay down next to me. And then I had four hands all over my body, giving me tasty sensation after tasty sensation until I couldn't take it anymore. I moaned and felt one of their mouths on my wet pussy. I moved a little and decided it was Wes down there. Each of them had a distinct technique.

Hands all over me. Hands in my hair, tracing lines across my face, across my belly, across my breasts. Hands teasing me, bringing me intense pleasure.

One of them turned me over and my ass was in the air and I knew, just knew what they were going to do. They were going to give me double the pleasure. They were going to double penetrate me. We had never talked about it and we pretended not to think about it. I had always wondered *when* they would do it. I had never wondered *if.*

To be honest, I didn't know if I could take it. But I didn't have much choice. I wouldn't know which orifice either of them would take, but I had a feeling Wes would take my pussy and Zack would take the other less charted area. He and I had done that only once but I knew we'd do it again. Today seemed to be the day.

Wes fucked me for a long minute which made my juices flow even more and then I felt the Zack's dick. It was slowly easing into me. It took its time, took time to take care, to make sure it wasn't a sudden entry, a sudden jerk which might bring me pain. No, it wanted to make sure it was *all good.*

And it was. It was all good. Zack's hard cock was almost all the way in and combined with Wes's hard cock and the intensity of the moment, I could barely do anything but pant. It was all this feeling, all this feeling combined with just a touch of pain, which soon eased into euphoria as I realized I was going beyond the limits. I was doing something purely for the pleasure of doing it and it was such a deep, intense pleasure, I don't know why I hadn't tried it before.

They began to fuck me then, both of them, at the same time. I had both of them in me simultaneously, together, and that thought of having both of them at the same time turned me on beyond belief. Fucking me like the woman I was; fucking me like the men they were. The strong men who wanted nothing but to bring me pure satisfaction, pure delight. They liked doing that to me; they liked fucking me like I was a piece of meat. I liked being a piece of meat. It added to the dirtiness and made me feel more human, more vulnerable, more susceptible to pleasure.

I don't know how long it went on, the fucking, all I know was that I couldn't get enough. It was the most intense sexual experience I had ever had, probably ever would have and I wanted to enjoy it until the utmost, until the umpteenth time, until I could not take anymore, until my body would not take anymore. Until I exhausted. Until they were exhausted.

I felt Wes's lips on mine and he was kissing me, sucking the life right out of me, like he couldn't get enough. We kept fucking, slamming into each other and Zack was sucking and biting at my neck and Wes's hands and mouth were on my tits, biting at them until I threw my head back and came in a rush. It was all over me, all this sensation and my body was in a flush, a red hot flush from the pleasure. It was all over me, the pleasure, just like their hands were all over me. It was forcing me to succumb to it and to eat it and take it for everything it was worth. I couldn't stop coming. I kept coming and coming and just as I thought I was done, it would come back at me stronger, with just a slight more intensity that kept me hanging on until the next sputter.

But it didn't last forever. If it had of, I might have collapsed. I did collapse just after they both came and were pulling away from me, breathing heavily, trying to get their senses back. It took me a good five minutes before I could even utter a word and then the only thing I could say was, "Damn."

★★★★★

Tony yelled, "You never did that with me!"

"So what?" I said offhandedly. "You never did it with me either."

"You never asked me to!"

I sighed and stared at my fingernails, then said, "Whatever."

"How could you?" he asked. "I mean, *how could you*?"

"Tony, you hypocrite. You divorced me, remember?"

"Yeah, but you weren't this worldly woman then."

"Maybe you didn't know me all that well."

He grunted, "Maybe you didn't know yourself."

And maybe that was it. I didn't know myself back then. Maybe I was no nearer to knowing myself now than I was then but I knew one thing, I was having a damn good time.

"You need to marry one of them," he said.

"You're not getting out of paying alimony, Tony."

"I mean, I just don't think you can do that."

"Do what?" I asked.

"Have two boyfriends at the same time."

I rolled my eyes.

"You know," he said. "You're getting turned out."

"What's that?"

"When a woman starts enjoying sex, she starts wanting it all the time."

I thought about that. Maybe he was right. Maybe I was getting turned out. But I knew it was just my dirty thirties.

"Why couldn't you get turned out when we were together?" he asked.

I stared at the phone and wondered why I still called him. He really got on my nerves sometimes.

"Fuck off, Tony," I said and hung up on him.

Two-times over.

I wanted my fun, but I didn't let my boys "run" over me. I wasn't a doormat. It was all in good fun. I was having the time of my life. I was in La La Land most of the time. My clients at the gym even noticed. I wasn't as much of hard-ass as I had been before.

"Only ten lunges?" Sara, whom I'd been training for years, asked. "Are you sure?"

I nodded and smiled at her. Then I realized what I'd just done. "No, I was just kidding. Give me fifty."

She started to do it then said, "What about pushups?"

I was already back in La La Land when she said this. I muttered, "Give me five."

"Five?"

"No," I snapped. "Forty."

"Girl pushups?" she asked hopefully.

"You know better than that."

She groaned and got to it. I looked across the room to see Zack, who had suddenly appeared. He smiled at me. I smiled back and he came over and said, "I just dropped by to take you to lunch."

"Great," I said. "We're almost through here."

"Not quite," Sara muttered and lunged.

"Ten more, Sara," I said.

"Bitch," she muttered.

"Just do it," I said and turned to Zack. "It'll be a few minutes."

"Okay," he said and kissed my cheek. "I have a few calls to make, so I'll be in the car when you're ready."

I smiled at him and then he walked back out of the gym.

"Done!" Sara exclaimed, and then rubbed her thigh. "That hurts."

"Do your pushups," I said.

She leaned over and whispered in my ear, "Is it just me or do I detect that you have a new boyfriend?"

I just stared at her and said, "Something like that."

She smiled at me and said, "Go ahead and leave. I'll finish up on my own."

"No, I can't do that."

"Do it for me," she said. "Go on."

"Promise me you'll finish your sets?"

"I promise."

"Really?" I asked.

"Yeah."

"Gee, thanks Sara," I said and patted her shoulder. "I owe you one."

She stared after Zack and said, "Just tell me where to get one like that."

"I got him from a factory," I said. "But his model's been discontinued."

She laughed and said, "Just go."

I raced into the bathroom and changed, then raced out to Zack's SUV and then we were off to a little diner down the street. Once we had ordered, Zack said, "I have a surprise for you."

"Oh great," I said and leaned over and kissed his cheek. "I love surprises. What is it?"

"I want to take you to Hawaii," he said.

"Really?" I squealed. "I've never been to Hawaii."

"Well, you're going now," he said, smiling. "You know, I used to surf a lot. I want to teach you and Hawaii has the best waves."

"Cool," I said. "But I'll have to check with Wes first."

"Oh," he said casually. "I already have."

"Excuse me?"

"I already got it cleared with him," he said and gave me a big, old smile. "He's cool with it."

He was? *What the hell?*

"But you didn't even ask me first," I said defensively.

"Well, it's not like I *wasn't* going to ask you," he replied and took a sip of his coke. "Why are you mad?"

I crossed my arms and hissed, "Because you two are going around behind my back talking about me."

"Well, it's all good, baby," he said and nodded. "We both think you're the best."

I glared at him. "I don't give a shit. It's like you're becoming best friends. I feel ganged up on."

"We're not ganging up on you," he said and shook his head. "Why are you pissed?"

"I don't know," I snapped. "But I am."

The waitress just then slapped our plates down on the table. I ignored her and the food.

"You know," Zack said and shook a bottle of steak sauce. "You're taking this way too seriously."

"I'm taking this way too seriously?" I asked and thought about it. Oh, shit I was. What was wrong with me? Maybe because of them talking without me around made me feel I was losing some of the control in the relationship. I didn't know. Maybe it was just PMS.

"Yes, you are," he said and sighed. "Now, let's get this straight. We're going to Hawaii and you're going to let up on the bitching."

"You're pushing your luck, buddy."

He just stared at me. "I'm serious. Let up a little, would you?"

"I'll consider it."

Of course, I went to Hawaii. I wasn't about to turn down a free trip.

It was great. Zack taught me how to surf—i.e. how to fall off a board and into the water without drowning myself. We went to a luau. We frolicked in the sand and drank mai tai's. Then we'd make our way back to our room and have all this hot, island sex. Sex with him in Hawaii was some of the best we'd had.

We'd just finished doing just that when he turned to me and said, "I'm going to surf the pipeline tomorrow."

"What?"

"The pipeline," he said. "It's this enormous wave."

"Yeah, I know, I saw a thing about it on TV," I said and studied him. "It's an enormous wave that can get you killed. Even professionals say it's dangerous."

He nodded. "I've always been a daredevil."

"Or an idiot."

"Wanna come?"

"Hell no," I said and shook my head. "I do not want to witness your demise."

"You're not going to witness my demise?" he said and laughed. "Where do you come up with this shit?"

"Don't know."

He leaned over and kissed me. "Are you sure you don't want to come? It'll be fun."

I leaned back and stared at him. "And please tell me how *that* would be fun."

He shrugged. "Just would be."

"I don't think you should do it."

"Why not?"

"Because it's stupid," I said. "And I'll be by myself all day tomorrow."

"You can come."

"Don't want to."

"Ah," he said and grabbed my hand. "Come with me."

I shook my head. "You can go by yourself."

So he did, leaving me asleep in the early morning. I awoke disoriented and stared around the room until I figured out where I was. Then I fell back to sleep for another three or four hours.

I didn't really have any plans so I took a long shower and ordered room service, and then ate on the terrace. I stared out at the ocean and wondered why I, of all people, was so lucky. I had two—not one but two—great men, a great job, a great house and a great life. Here I was on a great vacation. Well, if Zack came back in one piece, it would be a great vacation.

How did I get so damn lucky? What did I do to deserve all this? Well, for one thing, I took a chance. I smiled, thinking about our last threesome. Now that had been nice. We were all so turned on, it was like we would never be sated, but then we were and I fell asleep between them. When I awoke, Zack was gone and had left a note, "See you soon." Wes was still cuddled up next to me.

I was one lucky bitch. I just was. I should just accept it and go about my business. I stared out at the beach. That was my business. No worries today. Hopefully, Zack would be okay and then I would see Wes first thing day after tomorrow and then my normal life would resume.

Would it always be like this?

I almost panicked at the thought if it not being. What if they both left me? What if I got bored with them? What if? What if? What if? So fucking what? That was life. Things changed, people changed, and the world stayed the same. Not much you can do about it.

I got ready and headed down to the beach wearing my big, floppy beach hat. I settled in a lounge chair and took a deep breath. Hawaii had to be the most perfect place on Earth.

I lay there for a while until this guy came by and sat down in the chair next to mine. He gave me a little smile before settling back and closing his eyes. I smiled back and turned over. But then, I realized he looked familiar. I turned back around and I'll be damned. It was Trey Ellison! The movie star! He was sitting right next to me!

I turned back to check and sure enough, it was him. Oh. My. God.

"Hot out here, isn't it?" he asked without opening his eyes.

I mumbled something, I don't even know what it was. I think, it was, "Uh, uh...umm..."

He smiled and squinted at me. "I'm Trey."

Yes, you are.

"Who are you?" he asked and shielded his eyes.

"Katrina," I managed to get out without stuttering.

"Nice to meet you."

"And you," I said as casually as I could. *Trey Ellison was sitting right next to me!* And, oh, he was cute! He had light brown hair and beautiful brown eyes. He was as brown as a nut, too. He was tall and lean, like a surfer. Needless to say, he was my type. But then again, a guy like him was every girl's type.

"Would you like some lunch?" he asked. "I was just going to grab a bite."

I stared at him and bit my lip before I responded, "I would like that very much."

We went to the hotel restaurant and everyone made a big fuss over him. I just sat there and smiled, star-struck. Trey Ellison and I were eating lunch together!

We made mild chitchat and he told me a few things that weren't very interesting about himself. He was from Indiana and he was this and he was that. I just sat there admiring him and when our food arrived, I couldn't eat. He ate heartily and even reached over and ate some of my food.

"Oh, you can have it," I said and pushed my plate over to him. "I'm not hungry."

"I see that," he said and picked up a French fry. "How do you like Hawaii?"

"I love it," I said and couldn't get over the fact that I was sitting there with him. Trey Ellison! Trey Ellison was buying me lunch! How fucking cool was that?!

"Me too," he said. "I could live here. Where are you from?"

"I live in Vegas."

"Now that's a great place, isn't it?" he asked and chuckled. "I love to play in the old part, on Fremont Street."

I nodded and smiled.

He leaned in close to me and said, "Now I might have to make a point to get to Vegas more often."

Did he just say that?!

"You're not taken, are you?" he asked.

I just stared at him.

"A girl like you is always taken," he said knowingly. "Right?"

I smiled shyly and muttered, "I am, actually." I didn't say, two-times over. Yeah, I was taken, two-times over. He didn't need to know that.

"Figures."

I couldn't help but grin like a fool at him.

"Wanna come up to my room for a drink?" he asked.

I stared at him and got his meaning immediately. Why not say, *Wanna come up to my room for a fuck?*

I felt that simply nodding was the best answer. Sure, why not? I knew he did stuff like this all the time but I couldn't help but follow him upstairs. I don't know why, I just did it. When he handed me a drink, I took it and sipped it, feeling nervous and wondering what the hell I was doing. I didn't have to wonder long because he took the glass out of my hand and kissed me. Just like that.

His kiss was soft; it wasn't fiery like I expected it to be. Nevertheless, it felt good and soon I found myself responding to him, going with him as he led me over to the bed and pushed me back on it.

I shoved everything out of my mind, even though I felt a little weird about doing it with him. Why shouldn't I enjoy it? But for some reason, I couldn't relax enough to. I knew it was guilt. I knew I was cheating on my guys and I knew it was wrong. I should just get up and leave.

"Relax," he said and moved over me.

"No, I really need to—"

"Shh," he murmured and kissed me. "Just relax, baby."

I nodded and tried to. I felt out of myself as he undressed me and kissed me all over. It was only when he pulled my legs apart did I finally start to get into it. I closed my eyes and felt him moving down there, between my legs, kissing and licking at me. All of a sudden, nothing mattered but him kissing and licking at me.

I couldn't take it anymore. I wanted him to fuck me. I pulled him up and kissed him and he shoved his hard cock into me. I smiled a little as he began to move, realizing that he wasn't that great, that I was probably a better lover than he was. I could show him a few things, if I wanted to, but for some reason, I didn't really want to. Maybe it was because this was more of a novelty, the pleasure of fucking someone like him.

"You are so hot," he muttered as he fucked me.

I nodded and began to move. I'd at least show him what a good fuck was because, apparently, he didn't know. As I moved, he stared at me, then smiled as I wrapped my legs around his waist. I sucked him into me and clamped my mouth on top of his. He responded by grunting and holding my head still as we kissed.

I kept moving and he slowed down to let me move. I ran my hands through his hair and really began to grind against him. He was having trouble holding it, I could tell, so I let everything go and just concentrated on myself. I might as well get an orgasm.

And I did. As soon as I let myself go, it came at me, tickled me and then burst. I moaned with it as it hit me and he was pumping into me, fucking me with everything he had. He gave one last thrust and it was all over for him. He filled me up and then he collapsed on my chest, breathing heavily.

"Wow," he muttered. "Now that was hot."

I nodded, wishing he'd get off me. He didn't. He turned and kissed my cheek, then pressed his next to mine. What the hell was that about?

"We should do that again," he said and propped himself up on his elbow to stare at me.

I nodded lamely, feeling a little weird. What had I just done? I'd fucked Trey Ellison! I was a star-fucker! I had fucked a star. That's what I'd just done. I had star-fucked. Is this was groupies felt? If so, I was never going to be a groupie. I was feeling a little weird, then I realized it was just guilt. And the guilt was going to eat me alive.

"Just give me a minute," he said and kissed my cheek again. "And we'll do it again."

Like *hell* we would.

"I'll be right back," he said and got up and went into the bathroom.

As soon as the bathroom door closed, I jumped up and pulled on my clothes and ran all the way back to my room, feeling weird about what had just happened. Feeling weird about what it meant.

I stayed in the room all afternoon by myself, flipping channels on the TV. I was in one of the most beautiful places on earth but I couldn't force myself out of that room. I was at odds with what had just happened and it bothered me because I should have enjoyed it more. But I realized I didn't because I was being used and you don't usually enjoy things when someone's using you. But Trey had really been into it. Well, good for him.

And that's why I enjoyed Wes and Zack so much. We weren't using each other. Each experience was unique and different. We were playing and having fun and experiencing each other. And that's what made it different.

I realized I didn't have to fuck anyone else. Having fucked Trey Ellison was enough to teach me that. I had everything I wanted and could ever need with my boys. I was one lucky bitch. I really was.

Zack came back before six looking exhausted.

"How did it go?" I asked and grinned at him, happy to see he was all in one piece. And glad he had come back early so I could distract myself from the thoughts of what'd I'd done earlier.

"I didn't do it," he said sadly.

"You didn't? Why?"

He looked at the wall and said, "I didn't want to meet my demise."

I grinned and walked over to him, pulled his lips down on mine and once they made that initial contact, I knew Trey Ellison would be nothing in my memory but a sad mistake. This, what we had, was *something*. Something I never wanted to lose.

Coming home.

When I got back, Wes was waiting on me at my house. He jumped on me and fucked me before I could even get out a hello.

"God," he murmured. "I've missed you so much, baby."

"I missed you, too," I said and stared into his eyes as we fucked. "I've missed this."

He grinned and took my face in his hands and kissed me. "I love you so much."

"I love you, too," I said and arched away from the bed. "I love fucking you so much."

"Whenever I fuck you," he muttered. "It's like coming home. I get homesick when you go away."

"Mmm," I moaned and grabbed his face, kissing him. "I've missed you, too."

He began to eat at my lips, at my face and at my breasts. I lay there and squirmed against him, sucking him into me. I loved the heaviness of his body on mine. I thought briefly about Trey Ellison collapsing on me. I shuddered with guilt and pushed him out of my mind and concentrated back on Wes, who was so far gone, I had to catch up or there'd be nothing left for me.

I wrapped my legs around his waist and pressed against him. Soon we were slapping up against each other, as our fucking took over our bodies. We held onto it for a long time, just enjoying the sensation, and then I felt the orgasm.

"Oh, God, yeah!" I cried and felt it grip me and rip through my body. "Ahhhh... YEAHHHH!"

He was close behind. He pounded into me and I felt his hot cum fill me. I moaned and licked at his face and then he collapsed on top of me and was quiet. I kissed his temple and pressed my face next to his.

Phew. That was quick. I'd been home less than five minutes and I had already been laid. I'd have to go away more often if this was what I was going to get when I came home.

"Next time," he said, pulling back to stare into my eyes. "We all go and we get two separate rooms."

I grinned. "And I can scurry back and forth?"

"Yeah," he said but then his smiled dropped. "How long is this thing going to last?"

"What do you mean?"

"I mean," he said and sighed. "How long with this threesome or ménage a trois or whatever it's called... How long before... You know?"

I didn't know. It couldn't last forever. Things like this didn't last. They never did. I mean, you never hear of anyone being in a relationship with two guys and having divine threesomes. I'd never even heard of it even happening at all. I guess we were just unique. Or we didn't know much about how other people lived.

"It'll last," I said and smoothed the hair back from his forehead. "Until one of us gets bored with it or one of us doesn't want to do it anymore. That's how long it will last."

He nodded, liking my answer. "Okay. I was just wondering."

I smiled and kissed him, pulling him back on top of me, opening my legs to him, myself up to him, missing the way his cock filled me and feeling whole once it was replaced.

"God, I love you," he said and began to fuck me. "I love you so much."

"I love you, too," I said and moaned, kissing and licking at his face and neck. "I love you so, so much."

He fucked me for a moment, then held my head still and forced me to look into his eyes. He resumed like that, fucking me, taking me, staring into my eyes, not letting them waver for one second. He had me then and he knew it. And I had him and I had the world and I loved it. I loved having everything I had and wanting all of it, being glad that this was where I was at that exact moment, being glad to be alive.

"Let's stay like this forever," he said. "You and me."

I nodded and felt him, all of him at that moment in time. And then I felt a pang of guilt. Guilt because I had cheated on him and on Zack. It didn't mean anything. I could have done without it but then I had done it, mostly due in part to see if I *could* do it.

"Wes," I said. "I need to tell you something."

"Shh," he said and fucked me, grinding himself into me. "Just feel it."

I pushed all thoughts out of my head and felt what he was giving me then. I felt all of it, all of the love he had for me and because of that feeling, I began to come, I began to orgasm and it was a sweet one, a sweet one that was a little bitter because I had done something I shouldn't have.

He was coming too and as he came, he moaned a deep moan that told me he loved me and that what we were doing was more important than anything else we could ever do. We were giving ourselves to each other and because of that nothing else mattered, nor would it ever matter.

So I decided to keep my big mouth shut.

Honesty.

Of course, I wrestled with it for days. I would decide to tell them, and then would decide against it, and then I would go crazy for a few minutes before I always came to the exact same conclusion: I didn't know what I was going to do.

So I kept my mouth shut, decided that was the best thing to do. But I felt, in a way, I had betrayed them. On the surface, it really wasn't that big a deal. But underneath, it was eating me alive.

I knew I was wrestling with it because I was having so much fun with them. I knew something bad might happen if I told them and maybe I was setting myself up for failure. Maybe I didn't want to be happy. Maybe I couldn't stand it. Why did I deserve all this? What was so special about me anyway?

It was guilt, pure and simple guilt. I hated it and tried to shake it off and get back to the moment, but I couldn't. I knew I was punishing myself. Punishing myself because, I suppose, it was time. I'd been happy for too long. I'd been content and blissful and that stuff can't last forever. Something had to ruin it. I suppose I was the one who was going to ruin it for myself.

Self-sabotage is a bitch.

This went on for days until I decided I would tell them. I wanted to tell them because... Because I was part fool and part optimist. I thought if I told them, we could all laugh it off. And then, I could move on from it. I could free myself just by being honest.

But then I remembered Wes's extreme reaction when he'd found out about Zack and me. I didn't want a repeat of that. And what would Zack do? He might throw something through the window. Even though he was extremely laid back, he wasn't laid back when it came to me. He was very protective and once when we were out and this guy accidentally pushed me, he threatened to kick his ass until the guy backed away apologizing.

No way was I telling them. Fuck 'em. It would be my secret and eventually I'd get over the guilt. Until then, I'd suffer in silence. I was never cheating again. I wasn't built for it.

A few days after we got back from Hawaii, I invited them both over for dinner and then a little later on, a little something-something. And then after that, we could do it again.

After we'd finished eating and were sitting around sipping wine and talking, the phone rang. Wes got up to answer it. I didn't bat an eye because he always answered the phone at my house and I always answered it at his. It was just one of those couple things we did.

"Hello," he said.

"Oh," Zack said and leaned over towards me. "I forgot to tell you that you packed a pair of your shorts into my suitcase."

"Why didn't you bring them?" I asked and sipped my wine.

"I forgot until now," he said. "I'll get them to you tomorrow or the next day."

I nodded and glanced at Wes, who was on the phone, a look of consternation on his face. He turned to me and his eyes narrowed. I sat up taller and asked, "Who is it?"

He turned away from me and said, "Yes, this is her house. Who is this again?"

What was going on?

"Who?" he asked. "I don't understand. What? Who am I? I'm her fiancé. Who are you? Huh? Her what?"

He turned to stare at me. I suddenly realized what was happening and what was about to unfold. I sunk down in my seat. Oh, no. This couldn't be happening to me! Not again!

"And why are you calling her?" he asked, still staring at me. "Oh, really? You met in Hawaii? Is that so? Huh. You've had a hard time finding her but now you have? Huh again. Can you talk to her? Yeah. Hold on."

I almost reached for the phone, but he didn't hand it to me. He hung it up and then turned on me, a look of fury in his eyes.

"Why the hell is Trey Ellison calling you?" he snapped.

I sunk down deeper in my seat, wishing I could just disappear. I decided to play dumb. "What do you mean? Trey Ellison? That must have been a joke. I bet it was Tony."

"It wasn't Tony," he said. "It was Trey Ellison. Why is he calling you?"

Stonewall, girl! Stone-fucking-wall!

"Katrina?" he asked.

I shrugged. "I bet it was Nick, from the gym. He's such a hoot! Pretending to be Trey Ellison! I'll get him for this!"

"Trey Ellison the movie star?" Zack asked looking at me. "I heard he was in our hotel when we were in Hawaii…"

I watched his face at it dawned on him.

"…oh," he muttered. "Oh."

One, two, three. Now all the pieces to the puzzle were in place. Thanks, Trey, you lousy fuck!

Zack stood up and pointed at me. "You fucked him!"

I jumped up and said, "No, I didn't!"

"Then why did he say you two were 'old lovers'?" Wes asked.

"Because we… We, uh… When I was a cocktail waitress, he was at the casino one night and—"

"Shut up," Wes said, shaking his head. "If you're going to lie, at least try."

"You were a cocktail waitress?" Zack asked.

"No, she wasn't!" Wes snapped. "Katrina, did you fuck him?"

I stared at Wes, then at Zack, then at my feet. I nodded lamely.

"You fucked him," Wes asked and shook his head at me like a teacher. "I can't believe you fucked him."

"He was just one guy," I said.

"One guy?" Zack said. "Aren't we enough for you?"

"Of course you are!" I exclaimed and suddenly felt defensive. "Why are you two so mad?"

They just stared at me, fuming.

"It wasn't that great," I said. "He was really terrible in the sack."

"Like that makes what you did better," Wes snapped.

"Come on, guys," I begged. "Just forget about it."

"Let me ask you this," Zack said. "What if one of us fucked some other girl?"

My stomach bottomed out. Okay, I know I was one big hypocrite but it did make me sick. I said honestly, "I wouldn't want to know."

"See!?" Wes exclaimed. "Now you know how we feel! Why did you have to give him your number?"

"I didn't!" I exclaimed. "I swear I didn't give him my number. I never even told him my last name! I don't know how he got it!"

"Whatever," Wes said.

"Wes—" I began.

He threw his hand up at me, grabbed his jacket and left the house quietly. I wanted to run after him but I couldn't. Mainly because I knew he didn't want me to. He didn't want to see me just then, maybe not ever.

Zack let out a sigh and stood up from the table. He wasn't looking at me either.

"Zack," I said. "It didn't mean anything."

"No," he said. "It might not have but I thought we had something special and I just don't think that anymore."

"But why?" I cried. "It didn't mean anything!"

He turned on me and yelled, "So does that mean I don't mean anything either?!"

"No, of course not!"

"Well, that's how I feel," he said and glared at me.

"I'm sorry," I said. "I'm just so sorry."

"Whatever," he said. "You trying to get a foursome going now?"

"No!" I exclaimed. "Zack, please, just stay and listen to me!"

He shook his head and went to the door. "I don't want to hear it. See you later."

"Zack!" I called after him. "Zack, don't leave!"

But he was gone.

I wanted to fall to the floor and die. Instead I fell to the floor and couldn't move. I just couldn't move. There was nowhere to go and nothing to do. I had lost everything.

Damn Trey Ellison anyway. He was my undoing!

Love, love and love.

They broke up with me. Both of them out the damn door. Who could blame them? *I* could blame them, that's who! I mean, come on, aren't we allowed at least one mistake?

I guess not.

I was devastated. What could I do to get them back? Apparently nothing. Neither would return my phone calls.

I knew I had fucked something really good up but how was I supposed to know they'd both react in that way? Maybe I was asking for too much. Maybe I was being *too* selfish. Maybe I didn't understand it was all about the love. The love I felt for Wes and the love I felt for Zack and the love I felt for myself. I did feel love for myself. I wouldn't have done any of that if I hadn't. It's good to love yourself. Even better when someone loves you back.

Maybe I had screwed it up on purpose. Maybe it was all about guilt, about loving too much, about getting too much out of life. Maybe I felt like I didn't deserve it. And that's why I had ruined it.

They let me stew in my own juices for a few days. I was about insane with needing them, so much I was going to get on my knees and grovel, beg, plead, do anything to get them back. At least one of them. But they both cut me out.

Tony said, "Well, since you're free now, why don't we get back together?"

"You've got to me kidding me," I said and rolled my eyes.

"No," he said. "I mean, why not? We were good together once, we can be good again."

"Tony?" I said.

"Yes?"

"You don't have a fucking clue," I said and hung up on him.

Then Wes came by one day and he wanted me back. I almost fell over. I was so happy, I cried as he hugged me.

"You made a mistake," he said. "I can forgive you for it."

I smiled at him. "Thanks."

"No problem," he said and pulled me over to the couch. "I want to ask you something."

"What is it?"

"I want to know," he said. "If you still want to get married."

I stared at him. Uh, uh… *what?!*

"I was just thinking about that is all," he said. "I mean why not? We've been through a lot and we've made it. Marriage isn't so scary when you know you can make it."

He was right. But... But... Yeah. But what?

"I'll think about it," I said.

"Please do," he told me and kissed the tip of my nose. "I really want to do it this time. And I want to buy you a new wedding dress."

I nodded and grinned at him. "Okay."

"And it can just be us, you know?" he said. "Me and you, like it was before. We're so good together."

I nodded. We were. I giggled and pressed my nose to his. "I am so glad you came back."

"Me too." He pulled back and stared into my eyes. "I knew the threesome thing wouldn't last forever, and that's okay, baby. We can always pick up another guy, if you like, before we get married."

And after we get married? No more threesomes, that's what. That's what he was saying. It would be okay before but after, not so much.

"It doesn't have to be Zack," he said.

A pain shot through my chest. But I wanted Zack! I didn't want some other guy. It wouldn't be the same. I wanted him! But then again, he didn't want me. Not anymore. Wes was right. It might just be better for me and him to be together by ourselves. I hated that but Zack didn't want me anymore. All because of Trey Ellison. Maybe it wasn't because of Trey Ellison. Maybe it was because he was looking for a reason to get out.

Well, now he had it.

Wes started to kiss me just as the phone rang. I pulled back and stared at him. He shrugged and I got up to answer it.

When I picked up, Zack said, "It's me. I've been going crazy thinking about what an idiot I've been. I have to see you."

I couldn't believe my luck. This couldn't be happening. But it was and it was all too easy. There had to be a catch. But if there was a catch, I didn't want to know about it for a long time. I just wanted to get back into the groove and do what I did best, which was fucking.

I knew the catch. The catch was marrying Wes. But maybe I could postpone it a little and we could do a few more threesomes. And then we could get married and it would all be over. But I didn't want to lose Zack either. I knew one day I would have to choose. I would just wait until that day.

Maybe we wouldn't go on as we did. Maybe they would grow apart from me and find someone else or maybe I would. But right now, right this day, I had both of them back and that was better than good enough.

"I'm glad to hear from you," I said to Zack and then smiled at Wes. My smiled widened as I realized I was going to get what I wanted and whatever that happened to be, it was the best feeling in the whole world. I couldn't stop smiling, for apparent reasons. I was one lucky bitch.

Zack sighed and said, "I was thinking…"

"Yeah?" I asked and smiled.

"I was thinking," he said and drew a breath. "That you…"

"Uh huh."

"That you and me… God, I've never said anything like this to anyone."

"What is it?" I asked and glanced at Wes, who was staring at me. He smiled. I smiled back.

"I'll just spit it out."

"Okay," I said.

"I think we should get married," he said hurriedly, then, "Oh, that wasn't so bad."

Did he just… No. He didn't just say that.

"What do you think?" he asked like this was the best idea he'd ever had.

What did I think? I'll tell you. It was the worst idea I'd ever heard! What was wrong with these men? Didn't they know that they'd given me a taste of candy and were now taking it away from me? Didn't they care that I loved our threesomes? I knew once I got hitched with one of them, then threesome land would be over. Things would change. It wasn't fair!

"I mean, the threesomes are great and whatever," he said. "But me and you, baby, that's what I want. Maybe later on, we can try that again."

"Uh…" I muttered. "Uh…"

"And Wes is a great guy," he said. "Don't get me wrong, but I just want... I just want it to be us."

I stared at Wes. He'd said the same thing.

"Katrina?" he asked. "What do you think?"

The gig was up. The gig was definitely up. It was over. And now I was even more fucked than I had been before. Damn it. So much for being lucky. I stared at Wes and got an idea. Why not? I didn't have anything to lose. If I could just get them both in the same room then we could all talk and then maybe they wouldn't make me choose, not just yet. We could also do something else to take our minds off it. And that something else was what I wanted. At least one more time. One last time and then we'd all move on.

"Uh, Zack," I said. "Why don't you come over and we can discuss it in a little more detail?"

Romantic Hedonism

Lucky that way.

"Hello, beautiful," he said.

I walked through the door and turned to him. "Hello, handsome."

He grinned, closed the door and grabbed me. Our lips found each other's and locked. We began to suck at each other's mouths almost instantaneously. I couldn't get enough of him. I wanted all of him over all of me. I wanted to be inside of his skin, feeling the way he felt. I wanted it all and I wanted it now.

"Mmmm," he moaned. "You taste so good."

"You do too," I moaned and licked and sucked at his neck as pushed me up the stairs and into his bedroom, where we fell on the bed with him on top and me on bottom. Then he undressed me. I shivered with delight as he began to rip off my clothes and paw at me feverishly.

He paused as soon as he had me naked beneath him. I began to squirm but he put a hand on my stomach and stopped me. He wanted to devour my body with his eyes before he devoured it with his mouth. As he stared at me, as he took in my entire body, I couldn't help but inhale deeply. The way he looked at my body, the way he looked at me, made me feel like a woman. It made me feel alive.

"God, you're so beautiful," he said.

I blushed, even though he said stuff like that all the time. He never failed to make me feel beautiful. He never failed to comment on how much he loved my long dark hair and my "mystic" blue eyes, as he called them. He loved the freckles on my nose and he loved every square inch of my "curvaceous and sexy" body. He loved the fact that I was short, that he had to bend down to get a kiss. He loved me. It was that simple.

"I worship you," he said and began to kiss my belly. "I worship at the fountain of Kora."

"Oliver!" I squealed and almost laughed. But I didn't. And I didn't because he was nearing my nether regions, my pussy, and that brought everything into focus. Everything in the world was put on hold when he was going down there. My legs spread to let him have a look. He loved to look at it. He loved it, he'd told me many times. He liked the way it held him tight as we fucked and he loved to eat at it until I came.

He was doing that just now, eating at me, slurping and then sucking at my pussy. He was fingering me, sliding one into me while resting his thumb on my clit as his mouth licked at the lips. I exhaled almost feverishly, which made my lips tremble. I was going weak. I was getting strong. He was doing it again. He'd done it yesterday and hopefully, he'd do it tomorrow, too. I couldn't live without this. I don't know how I'd survived before I had it.

And there it was. It was coming; the orgasm was coming to take me away. It was like I was being struck all over with this intense passionate wave of lust. It was like my whole body, mind and soul woke up. It was almost like a religious experience and I cried out as it hit me.

He didn't stop until I was spent and pulling him to me. I kissed at his lips, sucked at his tongue until I grabbed at his hard, throbbing cock. He was always so hard, always so ready to fill me.

"I want to fuck you doggie," he murmured in my ear. "Turn over."

I turned over and got up on all fours. He spread my legs and then ran his hand sideways between my cheeks. I shivered with delight and began to gyrate. I couldn't take the anticipation. Give it to me. Give it to me now! Give me all you've got and fill me with your love.

He gave it to me. He gave it to me hard, fucking me as hard as he could. I grabbed at the leather headboard and dug my nails into it. He slowed down and I began to grind against him, fucking him. He liked that and showed his appreciation with a hard slap to my ass. I moaned and ground against him harder. Another slap, which would leave an imprint of his hand, which I would look at later and blush over. Not that I cared now. I wanted another one, and then after that, I wanted one more. He gave it to me, slapping my ass so hard the fire in my belly erupted and I began to come. He was coming with me. He was coming so hard I could feel his cock throbbing inside of me. We were fucking so hard the bed shook, the windows shook. I believed the whole world shook as we came.

When we were spent, we fell to the bed without a word. I could feel his heart beating. I could feel mine. I never felt as alive as I did then. I was so alive, I was flushing. My whole body was flushed with our love and passion. His was red, too.

I rolled over and grabbed his face and pulled him to me, kissing him. He moaned and held my head as I kissed him, like he was never going to let me go. I pulled away first and stared into his eyes and then, as always, we cracked up. We were laughing so hard, tears formed in our eyes. I don't know why, but fucking always made us so happy we couldn't do anything but laugh. And then we'd fuck again. We'd fuck the afternoon away and then I'd have to leave and go back home, go back to my husband and pretend I was a good girl, pretend that I'd just been out with a friend. The next day, we'd meet again and we'd do it all over. But the moments between the fucks were the longest I'd ever spent. All I'd think about was him. And, of course, his cock.

"That was some damn good loving," I said.

"It always is, isn't it?"

Yeah. It always was. We were lucky that way.

London kills me.

I felt like such an ass. Here I was at one of the ritziest hotels in London waiting on my damn husband. I'd been waiting for over thirty minutes! We were going to have a nice dinner in the hotel's restaurant and then we were going to go back to our apartment and have sex. Maybe. I *was* going to have sex with him *before* he had made me wait. Maybe I should make him wait now. He should learn how it felt.

I looked around the lounge area and felt like such a loser. Everyone else had someone to talk to. I was all alone. Besides that, if there's one thing I hated, it was to wait. I didn't have an ounce of patience. Patience takes too long.

"Miss?" the host asked. "A call for you."

"Huh?" I asked.

He shook the phone and motioned me over.

"Oh," I said and got up, then took the phone. "Thanks. Hello?"

"Hey, it's me."

"Kevin! Where are you?"

"The meeting ran over," he said. "I'm not going to be able to make it."

"You told me…" I began then glanced at the host, who was listening intently to my conversation. I lowered my voice, "Well, when can you be here?"

"I don't think I'm going to be able to make it."

"Great," I hissed under my breath. "Just great."

"Sorry," he said. "Look, I am so sorry. I'll make it up to you."

"Whatever," I said, feeling like a big baby. "You said that last time."

"Well, why don't you go have a nice dinner on your own?"

"Are you out of your mind?"

"No," he said. "Why not?"

"Oh, right," I hissed. "And while I'm at it, I can talk with my imaginary friend, too!"

The host chuckled. I moved away from him.

"Is your imaginary friend male or female?" Kevin asked.

I almost smiled and decided to make a dig at him, "Kevin, you know I'd never have dinner with anyone else. Unless, of course, they were better looking and richer than you and we both know that would be near impossible."

"Thanks for the vote of confidence," he said and chuckled. "Listen, I'm sorry and I'll make it up to you. I promise."

"Okay," I said.

"Love you."

"Right," I said and handed the phone back to the host. "Thanks."

"Table for one?" he asked and smiled at me.

I stared back at him and considered something. Was Kevin not coming because he didn't want to pay for dinner here? I'd be willing to bet that was it! I ought to have known when he made the reservations that he'd never go through with it. He was such a cheap bastard. I was so sick of it, too. Fuck him. I was having a drink—somewhere. I looked around and spotted the bar. I was having a drink in the bar. And maybe even an appetizer!

"Miss?" the host asked.

"I think I'll just have a drink in the bar," I said.

He nodded. I nodded back and walked past him and into the adjoining bar. I looked around the room. Everyone was dressed very nicely. They all had these wonderful sounding British accents and all I had was my Southern one. I sounded like a hick and they sounded refined. It wasn't fair.

Why the hell had I let Kevin talk me into moving to London for a year? Oh, because it would be good for his career. Yeah. He was such a money-grubber, always working harder, doing more just to put money into the bank, which he would not let me touch. "We have to save money for the future," he'd always say.

"But I want a new car!" I'd whine.

"Your old car works just fine."

Bastard! It wasn't *him* driving around in an old 1993 Ford Escort station wagon. Sure, it did work fine but I wanted a sports car before I got too old. I'd be sixty before he'd relent and then I'd just look pathetic. Fuck him. As soon as I got home, I was buying myself a sports car. A cherry red gas-guzzling Camaro—a 1970 or '71 model, those were the coolest cars. With bucket seats and a killer stereo system. No. I wanted a black Camaro.

Shit. I wasn't going to get it and I knew it. I was surprised he didn't make me get a job over here as a shopgirl or something. But then I was struck with guilt. Oh, shit. I felt bad. He was a good guy and all that, it's just we'd been married so long I forgot to appreciate him. Yet, he'd changed over the years. We didn't have that much fun anymore. It was all about work and trying to get ahead. But that's what marriage was about, I guess. I'd changed, too. Nothing either of us could do about it except ignore it.

I might as well have gotten a job, though. We'd been here two months and I hadn't made a single friend. I didn't think I could do another ten months. It was too rainy, cold and dreary. I spent most of my time alone. I was going home. He was never around anyway, always putting in long hours, always telling me that this was going to help "make him." He could make it on his own. He probably wouldn't even notice I wasn't there.

That's what I'd do. I'd go back to the apartment, pack my bags and leave him a note: "I'm going home. You can go to hell. And I'm buying my Camaro!"

Ha! He'd flip out if I did that. Sounded like a plan. But first a drink.

"What can I get you?" the bartender asked.

"A Bass, please," I said.

He poured me one from the tap and I took it to a little booth that wasn't occupied, sat down and wished I had a cigarette. But I'd quit. Because I was trying to be good. Cigarettes were bad and, according to Kevin, they were too expensive. "Think of all the money we could save if we both quit!" So we had. I'd missed it ever since.

I drank my beer and watched all the other people who seemed to be having a really good time. Why didn't anyone ever talk to me? They seemed like nice enough people. Maybe I wasn't approachable. But I was approachable. I was always talking to new people back home in Tennessee.

Back home. Oh, God, I missed home so much. I missed my bed and my TV and… Oh, good God! I even missed my mother! I would have given anything to be able to go over to her house and force her to make me some gravy and biscuits. No one over here knew what the hell gravy and biscuits were. Or cared.

Maybe I'd sit here all night and get smashed. Instead, I sat there and got slightly depressed. All I ever did was walk around and ride the Tube around London. Mind the fucking gap! Sure, there was some good shopping and I liked the Tower of London and all that but how much sightseeing can a person do? I really didn't care for the food, either. The first day we were here, we went to a pub/restaurant and I ordered a hamburger but was served a *lamb* burger. Yuck. And bangers and mash? What the hell was up with that? I didn't even know what it meant, let alone want to eat it. At least they had Pizza Huts and McDonald's all over the place. If they hadn't, I might have starved.

I hated London. I hated my husband. And I hated my life. I was going home. Yes, I was. I was going to drink my beer, get my ass up out of this booth and go home. I'd walk if I had to. Well, I'd walk and then maybe try to find a boat or something to get me back across the Atlantic.

"I brought you another one."

My head jerked up. I'd been so enmeshed in my thoughts, I hadn't noticed the guy standing in front of me. He was cute, too. I stared at him, then away, then back. Our eyes locked for a second. His eyes were so blue, so deep blue that—

What the hell was wrong with me? I forced my eyes to the floor and said, "Excuse me?"

"You looked thirsty," he said and slid into the booth. "By the way, I'm Oliver."

What audacity! Did I look like a... A... Something... What was the word? Desperate? Did he think I was one of those women who go into hotel bars looking to get laid? And to think, not a moment about I was feeling sorry for myself because no one ever talked to me. Maybe I should be nice to this guy, whoever he was.

"And you are?" he asked, extending his hand.

"I'm Kora," I said and shook his hand.

"You're American," he said. "From the south?"

I nodded. Yeah, everyone always picked up on my Southern accent. I said dryly, "And you're English."

He nodded and smiled. "That I am."

"No offense," I said. "But why are you sitting in my booth?"

His smile faded and he stood up abruptly. "Oh, I didn't mean to... Uh—"

"No, no," I said. "Sit down. I'm not usually so bitchy but..."

"You don't mind?" he asked and sat back down.

"No, it's cool," I said and smiled at him. Oh, there were his eyes again... They were so... I shook myself and forced my concentration back on the floor.

"So what are you doing in London?" he asked.

I started to say something about how I was over here with my husband but something stopped me. I could be someone new, different. He didn't know me from Adam. Or even Eve. I could be anybody I wanted. I could project any image. I liked that idea.

"I'm on business," I said then thought about how that sounded. "Wait a second. Just so you'll know, I'm not one of those women, okay?"

"Pardon?"

"You know," I said. "Those women who troll bars looking to... *That.* I'm not here for that. I'm just having a drink."

He stared at me like I was crazy, then smiled again, this time more deeply. "You've been drinking, haven't you?"

"No!" I said, indigently. "I just didn't want you to get any funny ideas."

Funny ideas? What the hell was I saying? Why was I even talking to this guy? Perhaps because he was one of the few people who'd actually taken time to... Try to pick me up. But then again, it was the first time I'd been in a bar alone, drinking. I looked desperate and I knew it.

I stared towards him. He was *cute,* handsome even. He looked solid. Manly. I liked that. And he looked vaguely familiar. Was he somebody? I mean, I knew he was somebody, but who was he? His hair was almost black and those blue eyes... Wait a fucking minute. I was married. And I was no slut. I glanced at him again. I could be a slut. No. Yes! No!

"Cheers," he said and tapped his beer against mine.

"Here's mud in your eye," I replied and took a sip.

He cracked up and shook his head at me. "So what are you doing over here?"

"I work for this company called Phar-Cor," I said.

"Wow," he said. "I have a mate who works for them. Phil Goodman. You know him?"

That was Kevin's boss! He knew Kevin's boss! It's a small, small world, after all.

"Uh, yeah," I said offhandedly. "I met him right when I came over. I'm over here to open a new branch office."

I winced. That was bad. But it was true, at least of my husband. That's why we were over here. He was opening an office and I was losing my mind.

"So you're a business woman."

"That I am," I said and smiled, feeling very proud of myself. "What about you?"

"Excuse me?"

"What do you do?"

"Oh," he said and gave me a peculiar look. "Oh... I'm a record producer."

"Noooo," I said. "Really?"

He nodded, then leaned back to stare at me. "Actually, I used to be a rock star."

"No way."

"I did," he said.

"No way."

He sighed, then motioned at the bartender, who jerked his head at him. "Tell her who I used to be."

"Oliver Evans," he said. "He was in a boy band."

"I was not in a boy band," he said a little testily, his eyes flashing.

I cracked up.

"We played our own instruments for God's sake," he muttered. "Well, at first we did. How's that for boy band? So what if we were called Here's This? I didn't come up with the bloody name."

I shrugged.

He waved the bartender off and turned to me. "Well, I might have been in a band with a few other blokes, but I didn't dance. And I *never* shook my ass."

I just stared at him.

"I crooned," he said.

"Like Elvis?"

He snapped his fingers. "Exactly! Like Elvis."

I nodded. Exactly.

"You've probably heard of some of my songs," he said, puffing out his chest. "*Devil's Stamp?*"

I shook my head.

"*High Strung?*"

"No," I said. "Sorry."

"Well, we never did really make it in the states," he said. "We tried, like a lot of others. And we failed. Had one hit over there, though. *Up in the Night?*"

I felt bad for him but I had to shake my head. "When did you have the hit?"

"It's been about ten years," he said, nodding.

"Sorry," I said. "I was in a Tom Waits' phase then. I probably just missed all that."

"You like Tom Waits?"

"I *love* Tom Waits."

"Great," he said. "So he's your favorite singer?"

"Actually no," I said. "Dean Martin is."

"I love Dean Martin," he said. "What's your favorite song of his?"

"*Sway.*"

"No way!" he exclaimed. "That's my favorite song, too!"

"You're full of it," I said. "But anyway, this sucks."

"Why's that?"

"I always wanted to have an affair with a rock star," I said just to get him. "You might have gotten lucky tonight."

"I was a rock star," he said. "I really was."

"Dancer!" the bartender yelled.

Oliver started to stand up and go over there. I grabbed his arm and pulled him down. He pointed at the bartender who shook his head at him and leaned over a newspaper.

"Bastard," he muttered and turned to me. "I was never good enough for any of those bastards. So what if I did wiggle my ass a little? The girls liked it! And I got a few million out of it. It doesn't change the fact that I'm still an average bloke!"

"This is obviously a sore spot for you," I said and grabbed my purse.

"Where are you going?"

"I really need to get home," I said and stood.

"Wait," he said. "I was a kid then. Since then I've done a lot as a producer. I'm producing this band right now, all-girl, Sinatra. You heard of them?"

I shook my head.

"We might change the name to Baby Maker," he said. "Which one do you prefer?"

I thought about it. "Baby Maker."

"I kinda prefer Sinatra," he said. "Come on. Have another beer."

I stared at him, staring at me. He seemed a little lonely. Not desperate lonely like an old man drinking in a bar alone, but just like he hadn't taken the time to get to know anyone and now he wanted to. The person was me. Besides, I was a little lonely myself.

"Okay," I said and sat back down. "But just one."

"Fantastic," he said. "I'll get us another one."

I nodded and he got up and went over to the bar. I smiled and looked around. I don't know why I'd let him talk me into staying but this was kind of fun. I hadn't had a real conversation with anyone in a long time. Kevin didn't count because I was pissed off at him for standing me up at dinner. And for being so cheap.

I watched as he grabbed the beers, then jerked his head to the side, indicating the he wanted to go out on the patio. I sighed, grabbed my purse and followed him out to the covered area where a lot of people were sitting around smoking and drinking. He sat down at a table set the beers shoe, sat down himself and lit a cigarette. Everyone, it seemed, smoked over here. But not me. I had quit and I was going to stay quit.

I stared at the cigarette and found myself holding out my hand. "Got one of those for me?"

"Oh, sure," he said and lit me one.

I took it and inhaled. "Thanks."

He nodded and puffed on his cigarette. I had a sudden vision of us fucking. He was on top. It looked like fun. Oh, *shee-it!* Where did that come from?!

"So," I said. "In addition to producing girl bands, what else do you do?"

"Have affairs," he said. "With lonely women in pubs."

I slapped his arm. "Shut up!"

He cracked up and shook his head at me. "I'm just taking the piss."

An English phase I would never understand. Nevertheless, I didn't like him making assumptions under the guise of humor. But it did make me wonder if he was good in bed. Was he good in bed? I gave him a good look over. Damn, he looked good. His clothes were expensive looking and he had a Rolex on. His black pants fit him *just* right and his blue shirt showed he had some muscle. His black loafers had slightly thick soles and looked like they were made of the yummiest of leathers. He looked nice. I wondered how big his dick was.

He smiled at me, showing a nice set of perfect white teeth. I couldn't help but smile back. He was the kind of guy that made a girl smile. What was up with him anyway? I looked away, then back at him. He wriggled his eyebrows and we cracked up. I felt like I was high. He stared into my eyes. I stared back. His eyes were so blue.

"You know," he said, leaning in. "You're quite beautiful."

I sighed. That was always nice to hear, especially when you didn't always feel beautiful.

He leaned in closer and whispered, "And that body of yours is like walking sex."

I felt myself grow warm. But I couldn't... I couldn't. I was married. I *couldn't* do stuff like that. It was wrong. But wasn't I my own person? Couldn't I make my own decisions? It's not like I could call my husband and ask for permission to have sex with this very handsome and charming man.

But there was no denying it. I liked what he was doing. I liked that he was taking charge. I liked that he didn't beat around the bush. Maybe I was drunk or maybe I'd lost my mind, but suddenly I wanted what he wanted. I wanted him in my pants. I couldn't justify *not* doing it. It was wrong, but I was ready for a change. Being bored for months on end will do that kind of thing to your brain. You want something to happen to take away the monotony. Oliver, I knew, would take it away. Besides, I'd always wanted to have a fling. Now was a good a time as any to get that done. It was one thing I could check off my "to do" list. Buy a house—check. Live abroad—check. Have an affair—check. Still waiting on that Camaro, though.

"I don't do stuff like that," I said.

"Isn't it time you started?" he asked.

He had a room upstairs. We nearly ran to the elevator. I noticed the bellboy was nowhere to be seen. Good! We got in and waited impatiently for the door to close then we just grabbed at each other when it did. Our sexual attraction was that strong. We didn't waste time with any bullshit. It was time to get down to business.

And, oh, how sweet that business was.

A kiss. A stick it to 'em, weak in the knees, heart pounding kiss. A slobbering, wet, intense, beautiful kiss. I loved the way he cupped my face between his hands and held me there, like he wasn't about to let me go. I held on and pushed myself up to him, pressing against his body and wishing I was naked.

The elevator dinged.

We quickly pulled apart and stood face forward. An old man on the other side of the door asked, "Going up or down?"

"Up," Oliver said.

"Go on, then," he huffed.

Oliver leapt to the button, hit it and came back at me. We started it again. His face needed shaving, but I didn't care. I liked the roughness against my skin. I moaned as he buried his face in my neck and began to give me those kisses that sent shivers all along my body.

"Oh, I want to fuck you so bad," he muttered in my ear, then licked it.

"Yeah," I moaned.

The elevator dinged. We pulled apart and as soon as the doors were open, he grabbed my hand and pulled me onto the floor and to his room where he fumbled with the key as I sucked at his neck. As soon as the door opened, he bent, picked me up and carried me inside, slamming the door shut with his foot.

I started to giggle.

"What is it?" he asked.

"Nothing," I said and began to kiss his neck. "No one's ever done that to me before."

"Oh," he muttered, then, "Where's the bloody bed?!"

I looked around. "I don't know. Is this a suite?"

"Yeah," he said. "But I've not been in it before."

I stared at him then shook my head and pointed at a door. "Try that one."

He grinned, walked to the door, and kicked it open. It was the bedroom and in the middle of it was the bed. It was big and looked inviting. He walked me over and literally threw me down on it. He fell on top of me and it was all tugging and shoving and wriggling around until we were naked as jaybirds.

I pressed up against him, pushing his head towards my breast. His mouth eagerly found it and sucked on my nipple. *Ahh yessss!* Oh, yeah! I looked down at him sucking on my nipple and was turned on beyond being turned on. I pulled his face up to mine and sucked on his tongue, bit at his lips and kissed his face. He parted my legs with his knee. I stopped him.

"What is it?" he asked.

I shook my head and forced him onto his back and kissed my way down his body and to his dick. I grinned up at him and stared at his dick. It was a very nice size, to say the least. Well, he was about six-foot, so there. I couldn't wait to try it out.

When I took it in my mouth, he gasped and said, "Brilliant!"

I'd show him brilliant. I deepthroated him and then began to suck as hard as I could, moving my mouth up and down it, until he grabbed me by the shoulders and pulled me up.

"You wanna—"

He cut me off my pushing me onto my back. He began to devour my body with his mouth and when he got to my legs, he pulled them apart and dove in.

Oh, God! Yeessssss! He knew what he was doing, too. He didn't just go in there with the tongue, he used everything he had. His lips, his tongue, his fingers, his nose. I squirmed and before I knew what was happening, I had grabbed onto his head and was grinding against his face. I moaned, gasped and came like I had never come before. The orgasm just jumped out of me. I nearly screamed.

"Oh, yeah," I moaned and pulled him back to me. "Fuck me now!"

"You ready?" he asked and moved between my legs, teasing me.

I wrapped my legs around his waist and kissed him, moaning. He put it in. I gasped a little. Damn! I mean...*damn!* It wasn't just length, it was...girth. Width. My pussy fit it like a glove. All of it inside me, pushing its way in and giving me that AHHH feeling. Whoever said size doesn't matter didn't know shit.

As we started to fuck, we stared into each other's eyes and began to push against each other. My hips took over. They started to move on their own. I couldn't help myself. My hips moved backwards, forwards, sideways, up and down. He moved with me, keeping up with my every move. Then I lost control. I wanted all of him pouring into all of me. Every single inch. My toes curled.

He pounded into me and moaned, "Oh, yeah, oh, baby!"

"Umm," I muttered and pulled myself up. I kissed his shoulder and bit it a little. "Ummm. Harder."

"Harder?"

I nodded then gasped.

"Oh, God!" he moaned. "I can't hold it!"

I couldn't either. Suddenly we were slamming into one another. I held onto his shoulder and pressed up against him and then it hit me like a bolt of lightning. It swept through me and I let out a scream. He covered my mouth with his and I sucked on his tongue until we fucked all the orgasm out of us.

Then...I got a bonus. Another little one came at me and made me give a little gasp. That was first.

He stared at me in awe. "Did you just...*two* times?"

I grinned and nodded. He kissed me fervently, taking my mouth in his. We kissed for what seemed like minutes, holding onto each other. He pulled back, gave me a peck on the cheek and pressed his forehead to mine.

I smiled at him. "I need a shower."

He nodded.

"You wanna…"

He nodded and we went into the bathroom, jumped in the shower and began to feel each other up. Soon we were all soapy and ready to go again.

I grabbed the back of his head, pulled his lips to mine, kissed him and said, "I just wanna…I dunno…fuck you."

"The feeling is mutual," he told me and kissed me back.

We stepped out of the tub, he got on the floor and I got on top and rode him hard. The bathroom was all steamy and sweaty and smelled of sex. I loved it.

It didn't take any time for us to come.

After we were done, and thoroughly exhausted, I said, "I have to have a cigarette after that one."

"And a drink," he muttered and shook his head.

So we made a little drink and shared a smoke. As we drank, I stared at him from the corner of my eye. He gave my look back. We cracked up.

"What the hell is wrong with us?" I asked, laughing.

"We're idiots, I suppose," he told me.

"I suppose so," I replied and smiled at him.

He came over behind me and kissed my shoulder. I leaned back against him. He began to lick at my neck. And, of fucking course, the phone rang.

We glanced at each other.

"Let it go," I said.

"Okay," he muttered and started kissing me again, then bent down in front of me and began to kiss my belly then he went lower. I put my leg on his shoulder and he began to kiss my inner thigh. I moaned. His kissed all the way up my leg, then gave my pussy one big lick before kissing up my body. I just stood there and loved feeling what I was feeling and it was pure ecstasy. I hadn't had sex like this in…well, ever.

He pushed me up against the wall and fucked me. I held onto him as tight as I could and fucked him back. He grunted and drove it in harder. I didn't even have to tell him. I liked that.

"Don't stop," I whispered and sucked on his neck. "Oh, God, don't stooooppp!"

I came so hard I felt myself bucking against him. He was bucking too. We kept at it until we were both gasping for air.

As soon as he came, he turned away from me and fell against the wall, breathing heavily. I was breathing heavily, too. That was so good, it was exhausting. I glanced at the clock. It was almost eleven p.m. That couldn't be right. We'd just gotten into the room like ten minutes ago, hadn't we?

I pointed at the clock. "Is that clock right?"

He glanced at it. "Oh, yeah."

"Shit!" I yelled and ran to my clothes in the bedroom. They were everywhere. I couldn't find my panties.

"What's wrong?" he asked, coming into the room.

I stared at him and realized he didn't know anything about me. He didn't know I was married or anything! Fuck! What a mess I'd gotten myself into! What was wrong with me? The euphoria was gone and had been replaced with panic. I was dead! Kevin would kill me! Well, that was a little strong, but he wouldn't like it one bit.

"I have this thing to do tonight," I said and pulled on my shirt, still looking around for my panties. "Oh, shit! Where are my panties?"

"What?" he asked.

"Are you on drugs?" I hissed. "Underwear! Where is my underwear?"

He shook his head. I glared at him and dressed without them.

"Why are you in such a hurry?" he asked.

"I have this thing to do," I said and slipped my shoes on and ran to the door. I opened it and said, "By the way, that was a good fuck."

He grinned and came towards me. "I thought so, too."

"No!" I squealed as he began to lick at my neck. "I didn't have time for this! I have to go, Oliver. I have somewhere to be!"

He eyed me and stood up. "You don't want to skip it by any chance?"

Actually, I did. I wouldn't mind skipping going home and trying to come up with a hasty excuse/lie for my husband. I would like to stay here with him and fuck all night. But I couldn't. I was married.

I shook my head. "It's a work thing."

He nodded, bent down and pressed his lips against mine. Heaven! I was in Heaven! Oh, God, why did this feel so good? Why did it make me want to do something I knew was ultimately bad for me?

"I'll be quick," he said and pulled me back into the room.

"Well," I said. "If you promise."

When I got home, Kevin wasn't there. He'd left a message on the machine saying that he was "working late" and would "be home soon." I stared at the machine. What had I just done? And how the hell had I gotten away with it?

Get lucky.

It was because I'd hit my sexual peak, that's all. I knew it'd get me one day! I'd been so good, too. Not one cheat in almost thirteen years of marriage. My friend, Tracy, had told me she'd cheated and then blamed it on turning thirty.

"It's like I couldn't stop myself," she had said. "I mean, do you think I'm a bad person?"

"Yeah," I had said. "I do."

"Kora!" she screeched.

"Listen, girl," I said. "I'm not going to sit here and congratulate you on doing something I've wanted to do for years."

"What the hell does that mean?"

"It means," I said. "I want some of that, too."

"Well, go get some."

"I can't find anyone!" I half-yelled.

Besides that, I worked long hours and trying to have an affair on top of a busy work schedule... Well, it just seemed like a lot of work. In addition to that, I didn't want to hurt Kevin and... Blah, blah, blah.

That's what all this was about. It wasn't about Oliver. It was about hormones. Biology. Technical stuff like that. Sexual peak.

Everyone knows women hit their sexual peak in their thirties. I was no different. Thank God.

I walked around the apartment all morning thinking about what I'd just done, thinking about how I'd like to do it again. I could call the hotel... No. I wasn't doing it. It was wrong. What was so wrong about it? Kevin was busy, why shouldn't I find a hobby? He wouldn't mind if I took up knitting. What was so different from this and knitting?

I sat down on the couch and stared around the place. It was nice. Kevin's company paid for everything, too, which made it nicer. It was modern and sat on the fourth floor of an older Victorian building that had been completely remodeled. It was near King's Road which meant I could go shopping all the time. It also wasn't too far from the hotel if I took a cab...

No!

Fuck. Fuck it. Damn it anyway. What was wrong with me? I still couldn't believe I'd cheated. But then again, that's what happens when you get bored. And that's why I'd done it. I was bored in my marriage. Maybe I'd outgrown it or something. God knows there were times when I'd wanted to run away. There had been times we'd argued so bad I thought I couldn't stand it one more minute. But we always worked it out and we worked it out by ignoring it. We were good at that.

But I hadn't been getting something I'd needed for a long time and what I'd needed was what I'd had last night, that good fucking. I'd forgotten how nice it was to be with someone new. I'd forgotten how exciting it could be. I'd, simply, forgotten. Damn. It was good to be reawakened.

I decided I wasn't going to feel bad about it and I wasn't going to feel bad because I deserved this. I deserved to feel good about myself because I'd put up with a lot of shit out of Kevin. I'd bit my tongue and forced myself to play nice. I went along because it was just sometimes easier to go with the flow. A girl deserves something special for being so good, doesn't she? And I'd had it. I was done. One cheat doesn't equal a bad wife. Everyone should be able to get away with one cheat.

Jut then the phone rang. I picked it up, expecting it to be Kevin, who was the only person who ever called and said, "Hey, what's going on?"

"Kora?"

I froze. It was Oliver. I stammered, "How did you get my number?"

"Just did a little snooping," he said. "Besides, you had dinner reservations. I just called down to the restaurant and they told me."

I'd forgotten about that. Then he must know about Kevin!

"So what's going on?" he asked.

I couldn't help but smile. "Nothing. What's going on with you?"

"Nothing," he said. "I just… It's just that you left something behind yesterday."

"Huh?"

"Your knickers," he said.

My knickers? Oh, shit! He had my panties! That was incriminating evidence! For a brief moment, I imagined him reclined back on the bed twirling them on his finger. I didn't want to image what else he could be doing with them.

"You can, umm…just throw them out," I stammered, blushing.

"Why not come over and get them?" he asked. "They're very nice."

"I've got another pair just like them," I said, trying to sound casual. "Just throw them in the garbage."

"Come over and get 'em."

"Nah, that's okay," I said.

"Then…"

"What?" I asked.

"Just wondering…"

"Yeah?" I asked.

"If you want to come over and…you know."

I thought about that. I did want to…you know. I really, really did. But I couldn't. I wasn't a bad girl. I was a good girl. Being a good girl sucked.

"Actually," I said. "I'm busy."

"Come on," he said. "Don't you want to get lucky?"

I did. Damn it. I was so going to get busted. But then again, it was Kevin who insisted on moving to this place, not me. It was his fault I was alone all the time, wasn't it? No, not really.

"Oliver," I said. "I can't."

"Why not?"

I looked around the apartment. All I had to do was watch TV and there was never anything on during the day.

"I'll be right over," I said and started to hang up.

"Wait a minute," he said. "Do you want me to send you a car?"

I stood taller. No one had ever "sent" me a car. "Yeah, I'd like that."

"It'll be there in twenty minutes," he said. "I'll see you then, love."

"Okay," I said and giggled and hung up. Then I froze. Was I going to do this? What the hell was wrong with me? I was... I was having an affair! Me! Sure, I'd fantasized about it enough but I'd never done anything about it.

I stared at the clock. It was almost noon. If I didn't go soon, there wouldn't be that much time and if there wasn't that much time, we couldn't do that much stuff.

Oh, hell. What was one more fuck with this guy? I'd go, fuck him and leave. Then I'd never seen him again. And I'd have a nice little memory to tide me over during the monotonous times I knew I would be spending with Kevin. I'd use him and then I'd lose him. Everyone deserves at least two cheats in a lifetime.

★ ★ ★ ★ ★

He smiled as he opened the door. "Hello, beautiful."

"One fuck," I said and waved my finger in his face. "Then I'm leaving and we'll both forget this ever happened."

"I don't think it's that easy," he said and pulled me inside, pressing his lips against mine before he kicked the door shut with his foot. "Come on."

He grabbed my hand and pulled me into the bedroom. I fell down on the bed and he fell on top of me. He was already hard. I was already wet. It didn't take long before we were tearing at each other's clothes and getting down to business. He began to devour my body with his lips and tongue. I just lay there and felt so good. I couldn't get enough.

"I love your tight little body," he said and came back to my mouth and kissed. "So sexy."

"You're not too bad yourself," I said and he wasn't. He had a great body. Muscular and tight. I loved his ass. It was just right, a little rounded but not at all big. I loved to squeeze it as he fucked me as he was doing right then.

"Mmm," he moaned. "I love doing this to you."

I smiled and bit my lip. "I love you doing it to me."

He chuckled and sucked at my neck and pushed it in harder. I gasped and ran my hands up his naked back.

"Come on and fuck me," he whispered, licking at my ear. "Do that thing you did last night."

I almost blushed, then I did it. I squeezed my pussy around his dick. I rode him for a few moments, getting my groove on.

He let out a grunt and said, "Slow it down. You'll make me come."

"That's the point," I said and sucked at his neck. "Let me ride you."

He stopped moving and I began to grind against him. He let out another grunt as I rode him. He loved it but at the same time it was almost too much. He bent his head down and sucked at my nipple. It was too much for me. All the sucking and fucking was too much. I began to come then. I came so hard, I dug my nails into his back. He took over and fucked the orgasm right out of me.

"Oh, Gooood!" I cried. "Ooooh, Gooooodd!"

He kept pumping and then he pulled out and came all over my tits. I gyrated as his hot cum splashed onto my skin. I was headed into overload. I rubbed my tits as it shot all over me. Before the last ounce of cum came out of him, I bent down and put it into my mouth and sucked it dry. I was that turned on and it tasted *good*. After I was done, I realized that was the first time I'd ever done anything like that. Huh. Me? Swallowing? What came over me? Maybe I was turning into a slut or something.

I looked at Oliver. He stared at me with an unreadable look in his eyes. It was as if he couldn't believe what had just happened, but he wanted it to happen again and again.

"Wow," he said and fell down on top of me. "That was dirty, wasn't it?"

"Mmm," I murmured and held him tight. "It was. I like it dirty."

He chuckled and kissed me, sucking at my mouth. I kissed back and wrapped my legs around his waist. We kept kissing until he rolled off and let out a deep breath. Once he did that, I was suddenly brought back down to earth and the realization of what I was doing came at me. I almost leaped out of the bed as guilt and shame took over my mind. Damn good way to spoil a mood.

He propped himself up on his elbow and smiled at me. I glared at him. Why the hell did he have to be so cute? Why the hell did he have to be so great? Why the hell did we have to meet like this? Why couldn't I have met him before I met Kevin? It wasn't fair! I'd be willing to bet he wasn't a cheap bastard, either. That would make everything just wonderful.

"What is it?" he asked.

"I'm a whore."

"What?"

I stood and began to pace. "I'm a fucking whore! I'm a slut! I'm a...a... What's the word? Trollop! I'm a fucking trollop!"

"What the fuck are you talking about?"

"I've got something to tell you."

He smiled again and said, "You never told me where you're from."

"Where the hell did that come from?"

"I don't know where you come from," he said.

I gaped at him.

"Where are you from, Kora?" he said. "Obviously, you aren't from London."

"I *could* be from London," I said, indignantly.

"You have a Southern accent," he said. "And not southern England, either."

I just stared at him.

"Well?" he asked.

"Knoxville, Tennessee," I said. "But I'm originally from Cumberland Gap."

"Like the skiffle song?" he asked, his eyes wide.

"I guess," I said. "I don't know. Listen, Oliver—"

"That's so cool that you're from there," he said, nodding. "Never met anyone from Cumberland Gap, Tennessee."

"Whatever," I said, thinking I should just blurt it. Yeah, that's what I'd do. "Listen... I...uh..."

"Uh huh?"

"It's just…" I mumbled, then blurted, "I'm married."

"I am, too," he said and sat up.

I almost fell to the floor.

"So?" he said nonchalantly and lit a cigarette.

"Wait a minute," I said and wagged my finger in his face. "Wait a minute. You're married?"

"Yeah."

"Then what the fuck are you doing here, at this hotel?"

"Oh," he said. "She kicked me out."

"What?"

"She does that from time to time," he said. "I'm beginning to think she's having an affair."

I stared at him. He cracked up at himself, laughing so hard he ended up holding his stomach. There had to be something wrong with this guy. I liked him, though. A lot. He was audacious as hell.

"She really kicked you out?" I asked.

He shook his head. "No, I left."

I started to ask if they were getting a divorce, then realized this conversation wasn't going where I wanted it to. And it was really none of my business and I wanted it to stay that way. I had to tell him it was over. That what we did last night—and this morning—was a once in a lifetime thing. But I was dying to know what was going on with him, though I couldn't bring myself to be so nosey.

"But you're still married," I said, shaking myself.

"So are you!"

I frowned and narrowed my eyes at him. He mimicked me. I frowned deeper and narrowed my eyes more. He mimicked again. I did it again and again and he kept mimicking me.

"Oh, stop it!" I yelled and slapped at him. "I'm leaving."

"Why?" he asked.

I started to the door, then stopped and said, "Because I'm married."

"Oh, come on," he said and got out of bed and came over to me. "Let's not do this."

"Do what?" I asked and felt tears spill out of my eyes. Oh, great. I was such a crybaby.

"This bullshit of trying to justify it," he said and took my hand. "Let's just let it be what it is."

"What is it, Oliver?" I asked and stared into his eyes.

"Good fucking."

I cracked up and shook my head at him. He laughed a little, too and kissed my cheek and led me back over to the bed, where we sat at the foot.

"Tell me a little about yourself," he said and pushed the hair out of my eyes.

"Not much to tell."

"Oh, there has to be something."

I shrugged.

"What do you like to do?" he asked. "What do you like to eat?"

I thought about that and said, "Biscuits and gravy."

"Biscuits and gravy?" he asked and made a retching sound. "You put gravy on your biscuits?"

"Yeah," I said. "Why wouldn't I? Everyone does."

"Biscuits and gravy?" He still seemed perplexed. "Who puts gravy on biscuits?"

I stared at him and then got it. "No, dumbass! Not cookies—*bread*. It's like a… It's just a damn biscuit. Bread. Not cookies."

"Oh," he said. "That's weird."

"No, you're weird," I said.

"I'm weird?" he asked. "I'm not the one putting gravy on biscuits."

"Shut up," I said and almost laughed.

"Okay," he said and grinned at me. "This is kinda romantic, isn't it?"

I stared him down. "No, it isn't."

"Why not?"

"It's too hedonistic to be romantic," I said. "I think. We might have to do some partying, but still, it's hedonistic. And I'm a Baptist! We don't go for that shit!"

"I'm Catholic," he said and seemed to consider something. "Yeah, it is hedonistic. But it's also romantic. It's romantic hedonism."

"You're so full of shit," I said.

"I need to write that down," he said and leaned over to the nightstand and scribbled it down on a notepad.

I rolled my eyes and stood, looking around for my clothes.

"Where you going?" he asked.

"Uh, home," I said.

He sighed and said, "It's still early."

"It's almost four," I said. "I have to… Listen, I'm not explaining myself to you."

"I think you should."

"I think you should shut up," I said and pulled on my pants.

He got up and came over to me. I stepped away from him. He stepped with me then grabbed me by the middle.

"Ow!" I yelled. "Let me go!"

"Just one more kiss, love," he said and tried to kiss me.

I slapped at him and pushed and then his mouth somehow landed on mine. Oh, hell, what harm could one more kiss do? I had the time.

"Just one," I moaned as he kissed me. "Then I have to go."

"Yeah, I know," he said and pushed me back on the bed.

Cheating/lying thing.

"Where you been?" Kevin asked as soon as I got home that night.

I froze and stared at him. What *the fuck* was he doing home so early? I glanced over his shoulder at the clock. It was almost seven! How the hell could I have stayed that long? What was I? An idiot?! Yes, yes, I was.

"Kora?" he asked. "Where you been?"

"With Sally," I said quickly. *Sally?*

"Who?" he asked.

"Sally," I said, feeling like shit, like such a liar. Like such a *bad* liar. "I told you about her."

"Oh?" he said, smiling. "You've been spending a lot of time with her."

"Well, you've been spending a lot of time working," I snapped.

"Well, nothing," he said. "I'm not looking for a fight."

"Oh," I said, feeling deflated. I shouldn't try to pick fights with the man I was fucking around on. It wasn't right. Damn it.

"So who is this girl?" he asked and reclined back on the couch.

I stared at him and then around the room. I didn't know if I had it in me to make up a lie about a girl I'd never met. I decided to play it cool. I said, "She's just this chick."

"Where'd you meet her?"

"Piccadilly Circus," I said and then wanted to kick myself. Piccadilly Circus? I hadn't been there since I moved to London. It was too crowded and not really a place where someone would meet somebody unless you wanted to meet a pickpocket or a tourist. He'd never buy that! Think! Think quick! "No, I mean I met her at... On Bond Street."

"Have you been shopping on Bond Street?" he asked. "Did you buy anything?"

I groaned. I got so sick of him keeping tabs on my spending. Oliver wasn't cheap at all... I stopped myself and said, "No, I was window shopping there. No, I didn't buy anything so shut up."

"So, anyway," he said. "Is she from London?"

Phew, he bought it. I nodded and sat down beside him. "Yeah, I think so."

"I'm so glad you finally met someone," he said and leaned over and kissed my cheek. "Invite her over for a drink."

"Oh, no," I said. "I couldn't do that."

"Why not?"

"She's busy," I said. "Busy, busy, busy."

"Then how does she have all this time to spend with you?"

Fucking hell! I wasn't any good at this cheating/lying thing. Why did I even try? And who the fuck was he? Sherlock fucking Holmes? Always had to find an angle on everything, didn't he? I hated that he was so smart. And so cheap.

"Kora?" he asked.

I stared at him and sensed his radar was beginning to spin. If he thought about it hard enough, he'd figure it out in no time. Oh fuck. I'd come too far to get busted on something like this.

"I'll ask her," I said quickly.

He nodded, then leaned over and kissed the top of my head. He pulled back and stared at the top of my head, then leaned in and sniffed it. Then he started to sniff me, all of my body, like he was a dog or something. Or like...He sniffed me like... Oh, no! Oh, no no Noooooo!

"I can't believe you," he muttered.

Up shit creek. No paddle. Yup, that's where I was.

"I just can't believe you didn't say anything," he said, pulling away. Then he sighed. "I've been doing it, too."

Oh, *great!* Well, at least I wasn't the only cheater. Ha! And to think how I'd chastised myself over this when he was out doing the same thing!

"I wondered when you'd start," he said.

"Listen," I began, feeling my stomach fall to my knees. "It's just—"

"You've been smoking again," he said and laughed.

Smoking? I almost fell over with relief. He was talking about smoking!

"Phew," he said. "Me too. Ever since we moved to London, I started back."

Thank you, God.

"Everyone smokes over here," he said. "So it's easy to bum cigarettes."

If I hadn't been cheating on him, I would have slapped him over that. One day he was going to have to stop being so cheap! I just imagined what everyone thought of him when he bummed smokes all the time. *There he is again! Hide the cigarettes! No! Just run!*

"That's funny," he said and chuckled. "We've been hiding it from each other. Like what could you do to me if I found out? What could I do to you?"

I didn't want to find out.

"You could never keep a secret from me." He laughed to himself then smiled at me. "I love you so much."

I felt so much like shit. And I hoped to God I could keep a secret from him.

"Mmm," he said and tried to take me in his arms. "Come over here."

Oh, shit. He wanted sex. I'd just had sex! I probably smelled like sex! I pushed him away gently and said, "Mind if I take a quick shower? I've been on the Tube all day and…"

"Okay," he said. "Be quick, though."

Phew. As I went into the bathroom, I wondered how the fuck I was going to come up with a woman who would come over for drinks. Damn. What a mess I'd gotten myself into. And for what? I thought about Oliver. For *that.* That was worth a little trouble.

I got in the tub and turned the shower on. As usual, there was no water pressure. Why didn't I just start taking baths?

"Kora?" Kevin said at the door.

"Yeah?"

"Can I come in?"

"Uh, I guess," I said, wondering what he wanted now.

He poked his head in. I noticed he was naked, totally buck naked. Oh, *that's* what he wanted. Well, it had been a while. He deserved a fuck. But I couldn't help but laugh at him. He could be so damn goofy. Usually it got on my nerves but today... Well, it kinda got on my nerves.

"Is it nice and warm under there?" he asked.

"Not really."

"Can I see for myself?"

"Sure," I said. "I guess."

He chuckled and got in with me, grabbed the soap and began to rub it all over my body. I started to tingle but then... I felt weird. Like I was cheating on Oliver. *With my husband.* I shook it off and turned to him. He grabbed me and kissed me hard. I liked that and responded by wrapping my arms around his neck and pulling him close to me.

He moaned, "I've been so horny for you all day. I don't know why, but I have."

"That's good to know," I said and threw my head back. He was sucking on my neck. It felt so good.

He bent down and began to devour my tits, sucking at my nipple until I thought I'd die. It felt so damn good. And I'd just done this all day with Oliver. It must be those dirty thirties. Those hormones kicking in. It was like I couldn't get enough of him or of Oliver.

I stared at him, at his dark brown hair, at his perfect nose and full lips. He was so cute. He had big shoulders and was so strong. He was great and I was cheating on him. I was such a bitch.

I shook that thought off, too. Nothing I could do about it right now anyway. He pulled me out of the tub and pushed me down on the floor. I moaned as he began to kiss me all over, taking his time to slide his hand between my legs. I rose up and ground against it. He kept at it, watching my face as I got off on his hand.

As I ground against his hand, I began to suck at his neck. Soon, he couldn't stand it anymore and pushed me back on the floor, pushed my legs open and stuck his hard cock in me. I gasped. He was coming at me harder than he'd ever come. It was almost too much. It was too good. I wrapped my legs around his waist as he fucked me and began to fuck him back. Soon, I couldn't take it anymore and the orgasm hit just as he grabbed onto my nipple and gave it a little pinch. I gave myself over to it and the orgasm soared over me. I was shaking it was so good. He was coming and as he came, he gave a hard thrust and a grunt. Then we were done. He fell on my chest and was silent for a moment.

I smiled and kissed the side of his cheek. It hadn't been that good in a long time. Mostly because he worked so much, but still. Maybe fucking Oliver wasn't such a bad thing. If it brought this out in Kevin, it might even help our marriage. You could never tell about these things. I still wasn't going to tell him or anything.

"What do you want to eat for supper?" he asked, breaking the spell.

"Let's order in," I said. "Do that 'take-away' thing."

"Why?" he asked. "We have food here."

I rolled my eyes and said, "I don't care. Just do whatever the fuck you want to do, Kevin."

The phone rang first thing in the morning. "Hello?"

"Hey baby."

I sighed. "Not today, Oliver."

"Why not?"

"I have to find a friend."

"You have to what?"

"Find a friend," I said. "To cover for me being with you. I told my husband that I'd met a girl and we were friends and now he wants to meet her."

"Oh," he said. "What else?"

"Huh?"

"Tell me what happened. What did he say?"

"Why do you want to know?" I asked.

"Well, we're kinda in this together, baby," he said. "So tell me."

He was such a snoop! I rolled my eyes but explained every detail about what had happened last night, being careful not to mention that I'd had sex with my husband. Just like I didn't want Kevin to know I was fucking Oliver, I didn't want Oliver to know I was fucking Kevin. Which was weird. What the hell was wrong with me? I felt like a double-cheater. I was cheating all the way around. I was so bad. I knew when it was all over, Karma was going to get me good. I dreaded that day so much.

"So," I said, finishing. "You can kinda see how I'd be busy today."

"I'll take care of it."

"Huh?"

"I'll take care of it," he said. "Now get your pretty ass over here."

I thought about it. I really didn't want to go look for a friend today anyway. I'd just keep putting Kevin off and then tell him she ditched me or something. "It was like one day we were friends and as soon as I invited her over, she got weird. People can be so strange, don't you think?" He'd agree and the issue would be dropped. And I could see Oliver in the meanwhile.

"I'll be there in an hour," I said.

"I'll have the car pick you up," he said.

"Cool."

"See you then."

The car didn't take me to the hotel. It took me to one of London's nicest neighborhoods. The houses which lined the streets were tall and brick, and so English looking.

"Where are we going?" I asked the driver.

"Primrose Hill."

"Uh, why are we going to Primrose Hill?" I asked.

"I'm taking you to Mr. Evans' house."

"Oh," I said and felt a little uneasy. What if his wife was home? Oh, shit! Maybe he wanted a threesome or something. Well, he wasn't about to get it. Nope. Chicks were great and all that, but I didn't want to fuck one.

Finally, we pulled up to a house that had a Range Rover sitting out in front of it. As soon as the car stopped, Oliver came out of the house, ran to it, opened my door, said thanks to the driver and pulled me inside. I barely had time to catch my breath. As soon as he closed the door, I asked, "What the hell was that all about?"

"Nothing," he said and kissed my cheek. "Let me take your jacket."

I eyed him suspiciously and took it off. "Is your wife here?"

"My wife?" he asked. "No. Why?"

"I assume this is your house."

"It is," he said and hung my jacket up in the hall closet. "But I don't share it with her."

"Oh," I said. "You have two houses?"

"Something like that," he said and gave me a good look. "You look absolutely beautiful today."

"I'm dressed in jeans and a t-shirt."

"And I have to say, that t-shirt really shows your tits off well," he said and grabbed them.

"Stop!" I squealed and pushed him away. "Show me around this fancy old house."

"Certainly," he sad and held out his elbow. "Come with me, young lady."

I took his elbow and he showed me around the house. It was very nice. A huge living room or sitting room or whatever they called those rooms with a big, plush couch, two big plush chairs, a desk pushed against the back wall, as if it was about to be moved out of the room. There was also an old fireplace with an orate mantel painted white. The gigantic kitchen was painted all in white and had an island in the middle and stainless steel appliances. A big master bedroom with a huge bed with a leather headboard in the middle covered with a red silk comforter. *Nice.* Everything was modern and new.

"I just had it remodeled," he said. "Like it?"

"I love it," I said and looked around the gigantic walk-in closet with its built in shelves and nice clothes. "You're really rich, aren't you?"

"I get by," he said and winked.

"You should give it all away and be poor like me."

"Why would I do that?"

"I dunno," I said. "'Cause you're a super-nice person?"

He cracked up. "No one's that nice, love."

"What is this place?" I said.

"I like to call it the fuck pad."

I turned red and looked around, wondering, *How many girls...* I shook it off and said, "Who says you're getting lucky today?"

"I do," he replied and came over to me.

"Wait a minute," I said and held him off. "Why were you at the hotel?"

"'Cause this place was being remodeled," he said. "They just turned the heat on this morning."

"Oh," I said. "So you just keep this house because…"

He shrugged. "It's the first house I bought with the money I earned. I never wanted to part with it. My wife wanted another house, so I got her that one."

His wife. I hated that word, wife. It meant I was standing here alone with another woman's husband. It meant I was cheating. It meant I was a bad, bad girl.

I pushed him away and headed downstairs.

"Where are you going?" he called and came after me.

I stopped in the middle of the stairs and said, "Oliver, this isn't right. It isn't right to your wife and it isn't right to my husband. We need to stop it right now."

He trotted down to me and grabbed my hand. "Listen, Kora, my marriage has been over for years."

"Mine hasn't."

He swallowed hard and said, "Is this the first time you…you know?"

"Cheated on my husband?" I snapped and yanked my hand back. "Yes, it is. Obviously it's *not* the first time you've cheated on your wife!"

"It's the first time…" He stopped.

"What?"

"Nothing," he muttered.

"Oh, fuck off," I said and stomped down the stairs.

"Hey!"

I stopped at the front door, then turned on him. "I'm not a bad person. I'm just bored, okay? I'm bored. I don't know anyone in this city and you're the only person I've met and talked to. Sorry! I guess I was just lonely."

"No one is judging you!"

"That's because no one knows!" I yelled and opened the front door.

He trotted down the stairs, grabbed me, pulled me back inside and slammed the door shut. Then he pointed his finger in my face. "You listen here, we are good together. I don't care if we are married. We like each other and we liked fucking each other. What business is it of anyone else's?"

"They don't know!" I yelled.

"So keep it that way," he hissed. "Stop running away from this. And stop making it into this big problem when it's not one, okay?"

I thought about that. What you don't know can't hurt, can it?

"Come here," he said and grabbed my hand, pulling me into the living room. "I've got something for you."

I went with him even though I was sure I would be better off leaving. He went to the stereo and turned it on, pressed a button and then... Then I couldn't help but smile and let all those bad feelings disappear. It was Tom Waits' *Jockey Full of Bourbon*. How could he have remembered that from the bar where we met? Well, it had only been a few days, but still.

"I remembered you were a fan," he said and grinned, his eyes twinkling.

"Oliver," I said and shook my fists. "You are such a charming bastard! I hate you!"

"I am, aren't I?" he asked and held out his hands.

I grinned and began to dance to the beat of the music, smiling at him. I danced over to him and sang with Tom, "*I'm full of bourbon*."

"And you can't stand up. Yeah, I know." He grabbed me. "I told you not to hit the bottle so early in the morning."

I threw my head back and laughed. He laughed too. I stopped and began to dance around him, whispering the lyrics of the song into his ear.

"You women are so evil," he said, watching me.

"How's that?"

"Look at you," he said. "You can make a man do anything you like. And we'd do it willingly."

"And why do you do it?"

"Because we can't help it," he said and grabbed me again. "We can't stand to see you without having you."

"So have me," I said and held out my arms.

He grabbed me and pulled me to him. As soon as his lips were on mine, the whole world disappeared. I couldn't think of anything else but what he was going to do next with his hands and with his lips and with his dick.

He pushed me over to the desk. I moaned and went with him. He pushed me on top of the desk and pulled him to me. He began to tear at my clothes. I tore at his. As soon as he pulled off my jeans, he stopped and stared at me.

"What is it?" I asked and looked down.

"Where are your knickers?" he asked. "You didn't have knickers on yesterday, either."

I groaned. "Shut up!"

"But why?"

"Do you want to fuck me or not?"

"Yeah, I do, I just wanted to know," he said and slid his hand between my legs. "God, you're so wet."

"I just..." I said and then stopped and moaned. That felt *so* good. "It's just the other day I didn't wear them and it felt nice and then I didn't see why I should. It felt good not to wear panties."

"That's so sexy," he said and kissed me, licking at my lips. "Walking around with no knickers on."

"Mmm," I moaned. "Do that some more."

He did some more, playing with me. His finger grazed my clit for a moment then slid into my pussy. "I love your pussy," he said, bending down and kissing it.

He stuck his head between my legs and began to eat at me. I shivered with delight and couldn't take it. It felt too good. I humped him, rubbing myself up and down on his face, riding it. He moaned and began to suck at me. Oh, God! Oh, yeah! Yeah! I grabbed onto him as the orgasm exploded in my body.

"Come fuck me!" I moaned. "Come fuck me now!"

He got up and stuck it in. I gasped and stared him dead in the eye.

"Come on now," I said and began to move.

"Oh, Kora," he moaned and bit at my nipple. "I love your tits."

"I love your cock," I said and rode it.

"Slow down," he said.

"Hell no!" I said and rode him harder. It was coming again and it was coming fast. I grabbed onto his head and fucked the orgasm out of my body. I shook with it. He was shaking too.

"Oh, baby!" he moaned and pumped into me. "Oh, God!"

"Come on, Oliver," I whispered and nibbled on his ear. "Fuck me hard."

He fucked me hard.

"Oh, yeah," I said and squeezed his ass. "Come on!"

He grabbed onto the back of my head and forced his tongue in my mouth. I sucked on it and as he came, he shuddered a little.

We didn't move. I didn't want to move. I wanted to do it again. But first I wanted to ask him something. I wanted to ask him what I meant to him. I wanted to ask him if any of this meant anything or if I was just fooling myself while making a fool out of my husband. I wanted him to tell me the truth. I wanted to know so I wouldn't be too hurt if I found out later that he'd only used me.

"Oliver," I said, ready to put it to him. "Do you—"

"Shh," he said and kissed my shoulder. "Wanna go for another?"

I eyed him. A talk or a fuck? What was I? A sensitive chick or a cheater? I thought about that. I was a cheater. I was a girl who wanted to fuck. A fuck it would be!

"Come on then," I told him.

"Bend over," he said and pulled me up off the desk.

I bent over. He grabbed onto my hips and pulled my ass towards him.

"Ummm," I said and widened my stance so he could get in there good. He bent under me and began to kiss me there, sliding his tongue along. Then he got behind me and fucked me doggie style. Fucked me so hard my head nearly hit the wall. I pressed my hands on the wall and said, "Stop."

"Why?"

"I can't handle it."

He didn't stop.

"Oliver, I mean it."

"I can't," he moaned.

"Please," I moaned.

"Shh," he said and reached around and put one finger on my clit.

I moaned and moved against it. Ah, yeah.

"That better, love?" he asked.

"Much better," I said and he began to fuck me, ride me. I let him as long as he kept that finger in place. It tickled me, that finger. I moved against it, loving the pressure his dick was giving me from behind, loving the pressure of that finger.

I couldn't handle it anymore. I began to shudder as I came and came and came. It was the longest orgasm I'd ever had. It was like I was wrapped up inside it, trapped. But I liked being trapped and I loved being wrapped up. I didn't want it to end. He pounded into me as I came and then he came and fell on my back.

"Oliver?"

"What, love?"

God, I just couldn't bring myself to ask him. *Do you like me? 'Cause I like you.* Maybe I should give it up already.

"Nothing," I said.

He kissed the back of my shoulder and said, "Cup of tea?"

I froze and said, "What?"

"Would you like a cup of tea?" he asked.

"Do you have sweet tea?" I asked.

He chuckled and pressed his face into my back. "Uh, no. just tea. Hot tea."

I turned around and stared at him. He stared back and then we cracked up. We were laughing so hard, I had to hold my stomach.

"What is wrong with us?" I asked as I laughed.

"I don't know," he said. "Fucking must delight us."

I pushed him away and shook my head, then thought about it. It must because we always seemed to laugh a lot once we were done.

"So would you like a cup of tea?" he asked and pulled on his jeans.

"I would like a glass of sweet tea," I said and grabbed my shirt and pants. "With lots of ice and extra lemon."

"I'll see what I can do," he said and held out his hand. "Come along."

I grinned and took his hand. We walked into the kitchen. He didn't have any ice or any lemons. In fact, he didn't have anything in his kitchen that was edible. Besides the bottles and bottles of beer in the fridge. It was like he was having a party or something.

"You don't stay here much, do you?" I asked.

"I will be soon," he said and winked at me, smiling.

I decided not to ask and opened a cabinet door. "I'm hungry. What are we going to eat?"

"You like pizza?"

"I *love* pizza," I said.

"Let's order one," he said, pretending to be really excited. "We'll splash out!"

"Whatever that means," I said, laughing.

He went to the phone and ordered the pizza. I stared at him, then around the kitchen. I liked it here. It was nice and warm. I looked out the window. It was dreary and raining.

He hung up and said, "It'll be here soon. Let's go sit down and vegetate."

"Okay," I said and started to follow him.

"Hold on," he said and bent down. "Piggy back?"

"I haven't ridden piggy back in years!" I squealed. "And I could break your back."

He jerked his head. "Come on, love. Hop on for a pony ride!"

I stared at his face. "Are you kidding me?"

"No, come on!"

"This is almost perverse, but what the hell," I said and shrugged. I took a few steps back, then ran and hopped up on his back. He grabbed my legs and ran with me all the way to the living room. We were laughing so hard, he tripped and fell and we went skidding across the floor. My elbow hit the coffee table.

"Ow!" I yelled and held it. "Motherfuckingshit!"

"What happened?" he asked and pulled me to him, staring at my elbow. "Oh, you're gonna bruise."

"Ya think?" I asked and slapped his arm. "Damn it! That hurts."

He stared at me, smiling slightly.

"What is it?" I asked.

"You're...you're really something else, aren't you?"

"No," I said indignantly.

"You are," he said, then leaned over and kissed my elbow. "You are so something else."

"In a good way or a bad way?"

"Good, of course."

"Cool," I said and lay back on the floor.

He lay back with me and asked, "Is your elbow okay?"

"Yeah, it's fine."

"Would you like some ice for it?"

"You don't have any ice," I said.

"You're right," he said. "Let me kiss it again instead. That'll make it better."

I smiled and he took my arm and kissed my elbow, then licked it. It didn't take long before he was kissing his way up my arm, turning it over to kiss and suckled the inside of it before he kissed my underarm. I shivered in delight. I'd never had anyone kiss me there before. It was so sensual. It felt so good.

He made it to my mouth. I opened it as soon as he got there and we kissed, just kissed, not moving an inch away from each other. Our lips pressed against one another's and our tongues slipped inside the others mouth easily and with passion, but not with any sense of urgency. It was so sweet, that kiss; it wasn't urgent. It was just nice.

Suddenly, he pulled back and stared into my eyes.

"What is it?" I asked.

"It's just I want you to know," he said, touching my hair. "You are one special girl."

"Well, I am pretty amazing once you get to know me," I said and smiled at him. All of a sudden a flood of good feeling swept all over me. "I'd be willing to bet you're an amazing guy, too."

He grinned. "Thanks."

Just then, the doorbell rang and he groaned. I groaned too.

"Pizza," he said and stood. He held out his hand. "Hungry?"

I nodded and stood and grabbed his hand. We went to the door, he took the pizza, paid the guy and then we went into the kitchen and dove in. Fucking makes a person hungry. As we ate, we began to talk. I hadn't talked like this with anyone in years, not even with Kevin. We used to talk like this, when we first started going out, but the conversations had dwindled over the years. I hadn't realized how much I liked jabbering.

Oliver was a good listener and wanted to know all about me, every single detail. I told him about myself, the small town in Tennessee I was from, how I grew up with three sisters, how I had moved to Knoxville when I'd married Kevin. He told me he had one brother and a mother. His dad had taken off when he was young and his mom had to take a job as a maid to make ends meet. He thought the world of his brother and mother and insisted that I should meet them someday soon. I smiled and said I'd like that.

We ate, drank beer and talked about everything under the sun. Even astronomy, which he was quite passionate about.

"See, it's like this," he said, a cigarette dangling from his fingers. "I dig the collision ejection theory because, think of it, all the planets—"

"Matter," I corrected. "You know, we talk about some weird shit."

"That we do," he said. "So, matter. Anyway, all this matter floating around and bam! Suddenly together. See what I mean? They collide, they form planets."

"But what about God?"

He gave me a small, gentle smile, then shrugged, "I dig God and all, but the theory just makes sense, don't you think?"

"It does, but so do a lot of other things," I said.

"Yeah," he said.

I sighed.

"What did you say?" he asked quietly and put his cigarette out.

"Nothing," I said. "I didn't know I said anything."

He shrugged, leaned back and put his hands behind his head. I stared into his eyes, wondering if he was crazy then came up with a resounding *no!* He stared back, seemed to wonder the same thing about me then decide the same thing I'd decided.

A big smile for him spread through my mind, then through my body until it showed on my face. He seemed pleased with that smile because he began to smile back, a little slower, as if he were considering my sincerity. The smile lingered until he leaned forward and I leaned forward and our lips just touched. Just like that. A soft touch. I could feel the whiskers on his chin, I could feel the emotion in his body as the touch lingered and wanted to be explored.

Oh, baby, baby, baby...

Just as I began to open my mouth, the phone rang, sending fright shivers up and down my spine. We pulled away abruptly and stared at the phone.

He muttered, "I have to get that. I have to sorta do some work today."

"That's cool," I said. "I should get home."

He nodded. "When you come back, I will have you some sweet tea."

"And some biscuits and gravy."

He chucked me under the chin and said, "And some biscuits and gravy."

A good dirty.

Later that night, the doorbell rang. I glanced at Kevin. He shrugged.

"I'll get it," I groaned and got up and went to the door. When I opened it, I saw a woman dressed in a very short skirt and a red tubetop. She was blonde and just a hair short of being skanky.

"Yes?" I asked.

"Are you Kora Christensen?"

"I am," I said. "And you are?"

"Sally."

"Who?" I asked, still confused.

"Your friend?" she said and rolled her eyes.

"Who is it?" Kevin hollered.

"Sally!" she yelled.

Then I got it. Oliver had said he'd take care of getting me a friend and he had. He'd just sent... I looked at her. A hooker? I was going to *kill* him.

I whispered, "Listen, I met you on Bond Street and—"

"I know all that," she said, waving her hand. "Oliver told me what to say."

"He *did?*" I asked and imagined Oliver calling her, then laughing his ass off about it. He was so going to get it for doing this to me.

Just then, Kevin came trotting in and smiled at her, extending his hand. "Oh, Sally. It's so good to meet you."

"You too," she said and handed him her coat. "Nice place you got here. Kevin, is it?"

He nodded and glanced at me. I smiled and said, "Sally we were just about to have a drink. Would you care for one?"

"Well, yeah," she said and strolled in. "That's what I'm here for, isn't it? Drinks?"

I stared at her and shook my head. "Well, come in. I'm so glad you could make it."

"Not a problem," she said and stared around the apartment. "How long have you lived here?"

"Just a few months," Kevin said and motioned to the couch. "Please have a seat."

She smiled at him and sat down.

I nodded and sat down on the other end of the couch and Kevin took the chair. We didn't speak for the longest time. It was so awkward. Oliver was so going to get it when I saw him again.

"Oh, shit, I forgot. Let me get us all a drink," Kevin said and jumped up and raced into the kitchen.

I watched him go, then turned to Sally and smiled at her.

"What?" she snapped.

"Nothing," I said and leaned in towards her. "Are you a hooker?"

"Escort," she said haughtily, like there was a big difference. "And I don't do kinky shite."

"No," I said hurriedly. "We're not... We didn't... You're just here as my friend."

"That's what I heard," she said. "But if it goes anywhere else, you have to pay extra."

I just stared at her then shook my head and said, "Believe me, it won't go anywhere."

"Cute husband," she said, ignoring me. "Is he kinky?"

"No!" I hissed. "He's not!"

She eyed me like she didn't believe me, then said, "Well, if he is, it's extra."

"Well," I said, hoping to get a laugh so the ice would be broken. "Good luck getting it out of him. He doesn't like to spend extra."

She didn't laugh. She just eyed me and said, "Well, he won't be getting extra then, will he?"

"I guess not," I said and groaned. So much for breaking the ice. It was going to be a long evening.

As soon as Oliver opened the door the next day, I slapped his arm.

"Ow!" he said. "What was that for?"

I slapped his arm again. "You could have at least warned me!"

"About what?"

"Sally?" I hissed and slapped his arm again. "I almost died when she showed up!"

"Well did it work out?" he asked.

"I guess," I said. "Other than the fact that we didn't have a damn thing to talk about."

He smiled. "So, it worked out? See, I told you."

I slapped his arm again.

"You are going to have to stop doing that," he said and pointed his finger at me.

"I sat there all night with my 'friend' and looked like an ass! I can't even believe Kevin bought it! And she's a hooker!"

"She's an escort," he corrected. "I called the best agency in town. She's one of their most popular girls."

"How would you know?"

He stared at me and sighed. "No, I don't hire them. I might know some people who do, but *I* don't. So don't think that."

I slapped him again.

"This is your last warning, young lady."

I reached out to slap again, but he grabbed my arm and pulled me into the living room. I fought and slapped at him the whole way but he was stronger than I was. Then he sat down and pulled me across his lap. Then he proceeded to spank me! I could have killed him!

"Stop it, you asshole!" I screamed.

He kept at it, then he slowed down. "I think you like it."

"You bastard!" I yelled and tried to get off his lap. He wouldn't let me. He was strong, that was for sure, but as soon as I was up, he would regret this. But then...

"I love your ass," he said and began to squeeze it.

"Don't..." I moaned, though I meant, *Do!*

He kept squeezing it, running his hand up and down it and between the cheeks. He bent down and began to nibble at it. I squirmed and wanted him to do what I knew he was going to do. I'd never had that done to me before, either. But with him, I wanted to. He brought this wild lust out in me. It was almost scary, but I knew I'd do things I'd never consider before with him.

His hands were going under my shirt, moving along my skin. Goosebumps rose up all over as he did that. It felt so good. Just the thought of what he was about to do to me was making me crazy.

He took his time, pushing me onto the couch until I was up on all fours. He took his time to pull my jeans off and then he took his time to eat at my pussy until I was dripping wet.

"So wet," he moaned and licked at him back. "So hot..."

I moaned and began to grind against him. He spread my legs and ran his hand between the cheeks, then he slipped one finger in. I shuddered and heard his zipper. He was getting out of his jeans. I squeezed my eyes shut. The anticipation was driving me crazy. It seemed to take forever for him to get out of his jeans and settle back on the couch. Then I felt his cock against my skin. It was hard and it was going to fill me up. I couldn't wait for it. Give it to me, give it to me now!

He was delicate, gentle, as he eased it into me. It hurt a little, at first, but it felt wonderful. He gave a little push and then was all the way in and then he was fucking me up the ass. I felt so invaded and so alive in that moment. It was so tight and so dirty. It was a good dirty. A very good dirty.

He grunted and leaned over and grabbed at my breast. I moaned and grabbed his hand and helped him squeeze it. Then I took his hand and put it on my clit and as he fucked me, I fucked his hand. It was too much. It was like I was getting it from every angle. I was going overboard. I was taking it too far, doing too much. And I loved every minute of it.

It didn't take long before we were both coming and we were coming hard. The couch shook as we fucked on top of it. We couldn't get enough of this, of this feeling of being so joined, of being so in tune we'd do something like this. The orgasm was one of the most intense I'd ever felt and it filled me from the top of my head the tip of my toes with good feeling. When it was over, I was exhausted from it.

I fell to the couch, breathing heavily and he fell on top of me, then turned me over and kissed me. I kissed back for a moment, the buried my face in his neck. I breathed in. He smelled so good, like sex and masculine cologne. He smelled like a man. It was so sexy. I wanted to tell him something then, something I'd never said to anyone but Kevin. But I couldn't. It wasn't right. It wasn't the time. But I wanted to. I wanted to so bad.

"I've got you some tea made," he said.

"What?" I asked and shook myself.

"I've got some tea," he said. "Sweet tea."

I turned to him and said, "You made me sweet tea?"

"And I got you extra ice and lemon, just the way you like it."

"You did not!" I squealed and slapped him on the arm.

He held up a finger and said, "You want another spanking?"

I nodded and climbed on top of him. "I do."

He grabbed my hands and slid his fingers between mine. I smiled down at him and kissed the tip of his nose. He pulled me down to him and kissed me, then rubbed his nose against mine. I giggled and swatted at him.

"What was that?" I asked and rubbed my nose.

"Eskimo kiss."

"You know they only kiss like that because the other way would make their mouths freeze together."

He stared at me. "Are you serious?"

I nodded. "I am."

"You're full of shit."

"No, I'm not," I said and got up off him and bent over and grabbed my jeans. "Give me some sweet tea."

He got up and slapped my ass as I was bent over pulling my jeans on.

"Hey!" I yelled and slapped *his* ass, which he really seemed to like.

"You said you wanted one," he said and gave me another slap before grabbing his jeans and disappearing into the kitchen. "Besides an ass like that needs a good slapping."

"Asshole," I muttered and followed him. He already had everything on the counter. A big pitcher of tea, a bowl full of ice and a lemon. I watched as he poured the tea, put in a few pieces of ice and sliced the lemon.

"Didn't get round to the gravy and biscuits, though," he said. "Sorry, love."

"This will do," I said and watched him. "You really took some notes, didn't you?"

"I looked it up on the internet," he said and handed it to me. "Try it."

I smiled and sipped it. *Ick!* It was terrible. Way too sweet and strong. Ugh.

"Like it?" he asked.

I wriggled my eyebrows and pretend to drink. He grinned and got a beer out of the fridge. I watched as he popped the cap, threw it into the trash can then took a long gulp. After he swallowed, he winked at me and took another sip.

I said, "You're in an awful good mood for someone who just fucked someone else up the ass."

He spit out his beer and started to laugh. I laughed, too.

"You are such a bad girl," he said and gave my temple a quick kiss.

"You've never complained before."

"I'm not complaining now," he said. "What would I ever do without you?"

I chuckled and sipped my tea. It really wasn't that good. "Can I have a beer instead? This sucks, babe."

"Sure," he said and got me one. "I tried it myself and wondered how anyone could drink the stuff."

"You just didn't do it right," I said. "Don't try to make it again."

"Okay," he said. "I won't."

I winked at him and took a long sip of the beer. "And while you're at it, forget about the gravy and biscuits, too. You're probably not a very good cook, are you?"

"No," he said. "But I'm good at a lot of other things."

I grinned. That he was.

"Oh, here," he said and threw a key on the counter.

I picked it up and stared at it, then at him. I knew what it was for and I knew why he was giving it to me. I started to say something, but stopped. What did this mean?

"It's for the front door," he said, smiling.

"I kinda figured that," I said. "Why are you giving it to me?"

"So you can come in anytime you want."

"You're giving me a key to your fuck pad?"

"Yeah," he said.

"What if I used it for a fuck? With someone besides you?"

He glared at me. "You wouldn't do that."

"You do it."

"Kora," he groaned. "Don't start this shit. I just want you to have a key."

I took the key and promised myself that I would not put any meaning into it.

"Oh, I want you to listen to something I've been working on," he said and went to the CD player and put in a CD. "It's Sinatra."

"I thought it was Baby Maker."

"We still haven't decided," he said. "Just listen."

I smiled at him as the music began to play. It was really techno sounding and the lyrics were atrocious.

> "Ice SCREAM I'm going to a rave Don't care
> about nothing Gonna pave my own destiny
> (destiny) Gonna dance till dawn Gonna make you
> see I'm not just a pawn Have some fun, fun, fun
> Without the son Gonna made a score, life's a
> bore…"

Thank God it was over. I smiled at him and nodded.

"You hate it."

"No, it's good," I lied. "It's real good."

"You hate it," he said and took it out. "It's just…"

"Don't worry about it," I said. "It sounds good. The kids will *love* it."

He stared at me sadly. "Thanks for trying to be nice. I really hate this shit, too, but it pays the bills."

"I know what you mean," I said. "I worked at a job for nine years that I despised and I was only able quit cause Kevin got this opportunity to come over here. But look on the bright side. At least you make good money."

He sighed. "Yeah, I suppose."

I sighed, stood up and kissed his cheek. "Hate to cut this short, but I have to get home to the old man."

"Okay," he said. "So I'll see you tomorrow?"

"Oh, no, sorry," I said. "I have to shop."

"Why?"

"My husband's company is having a fancy dinner thing tomorrow night and I have to find something elegant and classy to wear. So he can show me off."

His face changed. "So he can show you off?"

"That's right," I teased. "You see, my fella knows what a fine piece of ass he's got and he likes to make sure everyone else knows it too."

"Well," he said. "That's nice. Where's the dinner?"

"Uh," I said. "Let me think. It's at this restaurant/bar and it's called the…uh… The Polka Dot?"

"I have no idea," he said. "You don't mean the Paradox, do you?"

I snapped my fingers. "That's it!"

"Nice place," he said. "You sure you can't stop by?"

I shook my head. "No, sorry. I really won't have time. Besides, we've seen each other every day this week."

"Are you getting tired of me?"

"Oh, no," I said and ran my hand up his chest. "But I do need to leave you wanting more. Otherwise, you might not pine over me as much."

"I don't pine over you."

"But you will."

"You bitch," he said and chuckled. "Tell you what. I know this girl who's a stylist—"

"No!" I exclaimed. "I want to shop. I like shopping. And I want to get the best."

"She could get you the best like that," he said and snapped his fingers.

"I don't need her," I said and glanced at the clock. "Now put that beer down. We don't have much time before I have to go home."

He put the beer down.

The best fuck ever.

"You ready?" Kevin asked, rushing into the bathroom, but then stopped short. "Good God!"

"What is it?" I asked horrified, wondering if my ass looked big. I looked in the mirror at it. No, it looked good. The long black dress I'd bought to go to the Paradox clung to every curve on my body. Maybe it was too much, though.

"You are so fucking hot in that," he said. "Damn, honey."

"Phew," I said and grinned. "I was beginning to wonder."

"No, you look great," he said, eying me. "You'll get hit on a lot tonight."

"Jealous?" I asked.

"I might be a little," he said. "How much did you spend on it?"

I groaned.

"How much?" he asked. "A dress like that—"

"Kevin, if you don't shut up, I will take it off and you can go to that fucking party by yourself."

He shut up. One day, he would have to learn to let go of a dollar. And if letting go of a dollar meant allowing me to wear dresses like this, then this could be the day. I felt hot in it, very sexy. But when we got to the restaurant/bar, I felt silly and stupid. Kevin left me at the bar alone right off the bat and stayed in deep conversation about something "important" with his boss.

I wished I'd never let him talk me into coming in the first place.

He always did shit like this, though. That was one problem I had with him. He always picked his work over me. Whenever I'd call him at work to talk about something, he would inevitably say, "Hold on, I have someone on the other line." I always felt like second best.

I felt like that sitting at the bar. I felt less important than his work. But at the same time, he always wanted me to where I was supposed to be. It was like I was at his beck and call. I was so sick of playing that tired game with him. Maybe that was one reason I didn't break it off with Oliver. Why not stick it to Kevin a little? He'd been sticking it to me for years. I'd been a very good wife up until now. I never overspent. I always worked full time and I never forgot to fix his favorite dinners. I deserved something for all my trouble.

However, I knew I'd have to break the affair off soon. But the more I tried, the stronger Oliver came on. It's like he knew what I was thinking and was doing everything in his power to keep my attention on him. It didn't help matters that the sex just kept getting hotter and hotter. How could it *keep* getting hotter? It didn't seem possible but it was.

I sighed and looked around the room. It was a nice party. They'd rented the entire restaurant out. It was big and extravagant, lots of champagne and caviar. There was a four piece band playing in the corner. If I had actually known anyone there, I could have probably partied down.

I sipped my drink and turned in my seat, wondering how much longer I'd have to stay before Kevin would let me leave. Where was Kevin now? I looked around for him but he was no where to be seen. I kept looking for him, then thought I saw Oliver, but that couldn't be right, so I looked closer and sure enough it was him. Oh, God! No! What the hell was he doing here?! He saw me and gave a slight wink.

Oh, shit! Shit, shit, shit! I turned in my seat and put my head in my hands. What *the fuck* was he doing here? I glanced over my shoulder at Oliver who talking to some tall, lanky guy. I was going to kill him. Even if he did look good enough to eat. He was dressed in a tux, his tie undone a little at the top. He looked movie star handsome. I knew what was under those clothes, too. I couldn't wait to get my hands on it again. But not tonight.

Just then, Kevin came back into the room, still talking to his boss. I had to leave before something bad happened.

I started to get up, but then glanced at Oliver again. He glanced back at me and smiled. Before I could help myself, I smiled back. He jerked his head in the direction of the bathroom. He had to be kidding.

I mouthed, "*Here?*"

He nodded.

Should I? Could I? I looked around and glanced at Kevin who was still talking to his boss. Suddenly, I *wanted* to do it. I think I wanted to get caught. I wanted something to change. I don't know what, just something.

"No!" I mouthed and jerked my head to the door. "Get out of here!"

He pointed towards the bathroom, mouthing, "Meet me in the loo."

"No!" I mouthed. "Get out of here."

He pointed to it again. I shook my head and turned back around fuming. Just then, Kevin came up with his boss and said, "Honey, you remember Phil."

"Hello, Phil," I said and smiled.

"Hello, Kora," he said and his eyes raked over my body.

I'd been getting those looks from men all night. I now wished I'd dressed a little less sexy. I didn't like all that attention. It made me feel uncomfortable. Phil kept looking and then it seemed as if he had to force himself to look away. I was never dressing like this again.

"Oh," Phil said, looking around. "There's Oliver! I asked him to sing for us tonight. We went to school together."

God, I prayed, *please don't do this to me.*

"I couldn't believe it when he accepted," he said and smiled at us. "He never does anything like this. Got quite a good voice, though."

I couldn't help but roll my eyes.

"Oliver!" he called. "Oliver! Come here!"

Oliver turned and acted like he'd just spotted us. Then he came over with the guy he'd been talking to, who he introduced as George, the former guitarist for his band.

"And you are?" Oliver asked me, extending his hand, facetiously formal.

"Kora," I said and shook his hand.

"Nice to meet you," he said, then turned to Kevin. "And you?"

"Kevin," he said. "What song are you going to sing?"

"It's a surprise," Oliver said and winked.

"I play guitar," George said out of nowhere.

We stared at him, then everyone went, "Well, okay, then…"

I sat there and silently fumed as they made little chit-chat. *How long have you been in London? The weather was nice today, wasn't it? Thinking of a solo career…* And blah, blah, blah.

Finally, Oliver said, "Well, nice to meet you. We have to sing now."

"Good luck," Kevin said and smiled at them.

They turned to go. I breathed a sigh of relief but was momentarily stunned when they went to the stage where the four piece band was. He was really going to sing! George took an acoustic guitar and Oliver took the microphone, said something to the band, who nodded and smiled, then he turned to the crowd.

Kevin touched my elbow. "You want a drink?"

I shook my head and gave him a tight smile.

"Sure?" he said. "It's an open bar."

"No, I'm fine," I said, resisting the urge to slap him. "You know, Kevin, I'm not feeling so good. I think I'll leave."

"Oh, don't," he said. "Stay and listen to the song at least. And get a drink."

"Kevin—"

Just then Oliver said, "Ladies and gentlemen, we'd like to sing a little song by one of my favorite artists. And, of course, I'd like to dedicate it to all the beautiful ladies in the room."

I rolled my eyes, especially when all the ladies in the room swooned. The band started up and I almost fell to the floor when I recognized it as *Sway*. I could have died! How could he have remembered I'd told him that was my favorite Dean Martin song? Oh, this guy was smooth. Too smooth. I was just a simple country girl. I didn't know what to do with all this.

I stared at him and realized he wasn't singing the song to the crowd. He was singing it to me. He was singing my pants—or dress—right off. The bastard. The charming fucking bastard. And his voice was beautiful, so self-assured. He was such a good singer. It was too bad that he had been relegated to producing girl groups. I hated that for him. But I loved knowing he was there singing to me so he could show me what he had. And he had a great voice. He really did.

All the women sighed with lust as he sang that very sexy song. He didn't care. He was concentrating on me. I was sure Kevin would catch on but he didn't. He smiled occasionally and once kissed me on the cheek. It was a beautiful moment, even if he didn't understand what was really going on.

Oliver finished with a flourish. The room erupted in applause. I clapped too and smiled at him. I couldn't hold it back. I was very proud of him and honored at what he'd just done for me. Even if it did kind of piss me off.

"Kora," Kevin whispered in my ear. "I have to go by the office."

"What?" I hissed and turned around to him.

"Listen," he said. "It's important. I can't explain it. I have to go."

I glared at him. "So you're just going to leave me here alone?"

"I will be back in half an hour," he said. "Stay here."

"Kevin—"

I shouldn't have bothered. He was gone. Asshole. I was so done with him doing this shit to me. He was so work obsessed that I could hardly stand him anymore. And he was working later and later. I was usually in bed when he came home at night.

Maybe he was having an affair. Nah. He was just money-grubbing, working so that he could have more money to put in the bank. More money, more money, more money to not have any fun with.

Well, if Kevin was leaving, so was I. I glanced at the stage. Several women were hanging all over Oliver. It made me slightly sick, especially when I saw his eyes dart down to a set of breasts. *Asshole!* I was done with men. They could all kiss my ass. I was going home.

As soon as I found the bathroom, that is. I got up, walked across the room and felt Oliver's eyes on my back. I didn't care. He could bite me. Coming here. Old friend from school, indeed. What a prick!

I found the bathroom and after I was done, I walked out looking in my purse for cab fare and collided with Oliver.

"Hey, baby," he whispered in my ear.

"Fuck you," I said and turned around, having every intention of going back into the bathroom. He grabbed my hand and halted me. I jerked it but he wouldn't let it go. I hated it when guys pulled that shit. *Look, little girl, I'm stronger than you.* I started to get frustrated. He pulled me to him. Now that was better. I almost gave in to the temptation, then found my senses and fought against him. He grabbed my hands and held them behind my back.

"Come here," he whispered.

"Let me go!" I hissed and struggled against him. Damn! He was a strong son of a bitch. "What are you doing here?"

"I told you," he said. "Phil called and wanted me to sing. He's an old friend."

"Right," I said. "You came to check out my husband."

"I did not," he said. "I'm a singer. I get asked to sing all the time. I can't help it if we know the same people."

"Whatever, Oliver," I said and pushed against him. "Now let me go."

"Shh," he whispered and then gave me a kiss.

The bastard. Before I could stop myself, I kissed him back. I took his head between my hands and held him still. He pulled away and glanced around, his eyes settling on the men's bathroom door. Yeah, that would do.

We went in. Thankfully, it was empty. Muzak played over the speakers. We found a stall, went in and grabbed at each other. Suddenly, I didn't care. Fucking did that to me. It made me not care.

"God, you look so hot," he said and squeezed my ass. "You look like you were poured into that dress."

"So take me out of it," I said and pushed myself against him. "Just get on with it. Come on, get on with it."

He complied by getting down on his knees and pushing his face into my crotch. I gasped. Then he grabbed my ass and pushed his face between my legs. I put a leg up on his shoulder and pulled him closer. He went under the dress and began to eat at me. I moaned. I couldn't get enough. I wanted more and more. I wanted his cock inside me.

"Oh, yeah," I said and pulled him back up. I started down to give him a little of what he'd given me, but he stopped me.

"I just want to be inside you," he said.

That turned me on so much.

"So, get in," I said and smiled at him.

I unzipped his pants and stroked his cock. He grunted and pushed me back against the door, then pulled up the dress. I wrapped my legs around his waist and he stuck it in. We fucked our brains out for a good four minutes. Then... Then someone came into the bathroom.

We stopped and stared at each other.

The person went over to the urinal and proceeded with his business. I started to giggle. He put his hand over my mouth. I kissed it off and began to move again, just a little bit. He moved too.

The person called, "Oliver? That you?"

"Shit," he muttered, then, "Yeah? George?"

"It's me!" he called. "You check out that American girl?"

Oliver glanced at me and smiled. "Oh, yeah. Nice looking, eh?"

"Nice?" George hollered. "More like hot! Too bad she's married."

I whispered in his ear, "I love having your dick in me."

He pressed his face against mine and called, "Uh, George, bit busy right now!"

This made George pause. And I just knew what he was thinking. And I just knew he knew what we were doing. Now this was just a little awkward.

"Which one you got?" he asked excitedly. "Oh, mate, I knew it! You've got Erin in there!"

Who the hell was Erin? I hissed, "That bastard!"

"Or is it Nikki?" he asked.

"*Nikki?*" I hissed. "Who the hell is *Nikki?*"

Oliver covered my mouth with his hand and said, "Neither! Just me in here."

"I'm glad it's not Erin. Got me eye on her myself!"

"George, mate, still a bit busy in here."

"Oh," he said. "Well, see you later."

"Later."

And he left. Finally.

"Oliver," I said, staring into his eyes. "I don't think we should do this. We could get caught."

"We did just get caught," he said. "And we're already doing it."

"Oliver—"

"Shh," he said and began to kiss my neck. He had a way with that, too. His mouth opened wide and as he sucked on it, his tongue flicked out and stroked it. It sent shivers up my spine.

I grinned and kissed all of his face. He started moving more quickly. So did I. He grabbed onto the back of the door and held on as we fucked. And fucked. Then, the bolt of lightning. The sound of thunder.

"AHHH!" I moaned.

"UHHH!"

"Oh, yeah, fuck me," I moaned.

"Ummm!"

He gave one last push then it was over for both of us. We pulled apart smiling at each other.

He kissed me and muttered, "That was fantastic."

I nodded. "It was, wasn't it? I have to go now, though."

"You're coming over tomorrow, aren't you?"

"Don't you ever work?" I asked.

"I work at night," he said, slightly perturbed. "If you ever bothered asking anything about me, you'd know that."

I felt bad. He was trying to be nice and he'd just fucked me good. I was such a bitch. I couldn't do anything right.

"Sorry, honey," I said. "It's just… All this is making me crazy."

"Well, are you crazy?" he asked.

I stared at him and said, "You're just now getting around to asking me that?"

He cracked up. "Yeah."

"I'll see you tomorrow."

He grabbed my hand and whispered in my ear, "I'll just say this, okay? You're the best fuck ever."

He walked away without another word. The best fuck ever. Yeah. I could believe it.

Charming bastard.

A week or so later, I went shopping. Oliver's birthday was coming up and I wanted to buy him a present—of me in lingerie. Guys loved that stuff. I hadn't bought lingerie in years. Kevin just liked me naked. He always said that lingerie was a waste of money because it didn't stay on that long. Which was true, but still.

I took a cab to Harrods. They had the best stuff. It was expensive but I didn't care. I'd just put it on my credit card and tell Kevin I got the pounds/dollar thing mixed up again. I could just hear him say, "You are going to have to learn to convert!"

I shook my head and smiled out the window of the cab. It was May, almost June. The weather was clearing and the trees budding. I smiled with satisfaction and couldn't remember ever being this happy, this content.

As soon as I got there, I found a little red push-up bra in the lingerie department. When I stared at myself in the dressing room mirror, I nodded with satisfaction. This would do it. It made my tits look so good. I'd tell him, "I've got something to show you." And then, the reveal. *Ta da!* Instant boner. With the little red panties, I would be stylin'!

I smiled to myself and heard two women chatting outside the door.

"Oh, no, Claire," one said. "Try that one instead."

"Not that I should care," she replied. "But maybe I can save it for someone else."

My ears pricked up. I was such a snoop.

"Is he doing it again?" the other one asked.

"Yeah," Claire replied. "Jen, I tell you, he's not worth the trouble."

"Oh, he is," she said. "He's rich!"

"Well, he won't be half as rich when I get through with him," she said. "This time, I mean it! And he won't stall me by promising we can work it out. I'm not falling for that again. He just doesn't want to part with any money."

"Oh, I like that on you," Jen said. "Turn around."

"It does look good," she replied. "In the closet, it'll look perfect."

They laughed.

"So do you really think he's doing it again?" Jen asked.

"I know he is!" Claire exclaimed. "He's sleeping with some tart. Always does, always will."

"Well," Jen said. "Oliver is such a charming bastard."

I froze. Were they talking about Oliver? *My* Oliver? Surely not.

"That's how he got me," she said. "And the fact that he's worth a lot of money."

"Well, when you married Oliver, you didn't know he'd turn out like that," Jen said.

"I know," she sighed. "When you get a rock star, you can't help but get the tarts, too."

I felt sick. It was Oliver's wife! The other woman, I assumed, was her friend. I was dying to see what a woman who would marry Oliver would look like, but I couldn't bring myself to take a peek. I knew she had to be tall, blonde and beautiful. An ex-model who was built like a brick shithouse. I felt so low then. I'd never felt that low before. I was so low, I almost hated myself. I knew I looked as good as she did, that men desired me, but I'd always had that twinge of insecurity that rode my back. Whenever I thought it went away, it always came back to jump on again.

"And the fact that all the other girls love him," Jen said.

"Yeah," she said bitterly. "You don't understand that when you meet someone like Oliver. You don't understand you're just one of the few in a long line of many."

I was going to throw up. I was going to throw up right here and now! But I knew she was right. I was his tart! I was a tart! I felt like such a whore.

"It's terrible," Jen said.

"It is," Claire said. "He's staying at the fuck pad again. Must have him a new one."

I couldn't take it anymore. I took the bra off, put my shirt back on and raced out of the dressing room, keeping my eyes forward so I wouldn't see either of them. I didn't stop running until I got home, almost an hour later. Once I was there, I fell on the bed and cried all afternoon.

After I was done, I knew I deserved this. I deserved to know, to be hurt. I was just a stupid woman who'd fallen for a charming bastard. I could have kicked my own ass. But that didn't take away from the fact that I had this incredible sick feeling in my heart. It felt like someone had taken a chunk out of it.

The phone rang all afternoon. I knew it was Oliver. As soon as the announcement message played, he'd sigh and hang up, not saying anything. He never left messages. He was discreet. He knew what we were doing and you don't leave messages on machines where the husband can hear them. It took everything I had not to throw the answering machine against the wall.

When Kevin got home, he asked if anything was wrong. I shook my head and said my allergies were bothering me. I went to bed early and slept late the next day. Oliver called all day again. I ignored the phone and stared at the ceiling, wondering why I was hurting so bad. Why did it have to hurt *this* bad? I mean I knew it would hurt; I just had no idea about how much.

On the third day, he broke the silence and left a message, "I don't know what happened or why you're pissed off. But have some respect for me and pick up the fucking phone so I'll know you're not dead!"

I glared at the answering machine.

"Kora!" he yelled. "I mean it! Pick up the phone!"

I glared at the wall.

"If you don't pick up the phone," he said. "I am going to come over there and bang on your door. What will your neighbors think?"

I snatched the phone up and then I couldn't talk. I had wanted to tell him off, to hurt him like he'd hurt me. But as soon as I had the opportunity, I was mute.

"Are you there?" he asked.

"Yeah," I muttered.

"Baby, what is wrong with you?" he asked.

"I..." I stopped and decided to lie. "I just... I'm sick. With allergies."

"Don't lie to me," he said. "You're pissed off and I want to know why."

"No," I said. "It's allergies."

"Then come over."

"No," I said. "I'm busy."

"What's wrong?" he asked. "I really want to know."

"Nothing," I said pitifully.

"Come on, Kora!" he yelled. "Tell me what's wrong!"

"Nothing!" I yelled. "I'm busy!"

I slammed the phone down and began to shake with hurt and rage and self pity. I picked up a vase and threw it against the wall. It shattered and fell to the floor. Great. Now I'd have to clean that up.

As I was bent over with a dustpan and broom, the phone rang again. It rang four times, then the machine picked up, then Oliver said, "What the fuck is wrong with you? Pick up the phone and let's talk, Kora."

Pause.

"Kora," he said. "I swear if you don't pick up the phone right now, I will come over there."

Was he trying to bluff me or something? I ignored it and kept sweeping.

"Kora," he hissed. "You don't know what you're doing to me right now. You're really pissing me off with this. I mean it. Pick up the phone."

I shook my head.

"PICK UP THE FUCKING PHONE!"

"Fuck!" I yelled and picked up the phone. "What do you want, you motherfucker!"

"I want you to tell me what the bloody hell is wrong!"

"I'll tell you," I hissed, nodding vigorously. "I don't want to see you! I don't want to smell you! I don't want to touch you!"

He sighed wearily and said, "Why not?"

"You're ruining my life!" I yelled.

I could tell that hurt him and I could tell because he let out a deep breath as soon as I said it.

He muttered, "Well."

"It's no good, Oliver," I seethed. "It never was and it never will be."

"Fine," he said. "Tell me what changed your mind."

"The hell I will," I muttered. There was no way I was telling him about seeing his wife and eavesdropping on her conversation.

"Tell me what changed your mind," he repeated.

"No!" I yelled.

"Tell me!" he yelled.

"Why?" I snapped.

"So I can know what happened. That's all I want to know."

"Fine," I said. "I was shopping at Harrods and I overheard *your* wife and *her* friend talking about the fuck pad and about how you always had a tart or two around and how you had a new one now. I'm not a tart!"

He took a deep breath and said, "Oh, great! You're taking life lessons from Miss Chastity! You wanna know something about her? I'll tell you! I caught her in bed with my roadie Jason two months after we got married!"

"Well, look at what you do."

"What the fuck does that mean?" he hissed.

"It means," I said. "If you can do it, why shouldn't she?"

"I don't know how to respond to that," he snapped. "What the fuck do you want me to do?"

Tell me something, I thought. Tell me I'm better than her, tell me I mean the most to you. Tell me anything but don't say a word. Somehow make it right again. But I knew anything that came out of his mouth would be a lie. It killed me to know that.

"Just leave me alone, Oliver," I said and started to hang up. "I don't want to get in the middle of your marriage."

"Marriage?" he scoffed. "Yeah, that's what I have, isn't it?"

"I have no idea and I don't care," I replied. "It's your marriage and if you don't like it, get out of it. But leave me alone. I'm not getting in the middle of this shit."

"Get out of it?" he asked. "Oh, it's that easy, is it?"

"I have to go!" I yelled. "This has nothing to do with me!"

"Listen, my hands are tied, Kora," he said. "I can't do anything right now."

"Yes, you can," I said. "You just won't."

"Why hand that greedy bitch half of everything I have?" he seethed. "You wanna know why I'm not divorced? Because she has every intention of ruining me financially!"

"Yeah," I said dryly. "I know. She said that. She said she was going to get half."

"The hell she will," he muttered. "Listen to me, Kora, I tried with her. I did everything I could, but I couldn't make myself love her."

"Then why did you marry her?"

"I don't fucking know," he said. "I was getting older and it just seemed like it was time. And I wanted kids. She didn't. She just wanted to be rich."

"Well, if she had no intention of having kids," I said. "You could get the marriage annulled."

He paused and said, "Really?"

"I think so," I said. "Fuck! I'm not giving you marital advice!"

"Listen," he said. "You don't pick who you love, Kora."

"What the hell does that mean?"

"You know what it means," he said. "And you are not just some tart."

"The hell I'm not," I said. "You're using me and then you'll get tired of me."

"I'll never get tired of you."

"Oliver," I said. "I can't do this anymore."

"Kora," he muttered. "Don't do this, baby."

I started to cry. "Listen, I have to go, Oliver. I hear someone at the door."

"I know you're lying."

"I have to go!" I yelled and slammed the phone down. Oh, God, I felt so awful. It was all so ugly and grown-up. It wasn't fun anymore. And poor Kevin! I'd made a fool out of him.

I started to pace, thinking of all the bad things I'd done. I kept pacing and kept thinking, almost getting sick. I couldn't take it anymore. If I didn't stop this obsessive stream of thoughts about the affair and Kevin, I was going to have a nervous breakdown. I went into the bathroom and got in the shower. I stayed in there a long time, just trying to feel the warmth from the water, wishing something could warm my heart.

As soon as I got out and wrapped myself in a towel, I heard the doorbell. Oh, shit. He didn't! He'd better not have come here! He wouldn't dare, though. I would kill him if he did. I opened the door. It was him. He dared. He was standing there looking so sad and hurt I wanted to cry.

"Hey, baby," he said.

"Get out," I said and tried to shut the door.

He held it open and shook his head. "If we're going to finish this thing, we're going to finish it right."

"Fuck you!" I hissed and tried to shut the door again. "Someone is going to see you!"

"I don't give a fuck!" he hissed. "You either let me in or let your neighbors find out."

I let him in.

He walked around the apartment for a moment, taking it in, nodding to himself, then turned to me. "I've missed you."

"Fuck you."

"Come on, Kora," he said. "Don't be like that."

"Be like what?" I asked. "I can't do this anymore. I can't see you and I can't... I just can't."

"Why not?"

"I just can't do this!" I screamed, shaking my fists. "I am not built for this shit!"

"Oh, come on!"

"It's all a lie!" I screamed. "A big fat ugly lie! All of it!"

He stared at me, then looked at his shoes. I sighed. I didn't even know why I was so upset. I was just a hair short of being hysterical. What was wrong with me? I was usually easy going and happy go lucky. I stared at Oliver. That's why. He was the reason I was going to these extremes. I didn't like him because of it. I had promised myself it was just an affair but now I knew it was more than that to me. And it made me sick to think of him not feeling the same way I did.

He stared up at me, a little sadly. "What do you have to lose?"

"My marriage," I said. "Every fucking thing I've worked for! Down the drain!"

"You'll have me!"

"Until you get tired of me," I said. "And then what will I have, Oliver? A nice memory?"

"Don't you dare discount me like that."

"Be honest," I said. "How long does it take for a guy like you to get tired of his conquests?"

"You were never a conquest."

"I was a conquest from the day you laid eyes on me. You know that and I know that. Don't make a fool out of me."

He grabbed my arm and pulled me to me. He was so pissed off, his nostrils were flaring. "And don't you make fun of what I feel."

"I'm not making fun of it," I said. "And let go of my arm!"

"No," he said. "Not until you know how I feel."

"And how do you feel?" I asked and tried to pull my arm out of his grip. He wasn't letting go.

"I love you," he said.

I glared at him and tried to slap him with my other hand. He then grabbed that arm and held it tight.

"Don't do that," he hissed and glared into my eyes. "I love you, I love you, I love you."

"Let me go!" I yelled. "You're just saying that so I'll fuck you!"

"No, I am not," he hissed.

"Yes, you are," I said, feeling so angry my entire body was heated up. "I know how you guys operate. I know what you'll do to get what you want! And let go of my arm!"

He didn't. I pushed against him. He held on strong. Suddenly I was even more pissed off. I got free of him and slapped him as hard as I could. His face shot to the side, then he shook his head and threw me down on the floor and fell on me. Oh, no, he wasn't! Fuck him!

"Stop it!" I yelled and slapped at him. "You're acting like an animal!"

He pulled me under him and said, "What do you want me to do? How do you want me to act? Huh?"

I glared at him. I hated him so much. And I hated him because I loved him. Why had I let myself fall in love with him? How could that have happened? I knew he was just using me, no matter what he said, and as soon as he got tired of me, he'd let me go. That would be hard to take.

"It's not my fault we met and hit it off," he hissed. "It's not my fault that I love you! It's—"

"Shut up!" I screamed. "And get off me!"

He stopped moving and just held me tight. We glared into each other's eyes as our breathing escalated and our hearts beat furiously inside our chests. We were so close then, it seemed as if we'd always been that close.

But I couldn't stand it. I was still hurt, still pissed off. I wanted to make him pay. I wanted him to hurt, like I'd hurt. I wanted to show him I wasn't a tart and I deserved better treatment. I didn't like being put in this position. So I bit his shoulder to illustrate my pain. He yelled, then pressed his lips against mine. I bit at them. He pulled back and shook his head, then went in for a kiss. I struggled against him but then...then... it was no use. I'd missed him as much as he'd missed me.

My feelings took over and I was pulling him closer to me, trying to kiss him as he tried to kiss me. I didn't care anymore. I didn't care if he was lying about loving me and I didn't care if I was screwing my life up. I just had to get that kiss of his. I had to have him.

He let me have it. He gave it to me, all of it, all of himself. He was at me, all over me, kissing me and murmuring my name softly, telling me he was sorry about things I didn't care about anymore.

I wrapped my arms around his neck and ate at his mouth, loving the way his kiss was taking the pain away. Then it took over, the sex took over and nothing mattered anymore. Ahh... Good sex. Nothing like it in the whole world. Nothing at all could compare as he pulled the towel off my body and kissed me, covering my wet naked body with long touches and desperate kisses. Touches along my back, my stomach, my thighs, my breasts, and between my legs, which opened to allow him to put his hand there and touch me however he pleased.

I tugged his clothes and pushed and pulled them off until he was naked like me. We rolled on the floor and I landed on top, where I started kissing his forehead. I moved on to his ear, down his chest and stopped at his dick. I took it in my mouth and deepthroated him. He nearly rose up off the floor as I sucked as hard as I could.

"I want to be inside you," he said and tugged at me.

I allowed him to pull me up, to flip me over and to settle between my legs. I kissed him, slipping my tongue into his mouth and he sucked on it, which was the most incredible feeling. That made me hold onto him so his hands would stay on me, giving me the caresses I wanted.

"I've missed you," he muttered.

"I've missed you, too," I moaned and licked his neck. I stared into his eyes and said, "Don't ever let me be that stupid again."

He grinned and nodded. I loved that feeling his body gave me, the pressure of it. He pushed my legs open with his knee. And he was in. He was home, with me.

Ahh. It felt so good, better than I had remembered it. It felt like a good connection had been established and all the bad ones broken. I wrapped my legs around his waist as he kissed me and pushed in deeper making me gasp.

Soon, I felt the orgasm creeping slowly up my legs, making me numb in a few places. I held on to him and pushed as it began.

"Kora!" he gasped. "Ahh...baby!"

"Hold on," I said, still clinging for the right movement that would make my climax linger so I could make the real pleasure last. "Hold on, please, hold on!"

"Kora!" he groaned and began to really fuck me.

I fucked back and squeezed my eyes shut as it gripped me, made me weak, made me strong, exploded...then filtered away bit by bit. I was sad to see it go.

He rolled off me and lay on his back, breathing heavily. I closed my eyes and thought about how much I loved him. I loved him so much it kinda scared me. I'd denied it for too long.

"Oliver," I said. "I'm going to ask you one question and you need to answer it honestly."

"Alright."

"Do you really love me?"

He stared at me sadly for a moment, moved closer to me and said, "Yes, I do. I love you. When you wouldn't see me, I could have died. Don't do that to me again. Don't put me through that again, Kora. I mean it."

I nodded and kissed his cheek.

"Well?" he said. "Do you have something to tell me?"

I stared into his eyes and said, "I love you, too."

About naked.

I stared at the cake, then back at Oliver. I looked back at the cake and smiled at the icing which read: *Happy 34th Kora!* It was red velvet cake, my favorite. I think he had to find someone to make it for him special as I'd never seen a red velvet cake in London before today.

It was my birthday, today, December 13th. I'd been in London nearly a year and Kevin's company had prolonged his stay for "a few more months." I'd been with Oliver for almost nine. It didn't seem like that long. It seemed as though I'd only known him a few days.

"Blow out your candles," he said.

I grinned and blew out the candles, then kissed his cheek. "Thank you, baby."

"You're welcome," he said and handed me a little box. "Don't forget this."

I grinned and tore it open. Inside was a beautiful platinum and diamond bracelet. It was heavy. It had to be more than a carat. One thing about Oliver was that he wasn't cheap. I *loved* that about him.

"Oh, it's beautiful!" I squealed and held out my arm. "Put it on me."

He slipped it on my wrist and smiled at me. I smiled back and looked down at it. Wow. I was never going to take it off. Ever.

"Like it?" he asked.

"I love it," I said. "You shouldn't have."

"Oh, I think I should have," he said and sat down at the kitchen table, pulling me into his lap.

I wrapped my arms around his neck and kissed his cheek. "I suppose you'll be wanting a blowjob for this?"

He threw his head back and laughed loudly. "Of course! That's why I buy gifts. Makes getting blowjobs easier."

I touched his cheek and said, "I'm still so sorry I was mean to you that time. I know it was months ago, but I still feel bad."

"Well, you did say you'd make me pine over you."

I stared up at the ceiling and said, "Yeah, I did, didn't I?"

"Bitch," he said and chuckled.

I stared at him. God, he looked so good in the morning. And in the afternoon and in the evening and…just about always. I stared at the bracelet. Damn, he had good taste. I knew I'd have to hide it from Kevin, unless, of course, I told him it was a fake and I got it from a street vendor, just like I had all the other gifts of expensive handbags, jewelry and shoes he'd given me. I could do that. I was getting better and better at this lying/cheating thing.

"Give us a kiss," he said and moved his head up so I could bend down and kiss him. We kissed for a few minutes until he pulled away and said, "Let me tell you a funny story. I think you'll get a kick out of this."

"Go on," I said.

"Anyway, we were on tour," he said. "And I was with—now don't get mad—a groupie in a hotel room. Anyway, for some reason George came in and asked if I had something of his."

"Yeah."

"I didn't," he said. "And then the drummer, Teddy, came in and asked George something. Soon, there were about ten people in the room. I don't know why, don't ask me."

"Were you fucking the groupie?" I asked.

"Not at that moment," he said. "So, anyway, Nick, the keyboardist, came in and looked around at all the people and said, 'Why are all these people in here?' I told him I had no idea and then he said it looked a bit weird. And then the groupie said, 'Why? Does it look like we're having an orgy?' and Nick laughed. Then the bassist, Roland, walked in and asked what was going on. The groupie said, 'We're getting ready to have an orgy.'"

I smiled and nodded.

"And then she asked him if he'd like to join us," he said, laughing. "And he said, 'Sure, why not?' and I'll be damned if the bastard didn't start taking off his clothes!"

"No way!"

"Yeah," he said. "We let him get down to his socks and then Nick stopped him and told him we were joking."

"What happened?"

"He just looked at us and said, 'Oh, you didn't...' then his face went red and he said, 'Got you!' and raced out of the room."

I cracked up. "Then what happened?"

"We had an orgy."

I slapped his arm.

"No, really," he said seriously. "We had an orgy."

"Oliver!"

He laughed. "No, we didn't. We came close a few times, but no cigar."

"You rock stars," I said and shook my head.

He took my hand. "It's a good life, isn't it, Kora?"

"I wouldn't know," I said and smoothed the hair out of his eyes.

"I want you to know."

"Huh?" I asked.

"I want you to live it with me," he said. "I want you to be here with me."

I pulled my hand away. "I can't and you know that."

He dropped his head. "What's he got that I haven't?"

I stared at him and thought about it. I didn't know. I loved Kevin but I knew I was in love with Oliver. Funny how that works. But Kevin had always been with me. It would be scary living without him. I also knew if I went with Oliver, he might tire of me and then where would I be? Alone, that's where. It was too big of a gamble.

"Nothing," I said.

"Oh, come on," he said. "He's got to have something."

"You wanna know what it is?" I asked.

He nodded. "I do."

"He's got my loyalty," I said. "I can't shake it."

"But he hasn't got your love."

I felt a flush of anger. "Fuck you."

"It's true," he said. "He hasn't got it. And I don't, either. Who's got it, Kora? Who's got your love?"

"You know who," I said. "So shut up."

"If it's me—"

"Let's don't do this," I said and stood.

"Go ahead," he said. "Run out, run away.

I turned to him and said, "Come on, baby, you know how hard it is on me."

"I just want you to know where I stand," he said. "I'm getting older and let's face it, if we don't do something soon, we might not ever have the chance to be together. We can't let it slip through our fingers. We can't keep playing with it like this."

I hung my head.

He came over to me and took my hand. "I want something more, I want you. I want a family. I want a life."

I shook my head a little, wishing he'd just shut the fuck up. He was bringing me down. Kevin wanted a family, too. We'd discussed it. We had told each other we'd try for a baby as soon as we got back home, maybe after we got a bigger house. When I'd promised that, I hadn't met Oliver and it made sense to start planning. Now I wished I'd kept my mouth shut. And time was running out. It wouldn't be long before Kevin said, "You better start packing. We're leaving in a few days." I dreaded that day so much. But I thought if I didn't think about it too much, it might not come. I'd never avoided reality as much as I had these past few months.

"It's okay," he said and took me into his arms. "Don't worry about it."

"But I'll have to someday, won't I?"

He sighed and said, "Yeah, you will."

I pressed my face into his chest.

"How about this?" he said, wriggling his eyebrows. "How about we go on a little weekend trip?"

"You know I can't."

"Come on," he said, "It'll be fun. I have a little cottage in Bath. Well, it's my mother's but she's going to be away for a few days…"

"Bath?" I asked. "How far is Bath?"

"Not that far."

It sounded intriguing, then I realized he'd almost talked me into it. I waved my hands at him and said, "No! I can't."

"Oh, come on," he said. "Tell Kevin you're going with Sally."

I pointed my finger at him. "No."

"Come on," he said and winked at me. "Take a chance. You said he works every weekend anyway."

I thought about that. Kevin did work a lot. He was working to give us a better life that I was trying to screw up.

"I'll think about it," I said and thought about it. I didn't know if I had the balls to pull something like that off or not. This was a big step, a big risk. A whole weekend…a whole weekend of fucking.

Oh, hell, why not? Life was too short to get hung up on details.

★ ★ ★ ★ ★

As we neared Bath, I began to get excited. I still didn't know how I'd managed to pull this over on Kevin, but when I told him "Sally" wanted me to go home with her over the weekend for some "fun," he bought it. Maybe because he was going to be working all weekend anyway. Maybe *he* was having an affair. And if he was? I didn't want to know. I had my own issues to deal with.

Bath was like no other town I've ever seen. There were all these houses on the side of this enormous hill that all looked exactly the same. It was so old, too. The Roman ruins and Georgian architecture took my breath away.

"And the Romans built those baths?" I asked Oliver.

He grinned and said, "Sure did."

"And you grew up in this neat place?"

"Yup," he replied. "Like it?"

"I love it!" I squealed and kissed his cheek. "I'm so happy I came with you!"

"I'm happy, too," he said and squeezed my knee.

I grinned and stared out the window at the darkening sky. We'd been driving since noon and I was ready to get out of Oliver's Range Rover and stretch my legs. I was also ready to see the town. I had to remember to buy some souvenirs to prove I was here.

He kept driving and soon we were on a little deserted road where we finally pulled up in front of his mom's cottage. It was two-story and looked like a ginger bread house. It was so quaint and English.

We got out and he took my hand and led me inside. I looked around at the old stone fireplace and at the pale yellow chintz covered sofa and chairs. "Your mom has great taste."

"She does," he said. "Let me show you the upstairs."

"Okay," I said and followed towards the stairs. I stopped at the foot and watched him walk up. Damn, his ass looked good. I raced up behind him and tackled him.

"What the bloody hell do you think you're doing?" he yelped.

I turned him over and made him sit on a step. "What does it look like I'm doing?"

I pulled his shirt over his head and covered his mouth with mine, pushing my tongue in until he moaned and held onto the back of my head and kissed me back. I took his hand and pushed it under my shirt, and put my hand on top of his crotch. He liked that. He told me so.

"Like this?" I asked and unzipped his jeans.

"Very much so," he muttered.

I stood and pulled my pants off, then he struggled out of his jeans, and I sat down on top of...him. He pulled my mouth to his and we kissed for a very long time, just tasting each other. And he tasted good.

I began to move. He moved some too. I pulled my shirt over my head and he ripped my bra off; it fell in shreds off my back. Ahhhhhh...I loved that. The way his wet mouth just took my nipple and his tongue stroked so lightly, so nicely. It was sheer enjoyment, sheer pleasure as I squeezed my legs around his waist and then...we almost fell off the step.

Oliver grabbed my shoulders and steadied us. We sat still for a moment and stared into each others eyes.

"That would be very embarrassing," I whispered.

"What?"

"To fall to your death while fucking someone," I said and thought about that. It tickled my funny bone. I threw my head back and laughed loudly. He covered my mouth with his hand.

"Shh," he whispered.

I got back on task. I kissed him again, this time less furiously, but not any less passionately. We began to move together. My body prepared itself. The climax began. Oliver pushed his face against my neck and held on so tightly.

"Ahh...*Kora*," he moaned.

"Ahh, Oliver," I moaned back and licked his ear. "I love the way you fuck me."

He liked that. I could tell. His movements became more concentrated. He murmured, "What else?"

"I love it when you stick your hard cock inside me."

He pushed my head back and sucked on my throat. Ahhh, *good God!*

"What else!" he grunted.

"I love it when you touch me, when you run your fingers inside of me, inside of my wet pussy."

"What else?" he gasped.

I could tell he was about to come. I began to ride him harder, finding my groove. I licked his ear and moaned, "I love it when you lick my pussy."

"Uhhh," he moaned. "What else?"

"I love it when—" I didn't finish. I couldn't stop myself. I was coming and coming hard.

"What else?!"

"Just fuck me!"

He fucked me. Mmmmmuuu…ohhhh… Yeah! I shook, feeling every single part of my body just then and I came, intoxicated by the moment and by him. I held his head to my neck and felt him pump himself into me with all his might, with all his energy, with all of himself. He pumped until he was spent then he slowed down and held me tight.

"Damn," I sighed and ran my tongue lightly up his throat. "You're good."

"Mmmm, so are you," he said and turned so I could kiss him. "In fact, you're the best ever."

"You told me that once."

"I meant it, too."

I giggled and grabbed my shirt and pulled it on. I started to grab my jeans, but he grabbed my hand and led me upstairs. It was filled with antiques and enormous old beds. Oliver flopped on one, put his hands behind his head and eyed me. I smiled and looked around, then back at him.

"Why don't you strip?" he asked.

I stared down at myself. "I'm about naked."

"You've still got your shirt on."

"Oh, do I?" I asked and winked at him.

"Come on, love," he said. 'Take your shirt off."

I pulled it off and threw it at him. "Satisfied?"

He nodded.

I shivered. "It's as cold as a witch's titty in a brass bar in here."

He chuckled. "Where do you come up with this stuff?"

I shrugged and stared at him. "You're making me uncomfortable. Like you're a pervert or something."

"I've been called that before."

"Somehow that doesn't surprise me."

He gave a slight nod. "Come over here."

"Where?" I teased and went over. "Here?"

He grinned and grabbed me. I smiled and accepted his kiss, his passion. Our bare bodies pressed against each others and gave off so much heat that the cold was gone and all I felt was warmth.

"Ahh…" he began as soon as he had his dick in me. "Kora."

I held onto him and whispered, "Please, not yet!"

"Kora! Oh, baby, I…ahhh…"

"Please, not yet, Oliver. Oliver!"

Too late. Just then he took me, held on tight and my hips rose off the bed and I pushed against him, and felt it. I held on to his head and muttered, "Oh, Oliver…oh, baby. Oh, Oliver!"

"Come on baby!"

He didn't have to tell me. I was well on my way by then. It didn't take long and then it was over.

"Oliver," I said.

"What?"

"Where's the bathroom?"

Bad.

The most blinding, brilliant light glared through the open window and directly into my eyes. I turned and shoved my head into Oliver's pillow. I yawned and yelled, "Where are you!"

No response. I could hear water running in the bathroom down the hall. I got up and went to it.

"Oliver?"

"Yeah?" he asked, poking his head out of the shower curtain. He grinned from ear to ear.

"You are such a happy, happy man today," I told him and stepped into the tub. I kissed the back of his neck and asked, "Why?"

"I just like coming home," he replied.

I got in and put my arms around his neck and he bent at the knees to kiss me. I nibbled on his ear and said, "I like being naked with you."

"I like being naked with you, too."

I stared at my body, then back at him. I had to ask, "Do you think I'm fat?"

He looked right in my eyes and said, "If you were any more perfect, it'd be against the law."

He was so good with that stuff! I threw my arms around him, knocking him off balance. He grabbed my waist and we fell out of the tub laughing.

I climbed on top of him and rubbed his chest with my hands. He watched me and grabbed my breasts with both hands and pulled me to his lips. We kissed and he rolled me over and put it in.

We began very slowly, staring into each other's eyes. I bit my lip and began to move. He followed my lead and we fucked like that for a few minutes taking our time to touch each other, to arouse each other. He licked my neck and sucked on it, which made me moan. I grabbed his head and pulled his lips to mine and we kissed as we moved. He began to move faster, just a little faster and so did I. The orgasm came to me very slowly, it teased me at first and then it began to build in sputters. I was shaking I was so turned on. He was shaking too. We came at the same time.

After it was over, he said, "I love you, Kora."

I kissed his cheek and said, "Yeah, I know."

He eyed me and his eyes narrowed.

"What?" I asked innocently.

"You know what."

I cracked up and yelled at the top of my lungs, "I love you, too!"

"You better."

"Yeah, yeah," I said and stood. "Come on, let's take a shower."

"Let's eat something first."

"Food and sex," I said. "That's all you want, isn't it?"

He considered and said, "Well, is there anything else?"

Downstairs, in the most pleasant little kitchen in the whole wide world, Oliver prepared a "full English" breakfast of rashers (bacon), eggs, and toast and lots of it. There was even a tomato on there. He served me and then went back to the stove and kept cooking. I was almost finished by the time he sat down.

"I thought you told me you couldn't cook," I said.

He cracked up and said, "I wouldn't necessarily call this cooking."

I nodded. "Neither would I."

"Bitch, keep talking," he muttered and smiled, shaking his head at me.

"What do you want to do today?" I asked.

"How about we go for a walk this morning?"

"Sure," I said and smiled at him. "When are we going to go see the baths?"

"Later today if you like," he said. "You know you can't actually bathe in them, don't you?"

I shook my head.

"A kid took a dip a few years ago," he said. "And got meningitis."

My mouth dropped. "No way!"

He nodded. "They're full of green, rank water."

"Why don't they drain them?"

He shrugged. "I don't know."

"Well, I don't know if I want to go now or not."

He shrugged and then finished eating. Then we got up and went on a walk in the countryside. It was so clean and nice. We held hands as we walked but didn't talk much. It was so nice to just be like that.

"Let's take a break," he said and sat down under a tree.

I sat down beside him and took his hand.

"I've got something to show you," he said and pulled a piece of paper out of his back pocket.

I eyed him and took it. "What is this?"

"Just a tune I wrote and hope to produce for myself."

I smiled at him. "You're going to cut a record?"

"I might," he said with a very self-satisfied look. "Read it!"

I grinned and began to read…

> "She walks on air most of the time
> Hasn't got a care the surface woulda shown
> A puritan's smile, a devil's laugh, an angel's cry
> She'll never be perfect, she might as well not try
> If she wants you, she won't let you know
> It might take awhile, she can be kinda slow
> I want to hide, but can't seem to run
> If I look around, my world's been spun
> She might not be perfect, she'll never be fair
> I wrapped up in her precious air
> I want to run, I just can't hide
> I want to sit down right by her side
> Sometimes she holds on for more
> Other days, I'm simply a bore
> Maybe she's perfect, and I'll never know
> Why can't I convince myself it's really time to go?
> She might not be perfect, she'll never be fair
> I'm wrapped up in her winsome air
> I wanna run, just can't care
> Yet I gotta stay there, right there
> She speaks in metaphors, she gives it her all
> She wishes she was about ten feet tall
> I love to love her, see me right clear
> I want her to love me but can't ask for the fear
> She's damn near perfect; she doesn't even try
> But the rest of us, we're just getting by
> She not a bit perfect, not a chance she'll be fair
> I'm wrapped up in her timeless air
> I just can't run; I've nowhere to hide
> So, I'm gonna stay right by…right by her side."

"Wow, that's good," I said and stared at him. "Really good."

"Thanks," he said and smiled sheepishly. "It needs work, of course, but I think it's the best thing I've written."

"I think so, too," I said and kissed his cheek.

"You mean it?"

"Of course, I mean it, baby," I said, smiling at him. "This is the best song in the world."

He grinned. "You think?"

"I know," I said. "What's it called?"

"Uh, no title as of yet, I dunno... I just call it *Kora's Song*."

Kora's song?

"You know," he said. "For you."

For me?

"I wrote it for you," he muttered, looking away.

"Get out of here! You did?"

He nodded, and smiled, seeming very pleased with himself. "I did."

"Why?"

His smile disappeared. "What do you mean 'why'?"

"I mean... *why?*"

He sighed heavily and rolled his eyes. "Because I love you, Kora."

I felt my heart flip-flop. Any time he said those words, it flip-flopped. "But, Oliver, I thought—"

"You thought what?" he asked and stood up. "That I didn't have any feelings? That I was just some asshole using you? That I was lying? Is that what you think of me? After all this time?"

"No," I said, then lied, "I mean, I never thought about it one way or another."

He took the song out of my hands and shook it at me. "You gave me this back. I couldn't write anything before I met you. Maybe it was all the drugs I did—I don't know. All I'm saying is that I'm so grateful for that you'll never know. Now don't shit on it."

"I'm not!" I screeched but then I knew that I was. I knew that when it was time to leave, I'd leave. I'd go home. I knew it'd make me sick, what I was going to do, but I hadn't thought about it much because it seemed so far away. But the fact was, it wasn't far away. It was coming more quickly than I anticipated. I'd just put off thinking about it, that way I wouldn't have to plan anything.

"I can't believe you," he said and stood. "I can't fucking believe you!"

"What are you talking about?" I said and stood. "Oliver, I think it's the best song in the world! I'm just a little overwhelmed by it."

He stared at me, his eyes narrowing. "I'm getting tired, Kora. I'm getting tired of dancing around this. I'm getting tired of not being able to tell you how I feel. I'm getting tired of waiting."

I looked away and felt the tears sting my eyes. It seemed as soon as we got back on track, something always came around to derail us.

"You know I love you," I mumbled. "It's just so hard for me."

"Well, it's not hard for me," he said. "I filed for divorce yesterday. If she takes half, she can fucking have it. I'm sick of waiting her out."

"Why didn't you tell me?" I asked.

"It was a surprise," he said and shook the paper. "Just like this. That's what I get for wanting to please you."

"Oh, please," I said. "Let's don't do this. Let's don't fight. It's not worth it."

"Whatever," he said. "Come on, let's go."

He walked off, leaving me feeling stranded. My heart began to twist in pain. Kevin or Oliver... Oliver or Kevin... Kevin. Oliver. Oh, God! What was I doing? My indecisiveness was killing me. But I knew I wasn't only hurting Kevin, I was hurting Oliver, too. And I was sick of hurting myself.

As I watched him walk away, shoulders slumped, I knew something had changed, something had shifted. He'd thrown it all out on the table and I'd failed to meet him half-way. I was a failure. I was a bad wife, a bad lover, a bad person. I never wanted to be bad, but I was.

I knew we'd make up. We'd find something to laugh at and then we'd forget about it, shove it under the rug and then stumble over it from time to time. I also knew it was going to end. I didn't know how, when, where or why it would end, but it would. And then I'd be back to the person I was before. Just drifting, not feeling like he made me feel. I knew he was a great love in my life, but was he the greatest one? I'd always thought Kevin was. Maybe they both were. I didn't know. I just knew it was hard, all of this, it was too hard to deal with.

Just then, he turned around and stared at me, thusly making up. I gave him a little smile and held out my hand. He trotted back over to me and kissed me under that tree, under that enormous sky that I wished would swallow us up and let us be free from all of this pain and nonsense.

"Just so you'll know," he said. "I'll never hurt you. I'll do everything in my power not to hurt you, Kora."

Yeah, I thought, *but it's not you that's going to hurt me. It's me that's going to hurt you. And I hate myself for it.*

But I didn't say that. What I said was, "I know you wouldn't, Oliver. I know that."

Nevermind.

"Come on," Oliver said. "Go with me."

"I can't!" I exclaimed.

"It's just a small place," he said. "Not many people will be there."

"I can't," I said. "What would I tell Kevin?"

"Tell him you're going out with Sally."

I slapped his arm. "That won't work."

"Why not?"

"Oliver," I said and crossed my arms. "You know why. I already went away with you for a whole weekend! I'm surprised I didn't get caught! We were lucky. Let's don't push our luck."

"But what's one night?" he asked.

I rolled my eyes.

"Please?" he begged. "I just really dig this group and I know you'll dig them."

"I think they suck."

He drew in his breath. "You're saying The Howe and Why suck?"

"Yeah, I am."

He rolled his eyes. "They are the best. Their music is—"

"Quirky?" I asked. "I mean, is it music? A person can never be sure."

"They have lots of fans."

"Yeah," I said. "And so do you."

"Come with me."

"No."

"Yes," he said and pulled me into his arms. "Please?"

"I'll see what I can do," I said and laid my head on his chest, listening to his heartbeat. "But if I can pull this off, don't ask me to do anything like this again."

"I won't," he said. "At least not until they come back into town."

Kevin wasn't even suspicious when I told him I was going out with "Sally" to the "Hippodrome." Maybe because I was becoming an expert at this cheating/lying thing.

"Have fun," he said and glanced up from a file he was studying. "You're going out like that?"

I looked down at my jeans and sweater. "Yeah, why?"

"I thought you had to dress up to get in the Hippodrome."

"No you don't," I said even though I knew I was wrong.

"Well, if you get turned away from the door, don't say I didn't warn you."

"I won't," I said, then added, "Ass."

"Watch it," he muttered and watched me walk to the front door. "Be careful. Is it going to cost anything to get in?"

I groaned. "No, Sally knows the doorman. She said she could get us in for free or something."

He nodded. "And if any guy—"

"Gets rough, get a guy that's bigger than him to tell him to fuck off," I said and groaned. "It's not like I've never been out before."

"Going out in Knoxville is totally different than going out in London."

He had a point. But I said, "Listen, this isn't Cotton-Eyed Joe's, okay? This is the Hippodrome. I think they have security and everything."

"Well, good," he said. "Have fun."

"I will," I said and shut the door. Phew. I couldn't believe I'd pulled that off. I raced to the elevator and then outside where Oliver was waiting on me in his Range Rover. I got in hurriedly.

"You did it!" he exclaimed. "I knew you'd do it."

"Shut up and let's go," I said. "I have to be back before midnight."

"Why?"

"I have a curfew," I said.

"Do you really?"

"No," I said and giggled. "Let's just go!"

We went. The small venue turned out to be standing room only in a small theater that was packed asshole to elbow with a crowd of about a thousand. The Howe and Why band certainly drew them in.

"Hey," some guy said in my ear. "Is that Oliver Evans?"

"No," I said. "He looks like him though, doesn't he?"

"A little," he said, giving him a good once over. "But what would a guy like Oliver Evans be doing at a concert like this? He's too pop."

Oliver's eyes flashed with anger, but he held it in and gave the guy a tight smile. "Yeah, Oliver Evans is probably shacked up with some beautiful girl right now drinking champagne. He hasn't the time for this."

The guy eyed him and cracked up. "He's probably snorting cocaine, too."

"I heard he doesn't do that anymore," Oliver said quickly.

"Yeah, he's in re-hab, last I heard," he said. "But can't seem to kick it."

"He was never in re-hab," Oliver said, almost seething. "And he kicked it years ago. It was a fad for him, nothing more."

"Well, I heard—"

I stepped in quickly and said, "So is this your first The Howe and Why concert?"

"Oh, no," the guy said and smiled at me. "I've seen them about four other times."

"Great," I said.

"They're the best," he said. "I really dig them, don't you?"

I nodded even though I didn't. I just didn't want to risk getting mobbed. The whole crowd was waiting in anxious anticipation for them to come on stage. I started to get excited, too. It was almost like we were about to witness something really spectacular. I felt bad about lying to Kevin.

Oliver gave the guy a glare, then grabbed my hand and we stared at the stage together. The lights went down and the crowd roared, then almost instantaneously quieted. I'd never seen anything like it in all of my life. Out of nowhere, the sound of a bell and then one single stage light.

Mesmerized, we watched as Howe—the guitarist dressed in a black suit and a black and white American-style wrestling mask—placed a couple of milk crates on the stage, put two laptops on them and turned them on. We watched as he hooked them to some speakers. He clicked the mouse around for a few seconds and then suddenly a loud, fuzzy sound came out, then an infectious beat. Then he plugged his guitar in, straightened his tie and strummed. The other member of the band, Why, also known as Theo, walked out dressed in a similar suit and he had on a many colored wild and crazy ornate Mexican mask.

Oliver and I glanced at each other.

Why/Theo took the mike and said, "Hello, ladies and gentlemen. Our first song will be *The Druggist*."

The crowd was motionless. They were as enthralled—confused?—as we were. Why/Theo began to talk/rap/sing about the druggist and spouted some of the silliest lyrics I've ever heard. I cracked up. That was a pretty good song. Howe played a slow, bluesy melody and with the words, music and fuzz from the laptop it made for a very interesting song. I was beginning to dig them, even if I wasn't sure what they doing.

The show went on for about an hour and had the crowd mesmerized the entire time. At the end of their show, Why/Theo stage-dove and fell on top of two pretty English girls, who helped him up, kissed his cheek then left with him through the crowd.

The audience took a moment after the show was done.

"Well, that was certainly a riot," the guy told me.

"As it should be," Oliver informed him.

Well said.

"Let's go meet them," Oliver whispered in my ear.

"But Why/Theo left with two girls," I said.

"He does that at every show," he said. "They'll be backstage."

"Oh," I said and allowed him to lead me through the crowd and backstage. Once we got to them, The Howe and Why were covered with fans who wanted pictures and autographs, but their faces were no longer covered with wrestling masks. They were both really cute and the girls loved them. We waited patiently until Howe looked over and spotted us. He grinned and held out his hand.

"You're Oliver Evans, right?" he asked.

"Sure am," Oliver said and shook his hand. "This is Kora."

Howe turned to me, his eyes sizing me up and smiled like he liked what he saw. "Nice to meet you, Kora."

"And you," I said and shook his hand.

"You're a Southern girl!" he exclaimed.

"I am," I replied and smiled.

"We're from the south, too."

"I know," I said. "Oliver's told me all about you."

"Where you from?"

"Knoxville."

"We're from Memphis," he said and smiled at me, then turned back to Oliver. "My little sister used to have such a crush on you. Mind if I get a picture of you for her?"

Oliver's smile faded. I wanted to smack Howe. *What* an insensitive bastard! But then, Oliver shrugged and nodded, being a good sport. In that moment, I gained so much respect for him. He wanted what Howe and Why/Theo had, that respect. He wanted it so much, but he knew that he'd never have it. He wasn't artsy-fartsy or avant-garde or any of that. He was just Oliver and that made him all the more special.

I stepped back as they posed for the picture, then Howe motioned me over. "Come on and get in one with us."

I shook my head. "No, thanks."

"No, come on."

I shrugged and said, "Okay."

I stood beside Oliver, who took my hand and kissed it, then we posed for the picture. Just then another guy came up with a bigger camera and started taking pictures. The flash was so strong it made me wince.

"Oh, damn," I said and rubbed my eyes. "What the hell was that?"

Oliver stood frozen and stared at the guy who'd taken the picture. Then without a word, the guy stopped taking pictures and stared at Oliver. Then he took off like a jackrabbit on a date. Oliver raced after him.

What the hell was that all about?

Without thinking, I ran after Oliver. He was chasing the guy through the theater and then outside. I ran, yelling for him to hold up, but he wasn't listening. He was after the guy like he was going to kill him.

"Oliver, stop!" I yelled as I raced down the street after him.

The guy took off around a corner and then so did Oliver. When I reached it, Oliver was stopped, looking around. Then out of nowhere a car took off. The guy was inside it. Oliver took off after the car but just managed to just slap it before it disappeared.

I bent over and tried to catch my breath. I managed to get out, "What the hell are you doing?"

He stared at me, hands on hips and caught his breath.

"Oliver?"

"He..." he said and took a breath. "He took our photo."

"So?" I asked.

"He took a photo of us together, Kora!" he yelled.

"He was probably a big fan of yours!" I yelled back. "What's the big deal?"

"What?" he asked as if he couldn't believe how stupid I was being. "He's from the tabloids!"

I shook my head, not understanding.

"You don't know how it works over here," he said.

"How does it work?"

He stared at me, then at the ground and said, "Nevermind. It's no big deal. Let's go."

The taco incident.

The next morning, I slept almost till ten, which was unusual for me. I was usually up with the birds. I finally got out of bed, pulled my robe on and went into the bathroom and brushed my teeth. Then I went into the kitchen and stopped abruptly when I saw Kevin sitting at the table pouring over a newspaper.

"What are you doing home?" I asked.

"Are you finally up?" he asked with his head in his hands.

"What are you doing home?" I asked again and yawned. "Are you sick?"

He shook his head and continued to stare at the paper. Must be some interesting stuff in there. I never read the paper. It was all so depressing to me and I figured ignorance was bliss.

"Are you okay?" I asked and glanced at the paper.

He didn't answer. I sighed and wondered what he was so pissed off about. I decided to ignore him and went to the fridge for a coke. Then he muttered something.

"What?" I asked, turning around.

"I said," he said, finally showing his face. "I can't believe you."

"Believe me?" I asked.

He snatched the newspaper up and threw it at me. I caught it and glared at him. What an asshole! What the fuck was his problem?

"Read it," he snapped.

I shrugged and put the paper on the table, flipping the pages.

He watched me for a moment before groaning, "No, let me find it for you."

"Huh?" I asked.

He grabbed it out of my hands and tore through it, then slammed a sheet on the table and pointed at it, "What is that?"

I looked down at it and felt my heart sink to my knees. I almost fell over. Now I understood why Oliver was so pissed off at that guy last night. He was from the tabloids, all right. It was a picture of Oliver, me and Howe, the guy from The Howe and Why. There was also a smaller close-up of Oliver holding my hand. Oh, fucking shit! It showed my wedding ring! I'd forgotten to take it off. The caption read: *"Oliver's new Lover! And she's married, too!"* The story went on to tell everyone that I was a homewrecker and that we'd been seeing each other for months.

That explained why Oliver never wanted me to linger outside his house. That's why he was always suspicious of anyone on the street. I'd never put two and two together before, never gave it a second thought. I just thought he was acting a little erratically because we were having an affair. But he had been trying to protect me, trying to keep me away from it all. He knew what it was like, what could happen, what damage could occur. He'd been through this time and time again. He was an old pro. I was a novice. And now Kevin knew. Now I realized what damage I'd done to him by having an affair.

Kevin pointed at the picture and hissed, "Is *that* Sally?"

For the life of me, I couldn't speak.

"Who was Sally?" he asked, shaking his head. "What the fuck was that all about? You've been sleeping with this guy since you saw him at my office party, haven't you?"

I didn't say one word about the dates not adding up. If he thought that's when we started, then let him.

"You were so smitten with him," he said. "I saw it that night! Fuck! What a fucking idiot I am! Right under my nose!"

"Kevin it's not like that!"

"Then tell me what it is!"

"Stop yelling at me!" I yelled.

He paused then shouted, "WELL, TELL ME!"

"DON'T YELL AT ME!"

"TELL ME!"

"TELL YOU WHAT!"

He paused, then said in a calm tone, "What this means."

"I don't know!" I yelled and sat down. "I guess it means I got caught."

His whole face dropped all emotion, just like that. "You bitch."

"Oh, come on," I hissed. "You never noticed because you never thought anyone else would want me! And that's because you take me for granted!"

"Like hell I do!" he snapped. "I'm over here working my ass off to give you a bigger house, a better life!"

"I don't want a bigger house!" I yelled, almost on the verge of tears. "I already had a good life! I didn't want to come here and I wanted to leave! Is it my fault I met someone who makes me feel alive?"

He looked as thought I'd slapped him. "And how do I make you feel? Dead? Is that what you're saying?"

"No!" I exclaimed and dropped my head. It had been so nice and now it was ugly. It was going to end and I realized for the first time that I knew it was going to end all along. It was like I had been stabbed in my heart.

I looked down at the bracelet Oliver had given me and touched it. I hadn't taken it off since he'd given it to me. I loved that bracelet. It meant so much.

"And this," he said and grabbed my wrist, ripping the bracelet off. "This! I should have known you couldn't get something like this on the street! Lying to me!"

"Give it back!" I cried. "Besides, you never gave me anything like that!"

"Oh, there it is!" he yelled. "Fuck you, Kora! You know, I *had* to be cheap. I had to be the responsible one! I had to work my ass off for what I got. I didn't have it handed to me like that prick! If I hadn't worked for what I've got, we'd still be living in a shitty apartment with no money!"

"No one has to be that cheap, Kevin!" I yelled and glared at him. "You're just cheap because you're cheap! Admit it!"

"Fuck you."

"Admit it!" I yelled and slapped my hand on the table. "Admit how cheap you are! Everyone knows already!"

"I do my best!"

"Bullshit," I said, almost to the point of seething now. "Do you remember that time I brought tacos home?"

"Oh, Lord!" he yelled, shaking his hands over his head. "Here we go again! Not the taco incident again!"

"Yes!" I yelled. "Here we go again! I think you need to realize how shitty you were! I was working, too, you know?"

"Oh, I know," he said. "Everyone knows how much you've sacrificed!"

"You're damned right they do," I hissed. "And that night I brought tacos home, I wanted to please you! I don't even like tacos that much!"

"We had twenty bucks in the bank," he said. "And you spent ten of it on tacos! Besides that, we had food in the fridge!"

"But why did you have to yell at me like you did?" I asked. "You made me feel so bad. Did you think I liked being that broke all the time? I didn't! All I thought was that I was doing something nice for you and you threw it in my face!"

"I just wanted us to be secure," he said. "That's all I ever wanted, Kora."

"Oh, please," I said, glaring at him. "You yelled at me for twenty minutes over the fucking tacos. You told me I was trying to break us! Do you know after that I didn't buy anything for years? Then one day I woke up and said, *fuck him!* I started buying shit and I snuck it into the house just so you wouldn't see it. Just so you wouldn't yell at me for spending a dollar!"

He glared back at me for an instant then threw the bracelet across the room. It was just us, wasn't it? Us fighting. It had always been just us. Me and him, fighting over money, fighting over tacos. Now we had Oliver, too. And that was one too many. Three was always a crowd.

I looked away from him.

"At least I didn't sneak around on you," he said. "At least I didn't deceive you. You've been dishonest."

I dropped my head, feeling so bad for us that I couldn't stand myself. All of a sudden, I burst into tears. He sighed and sat down in front of me. I kept crying and refused to look at him.

"Kora," he said gently. "He's only going to use you. When he gets tired of you, then where will you be?"

It wasn't lost on me that I'd said those exact words to Oliver. But then I realized Kevin was saying them because he was jealous. He was afraid of losing me. *Men!* Ugh! They were all the same. Once they got you, they ignored you but in the meanwhile, they didn't want anyone else to have you.

But he was right. I hated that he was right, but he was. I knew it was just my insecurity talking, but I couldn't ignore it. *What if he was right?*

"We're leaving day after tomorrow," he muttered.

My head snapped up. "What?"

"We're leaving," he said. "I guess you kinda lost track of time, didn't you? It's been over a year, Kora. It's time to go. I told you a few weeks ago we were leaving. Don't act like I didn't."

"You can't make me leave."

He sighed and shook his head. "Kora, I don't know what kind of bullshit a guy like that would feed a woman, but I can tell you one thing. He will use you until there's nothing left."

"You're wrong," I spat, hating for him to say that, my worst fear.

"No," he said. "I'm not. And you know that deep in your heart. Don't throw away your life over some guy who's only going to get tired of you."

I began to cry, big buckets of tears. I'd had my premonition about that. I knew I was going to hurt Oliver and I knew all along I'd go back home with Kevin once it was time. I just didn't expect it to turn out like this. I didn't expect it to be so crude and ugly.

"Start packing," he said and got up and left the room.

I watched him go, then raced over and found my bracelet. I stared at it and started to put it back on, but then slipped it into my pocket instead.

★★★★★

Oliver called the next morning. I didn't say anything. I didn't tell him I was leaving the next day. He asked if Kevin had seen the picture and I told him no, that Kevin never read the newspaper and that we'd got away with it. He told me there were several photographers outside of his house, waiting to get a shot of him.

"But that's the way it works," he said. "It'll blow over in a few days, baby."

I nodded but didn't say anything.

"It might not be a good idea for you to come over," he said. "Though I'd love to see you."

I nodded again.

"Are any photographers over there?" he asked.

I moved the curtain to the side and looked out the window. There was one; he was waiting on me to come out. He'd been there all day. I'd wait him out for a little while but I couldn't wait forever. We were leaving soon.

"Kora?" he asked.

I dropped the curtain and said, "No, there's no one here."

"Maybe I could come over, then," he said.

"No," I said. "Don't do that. It's too much trouble and they might follow you."

"You're right," he said. "I'm so sorry you have to go through this, baby."

"Me, too," I said.

"But it'll blow over in a few days," he said. "Then we can get all this sorted out, figure out what we want to do."

I stared at the wall, then at the window.

"Kora?" he asked. "Are you there?"

"I gotta go, Oliver," I said. "I'll call you tomorrow, I promise."

"Kora—"

"Oliver, I gotta go!"

I hung up and burst into tears. You can't have it all. Don't ever think you can because you're only lying to yourself. And I'd done that enough to know.

I didn't take my time packing. I just threw stuff in the suitcases. I labeled the boxes and waited on the delivery guy to pick them up so he could ship them back to my house. I waited those long hours by myself. I cried. I wrote Oliver ten letters, all full of dismay and heartbreak, then I tore them up. I didn't want to leave him like that. I didn't want to tell him how weak I was and how I didn't believe in him enough to take a chance.

The photographer finally gave up on me and left. But I still didn't go out. And then it was time to go. Kevin and I got into a cab early one morning with our suitcases and we took that long drive to Gatwick. The airplane would fly us over the Atlantic and then to Atlanta. There we'd wait a few hours and then board a smaller plane that would take us home to Knoxville, where his parents would pick us up. Once I was home, I told myself, I'd be better. I would lose all the hurt over the ocean as I flew across it. I'd get me back.

We made it through the airport, got screened and all that. Then we went to the gate and waited for them to tell us we could get on the plane. I stared at my feet the whole time. I was numbing myself to the pain of heartbreak. It was long process.

"Flight 627 to Atlanta now boarding first class."

That's when I broke. That's when I knew. That's when I stood up and stared wild-eyed at Kevin, who began to shake his head. I began to cry and said, "I'm sorry, Kevin, I am so, so sorry."

"Kora," he said. "Don't do this."

I backed away from him, feeling my heart break as I did. "Kevin, I can't leave. I don't know why but I can't. I don't even like London that much."

"Kora," he hissed under his breath. "It was a fling. Now get on the fucking plane."

"I can't."

"You can," he said and grabbed my elbow. "And you will."

I jerked away from him. "I'm sorry, Kevin. I couldn't help it. It just happened. I'm so sorry."

"Kora!"

"I gotta go!"

"Straighten up!" he hissed and jerked my arm.

I stopped crying for a moment, looked him in the eyes and nodded. Yeah, I could do this. Even if it felt like there was someone slicing and dicing my heart out. Even if it felt like I was going to die, I could do this. I had to do it. I had no choice.

I was such a stupid girl. On top of that, I was the world's biggest coward. As I boarded the plane, I knew I'd made a mistake but it was too late to get off.

Kora's Song.

It was Oliver, all by himself, singing my song, singing it to me, to the whole world. He was singing to me from the TV in my living room, in Knoxville. He was coming all the way from London to sing it to me. He was on the screen, looking so sweet and handsome I felt my heart twist in pain a little as I watched the video.

He didn't look at the camera and he didn't dance. He sat on a park bench in glorious black and white strumming an acoustic guitar. He sang softly, brilliantly. He was professional and beautiful and so wonderful it brought tears to my eyes. In that song, he was going to finally get what he wanted. He was going to get his hit in the States and he was going to get respect. His video was being played all the time on TV and the song was all over the radio. His album was titled *Romantic Hedonism*. He was going to make it again. He deserved to.

There he was, right there in front of me. If I reached out, I could touch him. I could hear him and that was good enough.

As always, he left me breathless.

I found myself moving slowly, moving over to the TV. I found myself touching his face, there on the screen, wishing I could touch it for real. I found myself wanting to make love to that television set just to be near him. I found myself bent down in front of him, staring at me, as he stared at the camera, as he stared at everyone who would see this video. He kept singing to me, singing my song to me, loving me from across the ocean, begging me to come home to him.

He was always such a charming bastard.

I realized I loved him so much it hurt. I was hurting with the pain of love, with the pain of loss. I'd lost so much. I'd thrown it away because I was too afraid to succumb to it. I was too afraid to hurt someone else that I had done myself the greatest disservice. I was so stupid. I was so sorry that I'd been so scared. I was sorry I couldn't believe what we had meant so much. I was sick of being quiet and of being good. I was sick of not being who I was and sick of listening to everyone else.

Oliver had gotten what he'd always wanted. I was going to get what I wanted, too.

Six months. Six long months of adjusting back to the Southern accents, to the Southern food, to the heat and the humidity and the storms. Six months of adjusting to a life without a lover. Six months of cleaning house, of staring at the wall, of pouring over the want ads looking for a job to occupy my mind. Six months of trying to quit smoking again. Six months of pain and torture and of not living. Six months of telling Kevin I was over Oliver, of pretending to be over him. Six months of Kevin not believing me but hoping I was telling the truth. All lies, all over nothing, six months worth of nothing.

Six months too long.

Before I could stop myself, I went to my closet, took out my suitcase and began to pack. I didn't stop until I had it full and then I went to the phone and booked the first flight to London I could get. Then I wrote Kevin a letter. I told him how sorry I was. I told him I was scared and I was weak and if all that meant I had ruined his life, then I was sorry about that, too. I told him all the things I felt and told him I was sorry about what I was doing but if I didn't do it, I'd never be able to live with myself. I told him I was sorry if he didn't understand that.

I got on the plane and once I arrived in London, I took a very long cab ride to Oliver's house. And there I stood on his doorstep and rang the bell and waited. As I waited I didn't care anymore. I didn't care if he didn't come to the door and I didn't care if he rejected me if he did. I was so sick of caring about everything, so sick of over-analyzing. Sick of it all.

Where was he? I looked at my watch, then around the street which was beginning to lighten up with a new day. Come on, come on, come on. Kevin was home by now. He'd read the letter.

He hated me now, hated me with every fiber of his being. My heart twisted in pain but it wasn't going to stop me from doing what I had to do. It hurt for something lost rather than something missing.

Where was he?

I looked around. *Come on, Oliver!* Oh, no. What if he had changed his mind? What if he didn't love me anymore? What if he hated my guts in the way I was sure Kevin did? What if he'd moved?

I was just being paranoid. He *was* coming. Surely he was coming. What if I'd come all this way just to find out my suspicions were true? That he didn't love me, that I was just a fling? Oh, God, I didn't think I could bear that.

I listened to a car whiz by on the street as I waited for him. Maybe fate did play a part in things. I never gave it much thought, but maybe it was true. Maybe it was just something that was out of our control.

Come on, Oliver. Don't disappoint me, baby.

Just then, I saw him. He was at the window, staring at me while one hand held the curtain back. He saw me the instant I saw him and we both broke out into big smiles for each other. *There was my baby!* I couldn't wait to hug and kiss him. My whole body just lit up. Yeah, there was a reason we'd met. And, as I heard his footsteps bringing me closer to him, my world changed. It went from sour to sweet in a second flat. All this love I felt just came at me. I was overcome with emotion. Such good emotion.

He finally came to the door. He was dressed in a pair of jeans and nothing else, like he'd just gotten up and thrown them on because they were on the floor next to the bed. When he saw me, he drew back a little, but then seemed to relax.

"You're here," he said.

"I'm here."

"Took long enough," he said and smiled. "I waited on you so long. But I knew you'd come back. Don't ask me how, but I knew you'd come home to me."

He knew me better than I knew myself. And that was a good thing to know, too.

"Shut up and kiss me," I said and pulled him to me.

He shut up and kissed me. It was as though no time had passed since we'd last kissed. It was the best feeling I'd ever had. I never wanted to lose it. If I had anything to do with it, I never would.